Foreword

The Ghosts of Glevum is set in the winter of AD 187. At that time most of Britain had been for almost two hundred years the northernmost outpost of the hugely successful Roman Empire: occupied by Roman legions, criss-crossed by Roman military roads, subject to Roman laws and taxes, and ruled over by a provincial governor (now Pertinax) answerable directly to Rome where Commodus still wore the Imperial purple and ruled with an autocratic and capricious hand. In fact, the Emperor's debauchery and excesses were renowned, and he had become so unpopular that there was continuous rumour of unrest. Following an attempt by his sister to assassinate him early in his reign, Commodus was particularly savage in his treatment of conspirators, as suggested in the novel.

The existence of Pertinax – and his promotion to the African provinces at about this time – is historical, although there is no reliable evidence to show the precise date of his departure or, interestingly, the name of his successor. In the absence of accurate information here, the story postulates that no immediate appointment to the post was made, and that Pertinax continued to maintain nominal control over both provinces at once, using local appointees until a new governor could be installed. This is entirely speculative, of course, and probably unlikely, but such an arrangement is not impossible and there are historical precedents elsewhere. The division of the province of Britannia into two for administrative purposes (suggested here as a temporary expedient) is not known to have occurred at this time. It was, however, a suggestion attributed to Pertinax by some authorities, and the arrangement was in fact implemented sometime early in the third century. (Thereafter the two regions had separate governors, so that by AD 219 Paulinus is described in an inscription as 'Governor of Britannia Inferior'.)

Official authority within the province was divided between local, provincial and Imperial government, which all existed side by side throughout the period. Glevum (modern Gloucester) where the story is set, was a *colonia* – one of only a handful of such high-ranking cities in the province – and was effectively a self-governing city-state, founded as a retirement settlement for wealthy veterans, and enjoying such wealth and status that any freeman born within the walls was automatically a Roman citizen. A chief magistrate and councillor, such as Balbus, represented the local tier of government and would necessarily have been a person of considerable influence and wealth. Indeed, the term of office for the highest magistrate was usually restricted to a year or two, largely because the cost of tenureship – which included the provision of civic works and games – was recognised as cripplingly high.

In addition, each province had a procurator (or, in the case of smaller regions, a sub-procurator) such as Mellitus. These were Imperial appointees, responsible directly to the Emperor, but otherwise effectively autonomous. They were the chief fiscal officers, entirely responsible for the financial administration of the province, and although extremely influential were generally disliked, probably because they

Rosemary Rowe is the maiden name of author Rosemary Aitken, who was born in Cornwall during the Second World War. She is a highly qualified academic, and has written more than a dozen best-selling textbooks on English language and communication. She has written fiction for many years under her married name. Rosemary is the mother of two adult children and has two grandchildren living in New Zealand, where she herself lived for twenty years. She now divides her time between Gloucestershire and Cornwall.

Acclaim for Rosemary Rowe's Libertus series:

'A brilliantly realised historical setting dovetails perfectly with a sharp plot in this history-cum-whodunnit' *Good Book Guide*

'The Libertus novels are among the best of the British historical detectives. The characters are well formed and the plots leave you guessing while giving you enough hints and clues to grip your attention' *Gloucestershire Life*

'The character of Libertus springs to life. A must for anyone interested in Roman Britain' Paul Doherty

'Lots of fascinating detail about what the Romans ever did for us . . . History with an entertaining if murderous twist' *Birmingham Post*

'Rowe has had the clever idea of making her detective-figure a mosaicist, and, therefore, an expert in puzzles and patterns. Into the bargain, he is a freed Celtic slave, and thus an outsider to the brutalities of the conquerors, and a character with whom the reader can sympathise' *Independent*

'Superb characterisation and evocation of Roman Britain. It transports you back to those times. An entirely compelling historical mystery' Michael Jecks

'Libertus is a thinking man's hero . . . a delightful whodunnit which is fascinating in the detail of its research and the charm of its detective team' *Huddersfield Daily Examiner*

'Cunningly drawn and the very devil to fathom until the final pages' *Coventry Evening Telegraph*

THE GHOSTS OF GLEVUM

Rosemary Rowe

headline

Copyright © 2004 Rosemary Aitken

The right of Rosemary Rowe to be identified as the Author of
the Work has been asserted by her in accordance with
the Copyright, Designs and Patents Act 1988.

First published in 2004
by HEADLINE BOOK PUBLISHING

First published in paperback in 2004
by HEADLINE BOOK PUBLISHING

10 9 8 7 6 5 4 3 2 1

ISBN 0 7553 0517 5

Typeset in Plantin by Avon DataSet Ltd,
Bidford-on-Avon, Warwickshire

Printed and bound in Great Britain by
Mackays of Chatham plc, Chatham, Kent

Headline's policy is to use papers that are natural, renewable and
recyclable products and made from wood grown in sustainable
forests. The logging and manufacturing processes are
expected to conform to the environmental
regulations of the country of origin.

HEADLINE BOOK PUBLISHING
A division of Hodder Headline
338 Euston Road
London NW1 3BH

www.headline.co.uk
www.hodderheadline.com

To John and Maria, with much love
(and thanks to Eric, who knew about eels)

were responsible for tax. Their co-operation was none the less essential to local government.

There were also the military authorities. The army in the second century was commanded by two different kinds of men: career soldiers, such as centurions, who were professionals; and the *legatus legionis* of each force, a senator or would-be senator, for whom a short period of military service was a necessary part of a political career. These so-called 'senatorial officers' were drawn from wealthy families and generally appointed by the provincial governor (who was the commander-in-chief of the army in his province) often as the result of representations from relatives or patrons. Once adopted in this way, a bright senatorial officer could expect swift promotion, appointment as soon as a vacancy arose, and a seat on the Roman senate in a year. Under Commodus, however, there was a dearth of willing candidates, especially for the legions in Britannia where there had been some disturbance and unrest, for which the officers were penalised. The pay of senior officers had recently been increased, and some of the existing senatorial officers – in particular those with real military prowess – seeing little hope of satisfactory political advancement in Rome under the increasingly unstable Emperor, elected to extend their tenure, sometimes for years, and held a variety of commands. Praxus, in the story, may be seen as one of these.

All these powerful men were Roman citizens, naturally. Citizenship – with its social, economic and legal advantages – was not at this time an automatic right, even for the freeborn. It was a privilege to be earned – by those not lucky enough to be born to it – only by service to the army or the Emperor, although slaves of important citizens (like Libertus) could be bequeathed the coveted status, along with their freedom, on their master's death. Power, of course, was invested almost entirely in men. Although women could be classed as citizens and might wield considerable influence, even owning and managing large estates, they were excluded from civic office. Indeed a woman of any age remained a child in law, under the tutelage first of her father and then of any husband she might have.

However, most ordinary people lacked the distinction of citizenship. Some were freemen or freed-men, scratching a precarious living from a trade or farm; thousands more were slaves, mere chattels of their masters, with no more status than any other domestic animal. Some slaves led pitiable lives, though others were highly regarded by their owners: indeed the lot of a well-fed slave in a kindly household might be more enviable than that of many a freeman struggling to eke out an existence in a squalid hut, like some characters in the narrative.

Even below the slaves, however, there was another tier – the outcasts of society, who had no official status, home or name. The present story hinges on the intersection of two social worlds: that of the politically powerful and that of this underclass, which was politically powerless and had no rights at all. Its existence can be deduced, in particular, from the accounts of trials and lawbreaking. It is clear that old, ill and injured slaves were sometimes jettisoned and turned on to the streets, since legislation repeatedly attempts to outlaw the practice. Equally, the existence of the law forbidding a slave to run away (except to another master to seek sanctuary), and the severity of the punishment if he did, suggests that there were those who attempted it. It is also evident from contemporary accounts that there were thieves and vagabonds, that beggars often frequented the tombs beside the road, and that freak children who escaped the normal fate (of being exposed at birth until they died) were sometimes dragged around the fairs and exhibited by travelling showmen for a fee. There is some information (as to age, injury and sex) to be derived from common burial pits, but history has left us little evidence as to how such people lived, so the narrative in this regard is purely fictional.

The use of apparently modern nicknames such as 'Fatbeard' and 'Bullface' is historically apt. Such names were so commonplace that many eminent Romans are known by them today, rather than by their more official names. Caligula, for instance, means 'Little Boots', while Agricola was nicknamed 'Farmer' by his troops.

The Romano-British background to this book has been derived from a wide variety of (sometimes contradictory) written and pictorial sources. However, although I have done my best to create an accurate and convincing picture, this remains a work of fiction and there is no claim to total academic authenticity.

Relata refero. Ne Iupiter quidem omnibus placet. (I only tell you what I heard. Jove himself can't please everybody.)

I

It had been a long banquet. Course after course of exotic food, all disguised to look like something else. The final offering had consisted of a sow and nine suckling piglets, one for each member of the highest table, all made entirely of sweet almond bread and carried in on an enormous wooden plate by an equally enormous Nubian slave. That had earned a round of spontaneous applause, although it proved better to look at than to eat. Now the remains were being cleared away, the acrobats and jugglers had finished, and a dozen slaves were bringing out fresh bowls of watered wine. Loquex, an elderly poet, was ushered in to read.

I sighed. I knew his eulogies of old. Interminable banalities in lamentable verse. I was rather surprised that he had been engaged for such an important occasion, but of course it had all been organised rather hurriedly. Perhaps no one else was available. Loquex was almost overcome by the solemnity of the honour. He produced a depressingly large and densely written scroll of bark-parchment, and cleared his throat.

> 'Marcus Aurelius Septimus, just and fair
> Has hooded eyes and curly hair,'

he began – or words to that effect. (It is impossible to convey the full banality of the original Latin.)

In the obscurity of a corner, I shifted uneasily on my banqueting couch. Others, placed nearer the centre of the room, were forced to endure this without fidgeting. I looked at our host, the Marcus Aurelius Septimus in question: the provincial governor's personal representative, and by far the richest and most influential man for miles around. He was also my patron, so I knew him well, and I could already see the look of resignation glazing those 'hooded eyes', and detect frustration in the way that he was fingering the seal-ring on his hand. It was his own fault, of course; he had engaged the wretched local poet in honour of our two distinguished guests.

Loquex was just turning his attention to them:

> 'Gaius Praxus came from Gaul
> He's very brave and very tall . . .'

Someone on the second highest table – I think it was Balbus, the chief town magistrate, whose brother was rumoured to have served with Praxus's force – sniggered, but thought better of it and changed it to a cough. I had every sympathy. Of course, this poem was thrown together hastily for this evening, but Loquex did seem in even worse form than usual.

I glanced at Praxus – or Gaius Flaminius Praxus, to give him his full three Latin names. He was tall, one could not deny, but it was not the first word which would spring to mind. Praxus was tall in the way that – say – a small mountainside is tall and he was brave in much the same way – massive, unflinching and immovable, and about as impervious to anything as trivial as pain.

2

He was reclining at Marcus's right-hand side, in the place of honour, where he was the first to be served with everything – as well he might. Praxus had recently been transferred from northern Gaul to find himself, pending the arrival of the new provincial governor, the senior officer commanding most of the Roman forces on the western borders of Britannia, including the garrison at Glevum.

This mountain of a man was improbably dressed in a skimpy pale blue *synthesis* – that fashionable dining robe which was a combination of toga and under-tunic – and wore a floral banqueting wreath lopsided around his head.

The effect was utterly incongruous, but Praxus looked no less menacing for that. However, his square-boned face had for a moment lost its scowl and softened to a glazed expression of amused contempt, but whether that was the effect of the verse, or of Marcus's excellent Falernian wine, it was – at this distance – impossible to tell.

Loquex was just settling into his stride:

'And on the left is Mellitus, of course –
Who also earns our thanks and our applause.'

I heard a little ripple run round the room at this, and not just at the dreadful quality of the verse. Loquex had clumsily contrived to draw attention to the fact that Mellitus – the name means honey, but there was nothing remotely honeyed about his character – had been placed on Marcus's left-hand side, in second position to Praxus as it were. Mellitus would not care for that. I recognised him: a wizened little sub-procurator based in nearby Corinium, and the local expert on taxation and finance. He was famous for his grasping

3

hands and shrewd intelligence and had been a guest here once before. At that time Marcus had made an enormous fuss of him, but tonight was obviously different and Mellitus had been demonstrating his discontent by ostentatiously eating and drinking hardly anything, and greeting all the entertainments with a stony face. Now the unfortunate implication of the verse made matters worse. The sharp eyes narrowed more than ever and the thin lips pursed. It was an awkward moment.

Marcus, however, had seen an opportunity and risen to his feet. Taking his cue from 'our applause' he began to clap enthusiastically. I took the hint and did the same, and one by one the other guests joined in.

Loquex coloured, paused, and bowed – delightedly at first, but every time the claps and shouts slowed down Marcus began another round ('Well done Loquex! What a splendid attempt!') and after a few moments the poet understood. With a look of disappointment he put his scroll away, and – still bowing – allowed himself to be escorted from the room.

Gaius Flavius, the old ex-councillor seated next to me, gave an approving grunt. 'Well, let's hope that's the last of the entertainments for the night, so the important people can retire to do some serious drinking, and the rest of us can decently go home.' He sighed. 'I'm glad that I'm too unimportant to be part of that. It's obvious that those three aren't going to get along.'

His voice was not loud, but he spoke into a hush, and I was afraid that everyone would hear. He was drawing startled looks from everyone, as it was, by motioning to a slave to fill his cup, and draining it at a gulp. That was shocking behaviour, especially on a formal occasion such as this, but he seemed oblivious. I realised uneasily that he'd drunk a great deal of sweet watered wine with the dessert and the alcohol was loosening his tongue.

I murmured something non-committal, and tried to look as if these dangerous remarks were not addressed to me.

He refused to let the matter drop. 'It's easier for you, Libertus; everybody knows that you're Marcus's protégé. And you're a pavement-maker, anyway – people need mosaics, whoever is in power. But if those three up there start quarrelling, the rest of us will have to choose between them, and I for one shan't know which horse to hitch my chariot to.'

If there had been a hush before, there was silence now. You could have heard a breadcrumb fall on to the tiled floor. Even the slave with the watered wine, refilling the old man's goblet for the umpteenth time, paused in his pouring as if turned to stone.

Gaius plunged on, as unstoppable as a runaway cart rattling down a hill. 'I shall be glad when the new governor is properly installed, and things get back to normal again.' He drained his cup and held it out once more. 'What is the situation there, Libertus, do you know?' His speech was getting rather slurred by now. 'You've got your ear closer to the ground than most of us. Is it true that there has been yet more delay?'

I was aware of twenty pairs of eyes, at least, fastened on me expectantly. Suddenly I wished that I was anywhere but here. The Emperor doubtless had his spies in Glevum, as in every other city of the Empire, and the wrong choice of words could be disastrous. 'There have been a lot of rumours, Councillor Gaius . . .' I began.

That was the understatement of the season. Ever since it had been announced that Governor Pertinax had been promoted to the more prestigious African provinces, Glevum had been alive with rumour of all kinds. There were as many versions as there were inhabitants. You could take your pick. There had been a new governor appointed. There had not. Someone had actually set sail for Britannia, but had fallen overboard. Or had been pushed. A man *had* been selected by the Emperor, but had since been executed. Or proved to be a woman in disguise. Or both.

The only fact on which the gossips all agreed was that no new governor had so far appeared. The date for the expected handover had come and gone, amidst a flurry of Imperial messengers. Pertinax had finally departed to take up his new post, but in the absence of a successor it appeared that he was still nominally in charge, and interim running of the province had devolved upon his regional representatives. Hence this hurried meeting of the local great: Praxus, Mellitus and Marcus were the chief military, fiscal and legal authorities in the area. It was not a natural alliance, and probably one of them would emerge as paramount. No wonder my inebriated friend was worried about where to place his loyalties.

He looked at me contemptuously. 'Rumours! Huh!'

'Well,' that was the florid trader sitting on my left, 'someone told me only yesterday, in strictest confidence, that Jupiter has turned the governor-elect into a goat, and we are waiting for the gods to turn him back.'

'It can't have been Proconsul Fabius then,' another man chimed in. 'No point in turning him into a goat. No one could have told the difference anyway.'

There was a murmur of relief and mirth at this. It was safe to laugh. The Proconsul Fabius in question was securely dead. He had been a favoured candidate for governor – I

6

was fairly sure of that, from information I had gleaned at Marcus's – but he had been executed recently for an alleged plot against the Emperor. (Not all rumours are necessarily false.)

However, I did not tell my companions that. Instead I took advantage of the change of mood to divert attention to the honoured guests, who were showing signs of getting to their feet. 'Well, councillor, it seems you have your wish. The feast appears to be coming to an end, so you will be able to make good your escape.'

The last glass had gone straight to the old man's head. 'All right for you,' he grumbled indistinctly. 'The journey'll be colder and wetter than the Styx for all the rest of us.'

He had a point. This banquet was being held at Marcus's country house, but only Praxus and Mellitus – and their attendants, naturally – were house-guests here, able to stay at the villa overnight. Most of the other diners would have to make their way back to the city, several miles away. Of course (since wheeled carriages were useless in the town, where they were only permitted to move about at night) most would have hired litters awaiting them by now – the poor carriers already half perished with the cold – but travel on a winter's night like this was always dismal in the foggy damp and chill. I was glad that I had my cosy little roundhouse less than half a mile from here – so close that it had once formed part of the estate, until Marcus had given it to me as a reward for solving a politically embarrassing crime for him. I had no expensive carrying chair to take me home, but at least I would not have very far to walk.

'Beshides . . .' the old ex-councillor began, but he got no further. The house-party was already on its feet, and the newly appointed priest of Jupiter, a self-important youngish man with a face like a moon and a hairless head to match, was already making his way towards the portable altar in the corner of the room. I am not a believer in the Roman pantheon, preferring the older darker Celtic gods of fire and stone, but as a citizen I am expected to observe the formalities, and in any case one can never be too careful with the gods. I rose obediently to my feet with everybody else while the closing libation and food-offering were made. The deities do very well out of official banquets such as this, I thought: sacrifice and invocation to begin, the usual oblation to the Lares halfway through, and now – since the guest of honour was a military man and Jupiter is the army's patron god – this final offering to Jove. The household slaves would profit too, since they are traditionally permitted to enjoy any part of the sacrifice the immortals do not seem to want.

My tipsy friend the councillor was finding it quite difficult to stand by now, at least without the help of my restraining hand. And he was not the only one. Various guests were looking flushed, and either scowling with drunken concentration or smiling inanely as they swayed. Marcus's best wine was having its effect. Even the mountainous Praxus, ridiculous in his wispy pale blue robe, was clearly feeling the effects, and as soon as the solemnities were over he gave a brief nod to the assembled company and lurched off noisily towards the little chamber which Marcus had set aside as a *vomitorium* for the night.

Marcus caught my eye across the room, and raised his brows. He had visited the vomitorium earlier himself, of course, as many other notables had done, but only for socially accepted purposes – to tickle the back of his throat with one of the thoughtfully provided feathers and genteelly regurgitate his food so as to make room for more. Stumbling out to void your stomach because of too much drink is not the behaviour of a well-bred man.

Praxus had chosen an inconvenient moment for his exit, and there was an uncomfortable pause. It would be improper for the rest of us to move before the official party had withdrawn, and that was impossible until Praxus reappeared. The senior magistrate who had sniggered earlier, a corpulent decurion who notoriously enjoyed good drink, picked up his cup and sipped at the remnants of his wine, and after a moment more diners did the same. Others dabbled their fingers in dainty water bowls, removed their wreaths, untucked their linen napkins or otherwise made preparations to depart. Nobody was talking very much.

Mellitus, who was rumoured never to visit vomitoria – too mean to give anything away, the wits said – compressed his already sour thin lips into a firmer line and sidled up to Marcus. He gave his mirthless smile and murmured something – clearly disapproving, but inaudible.

Marcus nodded, and signalled to a slave. Then he appeared to reconsider and went out towards the vomitorium himself.

I knew the little room. Of course I did – I laid the pavement in there myself, in the days when the previous owner used it as a cramped and wholly unsuitable *librarium*. It was tiny, a windowless and charmless space, distinguished only by the heavy door which had once been fitted with a complex lock, and – if I may say so – by a fine mosaic floor.

Marcus – who had added extensions to the house, including a new study for himself elsewhere – had little use for that tiny room these days. It was generally used as an anteroom for slaves except on occasions such as this when it furnished a near-perfect spot for accommodating the huge glazed bowl on its stand, the supply of goose feathers in their great brass pot and the bucket of perfumed water for rinsing lips and hands when the purpose of one's visit had been fulfilled.

Even then, it was not quite ideal. Once a diner had arrived to use the facility, there was no space in there for anything else, not even for the usual attendant slave. The luckless boy whose function at such feasts was to stand by and periodically empty out the bowl and replenish the water in the pail was generally obliged to wait outside, in the verandahed colonnade which – as in many country homes built in the Roman style – ran round the courtyard garden and linked the series of individual private rooms in the rear wings to each other and to the central portion of the house. The colonnade was open on the inner side, so waiting out there in the biting draught must have been a cold and thankless task tonight.

Meanwhile, we were waiting too. Now Marcus seemed to have disappeared as well. The guests were getting slightly fidgety, and even the array of household slaves, lined up patiently beside the wall, were glancing at each other nervously.

Finally, it was Mellitus who spoke. 'What can have happened to our host? The vomitorium is just next door.'

There was a little rustle of undisguised relief. Mellitus was the senior man present and now that he had taken charge, the next step was up to him.

Mellitus frowned. 'They surely cannot have gone very far.' He picked up Praxus's goblet, sniffed at it disapprovingly and put it down again. 'Perhaps our military friend is taken ill? It would hardly be surprising, given the quantity he drank.'

There was another pause. Marcus and Praxus did not come back. More guests were perching themselves on the edges of their dining couches by now, though nobody had actually reclined again.

At last Mellitus did what we hoped he'd do. 'Well, we cannot be expected to stay here all night. You,' he indicated the nearest slave, 'go and find out what's happening.'

This time we did not have very long to wait. The slave was back in a moment, ashen-faced. 'Your pardon, Excellence,' he said to Mellitus. 'There seems to have been an accident. A serious accident. I am sent to request the citizen Libertus to come with me at once.'

II

This announcement caused a considerable sensation, not least in my stomach, which lurched alarmingly. What would the notoriously self-important Mellitus think of this – an anonymous citizen being specifically asked to join Marcus, when the sub-procurator himself was overlooked? However, there was nothing for it but to go.

I did not remain anonymous for long. Heads turned as I shuffled from my humble corner place and threaded my way towards the door. Five tables, with three couches each, meant that even this fine *triclinium* was packed and forty-two pairs of eyes were fixed on me. Mellitus, in particular, was staring at me with undisguised hostility.

I attempted to make my exit as unobtrusive as I could, with a brief required bow in his direction as I went, but before I had reached the doorway he called after me.

'Citizen?' That was all he said, but what he meant was: *Who in Mithras' name are you, and why should you be summoned? I am the most important person here.*

I made a proper obeisance, this time, as I replied, 'My name is Longinius Flavius Libertus, Excellence. Marcus is my patron and he sometimes calls on me if there's an . . . incident.' 'Problem' would have been a better word. That was another thing which worried me, in fact. If Marcus wanted me, there was something mysterious, and probably dangerous, afoot.

Mellitus looked even sourer than before, but he forced a little laugh. 'I see. Well, if your skills are so much in demand, pray do not let a mere sub-procurator delay you any more. Don't keep your patron waiting. Go.'

I went.

It was not difficult to see where I should go, even without the slave to lead me there. Outside in the colonnade there was a little crowd. Every spare slave from house and kitchen had evidently been called to bring torches to the scene, and they were clustered round the adjacent doorway with their backs to me, peering forward and holding their smoking lights aloft. The slave who had fetched me went ahead, parting their ranks to let me through, and a moment later I was standing outside the entrance to the vomitorium.

What met my eyes was not a pretty sight. Praxus was lying slumped across the bowl, his face submerged in that disgusting mess. His massive body blocked the entranceway, hairy legs emerging obscenely from the pale blue robe and protruding at an awkward angle into the passageway. Marcus had already squeezed past into the room, and now he looked up and gestured me to come.

It was not easy. I was obliged to step between Praxus's feet – huge sandals with the hobnails uppermost – and over the enormous bulk that blocked the door, before I could edge into the narrow space to join my patron.

'Libertus!' he cried, before I could say anything. Clearly there was no time for ceremony. 'I'll need your help. I don't know quite what's happened here, but anyway we'll have to move him first. I told the slaves to lift him, and several of them tried, but they can't. There's only room for one here at a time, and they can't get round him to grasp him properly. See what you can do, Libertus, before it's too late.'

I forbore to mention that it was clearly far too late already, or that – although Marcus could hardly be expected to lift Praxus up himself – I was also supposed to be a guest. However, I did suggest what the slaves would not have dared, that if Marcus were to move there would be more room to operate. He looked surprised. He didn't seem to have thought of that himself: shock seemed to have robbed him of the power of thought, though there was a degree of sense in his request to me. As one who handles heavy blocks of stone I have some expertise in lifting things.

Marcus nodded at me distractedly. 'I had to come and see what had happened. Have this, if it's any use to you.' He passed me the brass pot that had contained the goose feathers, which he'd been clasping to him like a talisman. 'Perhaps you could also . . .' He gestured towards the bowl.

Praxus's banqueting wreath had unwound itself and fallen off. It was floating bizarrely by his ear on the malodorous pool of half-digested delicacies and regurgitated wine. It seemed an odd thing to be concerned about, but these symbols are important to patrician Roman men.

It was my turn to nod. 'In just a moment, Excellence.' I put down the pot and waited until my patron had edged past me and picked his way distastefully back to the corridor, where Mellitus and half the company of guests – who had by this time followed me – were openly assembled, craning to peer in. Curiosity had evidently got the better of good manners in the end.

I endeavoured to ignore my audience and position myself for the lift by planting one foot on either side of what was, by now, undoubtedly a corpse. I had planned to slide my hands round underneath the arms: but, as Marcus had correctly observed, that was impossible – not only because of the angle at which Praxus lay, but also because my toga would not permit me to straddle that huge girth. I was obliged to give up in the end, and try to raise him from the side.

There was evidence of previous attempts to do this when I moved the drapes of his synthesis aside. A red line of bruise ran round the neck, under the edge of that ridiculous blue robe, and the material at one point had parted in a jagged tear, as if someone had grasped the cloth there in struggling to lift him up, and it had given way beneath the weight. I did not want to make the same mistake. I laced my hands round underneath his neck and hauled.

To no avail. I only succeeded in raising the head and shoulders an inch or two. Try as I would, I could do no more than that. Even then, it was an awkward lift, and in the end I let him go again. Praxus's head dropped back into the bowl, but at a different angle now, tipping some of the contents in my direction as it fell.

I scrambled sharply to my feet, but not quite in time. The splashing slime made contact with my knees. There was a murmur of laughter from the spectators, and in the torch-light I was aware of grinning faces watching me. Even the slaves who held the lights were having to suppress their smiles. Only two men did not seem at all amused: Mellitus, who was looking on with pained disgust, and Marcus himself, whose expression conveyed something closer to despair.

He was right to be dismayed. The death of an important guest during a banquet at one's house is always socially unfortunate. When the visitor in question is a senior member of the military and has just been appointed with you as a member of a regional triumvirate, it is also a political embarrassment – an embarrassment made even more acute if the man is drowned in vomit and gawped at by a crowd.

Poor Marcus. No wonder he had attempted to extract his guest before news of the manner of his death got out. He had intended, no doubt, to have Praxus moved somewhere a little more salubrious before announcing his in any case unfortunate demise.

I could feel some sympathy for Praxus too, although I had never liked the little I knew of him – unimaginative, inflexible and crass. The man who had so recently been a favoured appointee of the Emperor was subject to a double indignity: being sniggered at, as well as dead. And there was worse to come. There was only one way of moving him that I could see, and since Marcus was looking at me expectantly and something was obviously required, I voiced my thoughts.

'I think we'll have to drag him, Excellence. If I stay this end, and support his head, perhaps some of your slaves could take him by the feet? I think it might be managed then, without upsetting . . . everything.'

Marcus nodded. He turned towards his slaves. 'Six of the strongest among you do as he suggests.' The dinner guests reluctantly stepped back and half a dozen burly kitchen slaves came forward in their place. Three of them ranged themselves on either leg.

'Stand back,' Mellitus advised, and the crowd unwillingly complied. I seized the hair and raised the head again – without kneeling on the floor this time – and on my cry of 'Now' the servants hauled, and the unfortunate Praxus slithered and bounced, still face downwards, out into the passageway. His pale blue synthesis rode upwards in the process, displaying a pair of huge and hairy buttocks and an inadequate pair of leather underpants. His hands, which trailed behind him, slithered through the patch where I had knelt.

I watched him go, and then – mindful of what my patron had required of me – I went back and, using the brass feather-pot as an implement, carefully fished out the bedraggled festive wreath.

Feeling rather in need of the facilities myself, by this time, I put the pot down, then turned aside and scrubbed my hands and soiled toga enthusiastically in the water bucket – which by some act of the gods had remained standing upright all this time. However, the goose feathers, and a large potted plant which had been placed in the far corner of the room in some attempt to beautify the space, had been knocked over in the disturbance, and now lay with the rest of the noisome rubbish on the floor. It seemed that some of the plant had fallen in the water too – at least, I hoped it was the plant. There was something unpleasantly soft and slippery at the bottom of the pail.

I flinched as my fingers touched it, and dried them hastily.

By the time I made my way into the corridor, the group was crowding round Marcus and the body once again. The portly priest of Jupiter, who (despite Jove's connection with the army) was not supposed to see a corpse, was standing at the back, complaining loudly that this was a dreadful omen and portended woe, but at the same time stretching on tiptoe to get a better view. Only Mellitus kept himself aloof. He had been standing in the shadows, but suddenly he stepped into the ring of light from the torches and declaimed in his thin piercing voice, 'This is what happens when people have no restraint at feasts, and encourage other men to drink too much.'

There was a sudden hush. It was such an obvious attack on Marcus that I was surprised that my patron did not protest. Instead he met the procurator's eyes, and said in an expressionless voice, 'Praxus did drink rather more than was good for him tonight. I ordered the servants to water down his wine, but he drank so much of it that it made very little difference, in the end.'

Mellitus looked gratified. 'Perhaps it is a good thing for Glevum, after all. What sort of respect would such a man inspire?' People were turning to look at him by now and he adopted a posture like a politician, clutching the shoulder-drape of his toga with one hand as he spoke. 'A person who cannot govern himself is not fit to govern others. May the gods protect us from such leadership. See what his excess has brought him to, because he could not hold his drink. Ignominy. Desecration. Death!'

There was a little smatter of applause at this, as Mellitus had no doubt hoped, It was more oratory than conversation, but an assembly of magistrates and councillors enjoys such rhetoric, and the speech was certainly more polished than poor Loquex's verse.

Something that Mellitus had said, however, gave me cause for thought. I made my way over towards my patron, who was still standing by the corpse. The slaves had just rolled Praxus over, and as I approached I got my first glimpse of that distorted face, under the clinging wet festoons of Jove knows what.

If I had taken a moment to consider, I should not have uttered the words which were on my lips. As it was, I spoke before I thought.

'Your pardon, Excellence, but it occurs to me that it is rather strange that Praxus, of all people, should find himself so incapacitated by wine. He is such a giant of a man, and as a soldier surely he must be accustomed to drinking heavily.' Marcus was staring at me fixedly, but he said nothing and I blundered on, anxious to make him understand. Usually he values my ability to see the implications of events, and I assumed that this was why he'd called me from the feast, and also what he wanted of me now. 'He must have swallowed a prodigious quantity, don't you think, to fall into the bowl like that and be unable to help himself? Surely there must be some other factor at work here?'

My foolish tongue! Too late, I recognised my patron's warning frown. I looked down at Praxus's upturned face again. Blue lips, protruding tongue and bulging eyes. Marcus had realised what I had not. Praxus had not simply fallen in and drowned: someone had either poisoned him or – given that red mark round the neck – pulled a cord round his throat and throttled him. Perhaps even both – Praxus would be no easy man to kill. And all this here, in Marcus's house, after he had been drinking Marcus's wine.

I did my best to undo what I'd done. 'Possibly he had been drinking earlier? Or was he ill, perhaps? Did you have any inkling that he was unwell?'

'He was perfectly all right five minutes earlier!' That was Mellitus, who had moved forward now and was standing at my side with a calculating and gratified expression on his face. 'It is obvious, my esteemed . . . Libertus, is it? . . . why your patron wanted you. You evidently have a swift grasp of events.' The thin lips curved in an unpleasant smile. 'Did you hear, gentlemen, what this clever citizen observed? Praxus was hardly a man to be overcome by drink – however excellent the Falernian wine – and besides, he was the only one affected, it appears.'

Not quite the only one, I thought, remembering how swiftly my table companion had succumbed, but I kept that observation to myself. Around me my fellow guests were murmuring assent and distancing themselves from Marcus by degrees.

'Yet Marcus says he watered down the wine before it was served to Praxus, specifically.' The sub-procurator's mirthless smile widened. With his fleshless cheeks, his face reminded me obscurely of a skull. 'That is particularly strange. I wonder what he ordered it to be watered *with*?'

The mood was getting dangerous. There were distinct ripples of unease by now. I was aware of whisperings in the crowd. 'Marcus? Never!' 'Well, you can't be sure.' 'That pavement-maker's right – Praxus is too big simply to get drunk like that, and so quickly too. Besides, Marcus quarrelled with him only yesterday, I heard.'

I could have cursed myself for what I'd done. The fear of trouble, even by association, spreads like fire in a store of hay. Several of the more cautious councillors, I noticed, had already slipped back into the dining room and others were following one by one.

The small page-boy who had been in attendance at the vomitorium all evening had brought a bucket of water from the spring at the *nympheum*, the sacred pool within the grounds that formed the villa's chief water supply. Now, at Marcus's instruction, he bent and cleaned the face. It looked more grotesque than ever, and more guests withdrew. A moment later Marcus's Nubian slave appeared.

He bowed his head and murmured, 'Master, some of the councillors are asking for their personal slaves. Should I fetch them down?' Personal attendants, like my own Junio, having delivered their masters to the feast, are always shown to the servants' quarters at the rear and offered a more meagre supper of their own.

21

Marcus nodded his assent. The Nubian seized a torch and went, and very soon a huddle of attendant slaves was following him back down the colonnade, avoiding our corner even with their eyes. Marcus looked at me and raised his brows. He knew as well as I did what was happening. The first of his well-fed visitors had abandoned all pretence at dignity and were making a panic-stricken retreat into the night, like soldiers deserting a losing general.

He made an attempt to reassert control. 'This is certainly unfortunate. Praxus has sustained an accident . . .'

Mellitus interrupted him. 'Ah, but as this perceptive citizen points out, it does not seem to *be* an accident.' He addressed himself to the few guests who still remained. 'Now I have a problem, gentlemen, you see. I have the highest possible opinion of our host, of course. Yet Gaius Flaminius Praxus is clearly dead. If he was not simply overcome by drink, then – as our friend observes – there must have been some other factor at work here. Someone must have drugged him in some way, or given him something poisonous to eat, and then – when he came out here, already weak – managed to drown him in the vomitorium.'

There was a gasp of horrified assent.

'It must have been something of the kind. Praxus was too big to overcome in any other way,' Mellitus went on urgently. 'But hear me, citizens. Given that this is Marcus's house and that we have eaten Marcus's food and wine, *and* that only Marcus's slaves were in the colonnade, I cannot – unless someone can persuade me otherwise – see any other explanation but that Marcus, or one of his household, had a hand in this. Of course, it was cleverly designed to look like a mischance.'

There were mutterings of reluctant agreement now. Even

the priest of Jupiter joined in. 'It seems that the procurator's right. Now I come to think of it, Marcus was standing in there with the corpse. I saw him there myself.'

Marcus said sharply, 'This is preposterous. This death is as much a mystery to me as it is to you. I simply came out and found him lying there.'

Mellitus said doubtfully, 'Perhaps there is someone who can vouch for that? Where was the attendant at the time?' He whirled on the little page-boy with the water bucket. 'Well?'

'I was collecting water from the spring.'

Mellitus smiled. 'How extraordinarily convenient. And why did you choose that moment for your errand, so late on in the feast? Did you receive an order from your master, perhaps?'

The boy turned pale. 'I . . .' He stopped, and looked at Marcus helplessly.

Marcus said furiously, 'I did not send him!'

'But . . .' the slave began, and stopped again. He was sweating and clearly terrified, but none of the sub-procurator's savage questioning could make him utter another word.

'It does not signify,' Mellitus said at last, with a contemptuous laugh, giving the boy a push which sent him sprawling to the ground. 'We shall get the truth out of him in the end.'

I felt a chill run down my spine. I knew what that meant, and so did everyone else who witnessed it. When an important man is suspected of a crime within his house, his slaves are routinely tortured to discover what they know, since the authorities assume that loyalty to their master will otherwise drive them to lie in his defence.

'By Mithras, don't you dare treat my attendants so . . .' Marcus stepped forward to protect his slave, but then stopped in alarm. Clattering into the colonnade came half a dozen

Roman guards, in military uniform and armed. Before them they pushed Marcus's wretched doorkeeper, his arm twisted cruelly behind his back.

'Master, I attempted to prevent them . . .' he began, and broke off with a cry of pain.

'We are Praxus's personal bodyguard,' the biggest fellow said. He had a big, blunt square head and small eyes like a bull. 'One of the departing guests told us that he was hurt.'

'Dead,' Mellitus corrected, and stepped aside to let them see the corpse. 'And therefore it is my unpleasant duty, I'm afraid – and I call on these councillors and citizens to witness this – to formally accuse this man' – he pointed towards Marcus – 'of killing him, or, if not that, of having him killed by slaves in his employ. Balbus, have him seized.'

Everyone looked on, appalled. This was a formal indictment under law. Calvinus Nonnius Balbus was the corpulent decurion who had sniggered earlier at the poet's verse. As president of the town council he was also its senior magistrate, so during his year's term of office he was second in precedence only to Marcus himself. He was not sniggering now. He simply gave a little helpless moan and twittered indecisively, fingering his silver toga-clasp as though it were a charm. The few other guests who had remained glanced at one another doubtfully, uncertain what to do. However, the bull-like guard did not hesitate. He drew his sword and signalled to his men.

What followed was not a dignified affair. Marcus, after a startled glance at me, took to his heels and tried to run. He set off across the inner garden to the gate, while his slaves closed ranks to try to cover him. One of them, who was carrying a torch, lashed out with it, setting a soldier's beard and hair alight. He was instantly cut down. The visiting dignitaries, shocked and splashed with blood, huddled in doorways and under arches as if turned to stone – like the statues in their damp niches near the garden pool, where two of the soldiers had caught up with Marcus now.

We could just make out their burly silhouettes against the misty dark as they tumbled him to the ground, seized him none too gently by the arms and hauled him to his feet.

III

It was all over fairly quickly after that. The household servants were even now prepared to fight, but the soldiery had swords and they had none – and Marcus himself commanded them to cease.

He had been brought back to us at sword-point, his fine purple-edged toga mudstained and his wreath awry. He was panting and distraught, but he still retained his dignity. His face blanched when he saw his servant's bloodied corpse. 'There is some terrible mistake,' he said at last.

Balbus said weakly, 'There will have to be a trial, I suppose. Oh, Great Minerva! And when I had only a few months to serve!'

'I shall appeal to the Emperor, of course.' Marcus spoke angrily.

Even Mellitus was looking shaken now. He said, 'Of course you must. There was no need for that.' He rounded on the soldiers. 'This is an outrage, you confounded sons of dogs! Can't you see from his toga that this is a man of noble birth? From now on treat him with appropriate respect. I shall see that your new commander hears of this.' He turned to the still cowering dinner guests. 'As you are my witnesses, citizens, I asked only that Marcus be accused. I did not call for bloodshed or drawn swords.'

Bullface said sullenly, 'Wouldn't have been called for if he hadn't run away. And as for that confounded slave, it is an offence to strike a Roman guard – let alone set fire to his beard. He would have had worse coming to him from the courts.'

Balbus seemed to find his tongue. 'There is some truth in that. And, Marcus . . . Excellence . . . at the very worst, the court could surely only sentence you to be "deprived of water and of fire".' He was intending to be comforting. That sentence means exile beyond the Empire, effectively, since a man cannot live without fire and water for very long, and is a sub-capital punishment for the privileged. Balbus meant that Marcus, reputed to be related to the Emperor, would not readily be condemned to death, even if a charge of murder could be proved.

Marcus, however, seemed unimpressed by this. 'Balbus, do not be a fool.'

I frowned at him. I knew that he had little time for Balbus: in fact I had once heard him publicly describe the twittering decurion as 'more ambitious than his talents merited, and ready to lick anybody's feet if he thought it would advance him by an inch'. (Only, of course, Marcus had not actually said 'feet'.) But Balbus was now clearly in command, and this was not a moment to betray contempt.

Marcus however, seemed oblivious. 'I have done nothing! Nothing, do you hear?'

'There's . . .' Bullface began again, but he was interrupted by a female voice.

'What is the meaning of all this? Marcus, husband! What is happening here?'

All heads turned, and there was a sharp gasp from the assembled company. Julia Delicta, Marcus's young wife, had come through from the new wing of the house. She was always beautiful, but I thought that I had never seen her more lovely than now, standing there in her simple shift in that misty colonnade, her hair twisted up into a hasty coil, with only a thin cloak to shield her from the cold and flimsy embroidered slippers on her feet.

There was a general shuffle of embarrassment and shock. Respectable Roman matrons were not supposed to appear on banquet nights before the guests had all gone safely home, unless by special invitation of the host, and especially not in such inadequate attire.

'Madam citizen!' Mellitus reproved.

But Julia ignored him, and came on. It was extremely brave. She must have felt utterly vulnerable and alone: her husband was arrested, there were two bodies on the floor, the house was full of men she did not know, she was inappropriately dressed for company and it was only a few weeks since she had given birth – even now two of her serving women were at her side to offer her support. Yet she faced the armed contingent with a defiance and energy which put the rest of us to shame.

'How dare you treat my husband in this way? What has been happening here?' she cried. Her voice was firm but there were tears trembling on her eyelids and an anguish in her glance which would have melted a statue's heart.

Mellitus, though, was a Roman official of the most old-fashioned kind. Women, even wealthy and beautiful ones, were of no account. 'Lady, do not meddle in masculine affairs. Your husband has been formally accused of homicide and arrested. He will be taken to the garrison under guard, and now the law must take its course.'

'Homicide!' The lady looked as if she might collapse. 'But

that's absurd.' She looked down at Praxus and the slaughtered slave. 'Oh, dear Jupiter. What has happened here? That is poor Paulus, our attendant – who has murdered him?'

'Stand back, lady,' said Bullface, interposing dangerously and raising his sword again. 'You heard what the procurator said.'

Balbus attempted to intervene. 'You will be informed when a decision has been reached, and appropriate arrangements will be made for you,' he said, as though talking to a child. Of course, in the eyes of the law, he was.

'But, citizen . . .' Julia was about to protest again, but the guard cut her short.

'Lady, go back to your quarters and get dressed. No harm will come to you – provided that your husband will come quietly.'

It was a threat – unsubtle, but it did the trick. Marcus capitulated instantly.

'Julia, my dear, do not distress yourself. There is obviously some mistake. No doubt my old friend Libertus will help sort it out. In the meantime there is nothing you can do here. You are putting yourself in danger and will catch a chill. Go back to your quarters and take care of yourself – and of the boy.' Marcus was inordinately proud of his baby son.

Julia looked at the bodies on the floor, and murmured 'But . . .' again, and then lapsed obediently into silence.

'There has been an unfortunate accident, but I have done nothing wrong. All the same, it seems I will have to bow to superior force, and go with these soldiers to the garrison. Libertus, I leave matters here to you. I'm sure the truth will shortly come to light.' He turned to his slaves, who were still standing hesitantly by. 'Thank you, my servants, for defending me. I do not expect to be away for long. Obey your mistress in my absence.'

His wife looked helplessly at him. 'As you command, my husband,' she said reluctantly. 'Libertus, I would be glad if you'd attend me later on, when this is over.' And, leaning on her handmaidens, she left.

Mellitus watched her go. 'It seems you're very much in demand tonight, Citizen Libertus. Perhaps the lady will be in need of some support. We'll have to search the villa later on, and probably round the servants up as well.'

'The servants!' Marcus looked appalled. He knew, better than any of us, what lay in wait for them. A slave's testimony against his master is always sought in law, but is not valid unless extorted under torture. 'The servants could have had nothing to do with it. Search the villa if you like. I tell you my household had no part in this. You might as well suggest that you would check the guests, to make sure they're not concealing poison phials in their belts!'

Mellitus gave his mirthless smile. 'An excellent suggestion, citizen. I should be the first to volunteer to undergo the search. Or perhaps your slaves could tell us where to look?'

My patron flushed. 'My slaves are innocent! There were forty people here who can testify to where most of my servants were when Praxus died.'

'That is quite true, Excellence.' Balbus seemed suddenly concerned to support his erstwhile host. 'Those who were attending us in the dining room cannot have had any part in this.'

Bullface stuck his chin out and said nastily, 'It is my duty to take them in for questioning. Anyone who was serving here tonight. And I shall oversee the search myself. An army commander has been murdered here.'

Balbus was still trying to mediate. 'Perhaps it is not necessary to arrest them all – not straight away, at least. Only

31

those who were present in the colonnade after the final sacrifice to Jove. If His Excellence Marcus Aurelius Septimus would order the rest to stay here in the house . . .'

Marcus understood. This was an opportunity to save his slaves. 'Those are my orders. No slave is to leave the villa until I am released.'

'Or sentenced,' Mellitus put in. 'To cover every eventuality, that is.'

'Or sentenced,' Marcus said, unwillingly, and the deed was done. The servants were effectively incarcerated now. They would be classed as runaways if they tried to leave, and that was a capital offence. If they were caught and brought back, they could expect to be tortured to death, whether or not they had anything to tell. Interrogators merely extorting information generally stopped short of that.

Mellitus nodded slowly. 'Capital.' He turned to the apprehensive slaves. 'So who was out here at the time?'

Perhaps unsurprisingly, nobody moved. Mellitus looked furious. 'Then we'll take those who were out here holding lights. And those who were not here at all, but might have useful information – including that page-boy with the pail and that fool of a doorman over there . . .' He gestured to where the unfortunate doorkeeper in question was still shivering in the shadows of the doorway where he had been pushed.

I realised that I could not see the pail-boy anywhere. Presumably, in the disturbances, he had taken the opportunity to run away, and at any moment now his presence would be missed. And then . . .?

Suddenly my blood ran chill. Why the thought had not occurred to me earlier, I cannot explain (unless perhaps I too had been imbibing an unaccustomed quantity of Falernian wine, when I very seldom drink any wine at all, preferring the more robust ales and mead of my Celtic youth). If my patron and his household staff were taken under guard, then it might not be long before somebody decided to bring me in for questioning as well – after all, I was known to be his close associate and this evening had been singled out by name. Rather belatedly, I decided, as several of the lingering dinner guests had already done, that it would be conducive to my health to ensure that I was somewhere else as soon as possible.

Fortunately, Marcus's wife had furnished an excuse, and I could take my leave without appearing to desert my patron in his hour of need. Not that I could have done anything immediate to help, in any case: Marcus had been formally arrested by the authorities, and the best assistance I could render now was to find some way of persuading them that this was a mistake.

'If you will excuse me, gentlemen, I must attend the lady Julia,' I began, in my best ingratiating voice, but it was a waste of time. Nobody was paying the slightest attention to me.

Bullface had just noticed that the bucket-boy had gone.

'Where is he? Where is that confounded boy?' He had his dagger drawn by now as well as his sword, and was jabbing both of them in the air in front of the bewildered guests, as if by doing so he could prod the truth from them. 'Come on, if you know what's good for you. One of you must have seen something. Where's the boy?'

'Mellitus!' Gaius, the old ex-councillor who'd sat next to me, was sober now and had clearly been pushed forward to protest. He twitched at his toga to assert authority, but his voice had become high-pitched and wavering. 'This must be stopped at once. This sword-waving is an insult to our dignity.

We are not landless peasants to be treated in this way: we are councillors and magistrates, members of the *ordo* of the town – and not just a common town, but a military colonia with full republican rights! An affront to us is an insult not just to Glevum but to the whole Empire and to Rome.'

Everyone began to speak at once, and suddenly pandemonium broke loose.

'Where is the boy?' Bullface insisted in a roar.

'It isn't . . .' Mellitus, trying to keep the peace.

'I don't know . . .' The doorkeeper, as one of the soldiers twisted his arm behind him once again.

Balbus and the other guests were still protesting too. 'By all the deities . . .'

The high priest of Jupiter was muttering something at my side. He seemed to be invoking all the gods. It may have been an incantation or a prayer, but I interrupted anyway. I touched his sleeve.

He leapt to face me as if burnt and I murmured soothingly, 'I must attend the lady Julia at once, since Marcus has nominated me her guardian. I did try to explain, but they did not hear. If anyone asks for me, that's where I'll be. I'll look out for the page-boy on my way.'

I did not wait to see his startled nod. Taking advantage of the chaos created by the noise and the flickering shadows of the torchlit search, which was now beginning in the colonnade, I slipped away, taking the long route through the now empty triclinium and the central block, and through the side entrance to the even more opulent owner's wing beyond, which Marcus had so recently had built.

It was as well I knew my way. Eerily – for any mansion on this scale – there were few oil lamps burning in the corridors, and there was not a solitary slave in sight.

IV

Julia was waiting in her dressing room, a little ante-room next to the smaller of the two adjoining bedchambers which Marcus had constructed for their use. The original master of the house was not a married man, and all the bedrooms round the central colonnade – though luxurious – were self-contained: small individual rooms which opened off the court. This further wing had been my patron's fantasy, a tribute to his beautiful new wife, and he had showed me proudly round it when it was complete.

It consisted of this connubial suite (well-bred Roman couples always have separate rooms, a practice I have never understood), a nursery and a servants' room nearby, and a fine new librarium as well, all situated around another little walled enclosure containing a statue of Venus and a lily pond. The extension to the front façade, through which I'd just approached, also provided another small triclinium, an intimate dining area the family had used when the approaching birth had kept Julia from any public gaze, and where she could still dine in comfort and apart on purely masculine occasions such as tonight's. I still hoped for a commission for a floor in there – the current plastered one was only a temporary expedient, hurriedly laid down by the builder to ensure that the room was ready by the promised date.

'Libertus.' Julia rose to her feet to welcome me. She had

been sitting on a little gilded stool, surrounded by her maids, and was now demurely dressed in a warm dark-coloured Grecian robe with a cloak around her shoulders and her arms, and her hair obscured by its handsome hood. Of course, it was much more fitting garb, for both the climate and the company, but I was a little disappointed at the change. I may be an old man – at over fifty I am one of the oldest men in Glevum – but I am still susceptible to female charms.

She misinterpreted my glance and shook her head. 'It was foolish of me to come out like that, I know, but I did not stop to think. I was told that they'd seized Marcus, so I came just as I was. However, I have recovered my wits now, as you see.'

'I see that you have wrapped up against the cold.'

She gave a bitter laugh. 'And against the wagging of malicious tongues. With Marcus gone, there might be allegations of impropriety. Of course the idea is perfectly absurd, old friend – no one could imagine you in such a role – but those who have trumped up charges against my husband would no doubt gladly do the same against his wife.'

I nodded glumly. Her absolute discounting of me as a virile male was hardly flattering, but I did see what she meant. She was alone in private with a man at night and in her personal quarters too. It was most unusual for anyone but the spouse to bring charges of adultery, but it was not utterly impossible, and for those found guilty of the crime the punishment was cruel.

I said, 'Marcus has appointed me your guardian. It would be hard to make an accusation stick, even if there was anyone to bring a charge. Besides, you have your maidservants as witnesses.' This was thin comfort, as we were both aware: the presence of slaves – especially female ones – would hardly signify. However, my own words did give me an idea. 'Perhaps you could send one of your attendants to go and fetch my slave as well? He will be waiting in the servants' quarters in the main part of the house.'

She gave a wan smile. 'Of course. Cilla, see to it.' She nodded to one of the handmaidens, a large and rather lumpy girl, who trotted off at once. All the time that I'd known Julia, she'd always surrounded herself with unattractive maids, not out of compassion for their plight, to offer the poor things employ, but so that she could sparkle the more in comparison. It was an unnecessary and rather disappointing vanity. Julia would have sparkled in any company. Even now in the flickering light from the oil lamps, muffled in a cloak and looking tired and strained, she was astonishingly beautiful. If I did not have a dear and much-loved woman of my own, I might have envied Marcus his delightful wife.

One of the female slaves had brought a stool for me, but I preferred to stand. Julia, however, sank down again and muttered in a breaking voice, 'Libertus, what are we going to do? To accuse Marcus – Marcus! – of murdering a guest! And a senior officer in the army, too! Of course my husband hated Praxus, we all knew that, but Marcus would have contained his power in other ways. This is simply unbelievable!'

'Contained his power?' I must have been peculiarly dense that night.

Julia seemed to think so. She gave me a startled look. 'Of course. The three of them were to rule the area, under Pertinax's nominal control, until the new provincial governor is installed. Surely you were aware of that?'

I was, of course. I nodded.

'Praxus seemed to think that, since he had the army under his command, he was the one with ultimate authority. Obviously Marcus was not happy about that. He was the senior man, if anything – he was named as the governor's personal representative in Glevum long ago. And not only that, Marcus was concerned about the rule of law. Praxus has come here from Gaul, and his idea of exercising power there was always to use his forces first and ask questions afterwards.'

I looked at her with admiration. How many pampered Roman wives could give so cogent an account of their husbands' political concerns? Marcus was a lucky man indeed. I said, 'And they quarrelled about that? I heard that there had been an argument.'

Julia coloured. Even in the shadowy light I could see that the cheeks beneath the hood were flushed with red – and not merely from the brazier at her side. 'Not exactly that,' she muttered awkwardly.

'What then?' My mind was on disturbances in Gaul. There had been several recent instances of civilian unrest in that province, which the army had repeatedly put down. Perhaps Praxus's methods had been needed there. But in Britannia it had been the other way. Here it was a group of legionaries who'd rebelled, wanting to overthrow the Emperor and set up Governor Pertinax in his place, until Pertinax himself loyally subdued them, and denounced the ringleaders to Rome. The whole event had almost got him killed – one reason why he'd begged to be replaced. It had also won him mortal enemies among those jostling for Imperial regard and, since Marcus had supported Pertinax throughout, presumably my patron might be a target too. This was a seriously worrying thought.

Julia's answer to my question, therefore, astonished me. 'I was the cause of the quarrel, I'm afraid.'

'You?'

'Praxus had just come from Gaul. Marcus presented me to him – he was after all a guest in our house – but Praxus, well . . .! His behaviour was positively uncivilised. He started with lewd looks and ribald jokes. Then, when he heard that I'd just had a child, he made some extremely coarse remarks about what Marcus must have done to bring that about, and suggested that he'd like to do the same – with graphic variations on the theme. He seemed to expect Marcus to be flattered and amused. All this in my presence, too, as if I had no ears.'

'And Marcus took exception to all this?'

'Well, not at first, at least not publicly. He kept telling me that Praxus was a military man, and used to soldiers' ways, how he couldn't marry till he surrendered his command and very likely had to leave a would-be wife in Gaul, and that anyway we should forgive him because he was a guest. Oh, Marcus made every excuse for him at first. And then Praxus asked for a female slave to bring a phial of oil to his room, and used her when she came, without so much as asking our permission first. That did it. Marcus really lost his temper then. That was more than simply uncouth words, he said, it was a kind of theft.'

I nodded, closing my eyes in horror at the tale. My wife Gwellia had been a slave – captured into servitude with me when we were young – and though she never talked about those years, every time I caught a glimpse of what her life must have been it struck chill to my heart. I had been luckier: although I was mistreated for a while, I was sold at last to a just and wealthy man who had not only had me taught a trade, but bequeathed me my freedom when he died.

Julia, though, was typically Roman in her attitude. She nodded, misinterpreting my pain. 'Unforgivable, was it not? And Praxus seemed to feel that he'd done nothing wrong – that any slave was simply his to take, as if he was the Emperor himself. I think that is really what sparked the quarrel off. One thing led to another then, and harsh words were said, until Marcus threatened to take him to the courts. Then Praxus did calm down a little. He even apologised, after a fashion, saying that if a guest of his had asked for a female slave he would have known how to interpret it; and that he was sorry if he'd offended me, but he thought that as I'd been married twice before I was no shrinking virgin to be horrified by a man's carnal needs.'

It was true. Julia had been once widowed, once divorced, although that had not prevented her from marrying again: indeed it had simply increased her dowry. The Romans have a laxer attitude to these things than we Celts. As an apology, however, it left much to be desired. I found myself grinning slightly, for the first time that night, though there was little enough to smile at, even now.

Julia gave a tiny laugh. 'I know, old friend. It is bizarre. Then, in his anxiety to heal the breach, Praxus asked my husband – in all seriousness, it seems – whether he would be prepared to divorce me again, now that he had his son and heir, so that Praxus could marry me himself.'

'But I thought . . .'

'In a few months' time, of course, when this interregnum is over. Praxus would be old enough by then, and if he chose to do so he could draw his pension and retire. He was a wealthy man, he said, and he invited Marcus to name the "fee". He even offered to give him a substantial sum to ensure that no one else could negotiate for me between now and then! And when Marcus protested, Praxus looked surprised again, and said that people do this all the time in Rome. He didn't ask me what I thought.'

'And what did you think?' I asked, although I was pretty sure I knew the answer anyway.

'That hairy giant?' Julia looked appalled. 'I'd run a knife between his ribs – or mine – before I'd marry him. He cleans his fingernails with his teeth, and spits.'

'He did,' I said. 'He doesn't any more. And, lady – Julia – take care what you say. It was not a knife between the ribs, but someone did murder him. The Emperor has spies everywhere. I'm sure your slaves are loyal, but you never know who may be listening.'

As if on cue, a shadow detached itself from the darkness of the court. Another larger shadow followed it. My heart gave a lurch and Julia clutched my arm, but then a familiar voice said, 'Master?' and I breathed again.

It was my attendant, Junio, and the lumpy slave who had gone to find him from the house. 'Mistress, I am sorry if we startled you,' the girl said. 'And you too, citizen. But there is such a commotion in the house that I thought it better to come the long way round and bring the slave by the back gate. Even so, we just escaped the guards. They are hunting for Golbo. They have been everywhere in the main part of the house, and – oh, madam – I believe they will come here very soon and question you. What will you tell them if they do?'

'That he is not here, of course, since he very evidently is not,' Julia said quickly.

Too quickly. Suddenly my brain, which had been lulled to sleep by too much wine, struggled into consciousness again. Golbo was the bucket-boy who had disappeared. 'But he was here, wasn't he? Dear lady, do not attempt to deny the truth, especially to me. How can I hope to help you otherwise? Of course the boy was here. How else did you hear the news that Marcus had been seized? No one else left the colonnade after the guards arrived.'

'With respect, master, that is not entirely true,' Junio put in. 'A slave came from the banquet hall several times to fetch servants from the waiting room when their owners wanted to go home, both before the soldiers came, and afterwards.' He gave me his familiar cheeky grin. 'I was hoping you were going to call for me, but it was a long time before you did. In the end there were only a half a dozen of us there – apart from Praxus's and Mellitus's personal slaves, of course, but they were staying in the house.'

I had forgotten that. 'None the less,' I said, 'I saw those people come and go. I still believe that Golbo – is that his name? – came here.'

Julia nodded. 'You are quite right. The poor lad did come here. I think he hoped that I could shelter him.'

'And did you?'

'He changed his mind. He told me what had happened, then took fright and ran away. I'm not surprised.'

'Did you attempt to stop him?'

She looked at me. 'I did not. He has a legal right to flee, you know, if he fears ill-treatment.'

'Ill-treatment at his owner's hands,' I said. 'And only to another patron, then.'

She shrugged her lovely shoulders. 'I know. All the same, citizen, I let him go. I didn't have the heart to have him chased and caught. Especially when I saw what those guards had done to our other poor slave in the colonnade. Hacked him to death for attempting to defend his master, although the poor boy was doing no more than his duty. Golbo had prepared me for the sight, but even so I was shocked when I saw just how cruelly they had hewn him down. No wonder poor Golbo was so terrified. He was just obeying orders too. He was instructed to refill the pail, he said, and he went to the nympheum to get water as he was told. But he was afraid that he'd be killed for saying so – and more, that he would betray Marcus if he did.'

I frowned. If Marcus had sent the bucket-boy away, then things looked bad for him. Was that why he'd been uneasy earlier? I almost asked Julia to reiterate, but Junio seized the opportunity to speak.

'Killed? Hacked to death? Master, what has been happening here? I heard that there had been an accident and Praxus choked to death. But no one said anything about violence to the slaves, only that Marcus had been obliged to go down with the guards, to take the body back and explain to the commander of the garrison what had occurred.'

'That is one way of putting it,' I said, mentally applauding the discretion of Marcus's messenger. 'More accurately expressed, Marcus has been formally accused of homicide. Praxus's death was not an accident.' I gave him a brief outline of events.

'Great Mithras!' Junio exclaimed. He was clearly shaken: he did not often swear on Roman gods. 'Then, master, you are in danger staying here. By your own account you were the first upon the scene, and if Marcus did order the bucket-boy away, and then called on you, it might seem that you were an accomplice to all this.'

Julia rose to her feet again at this. 'He is quite right, Citizen Libertus. I should have thought of that myself. It was ill-judged of me to bring you here at all. It is important that you go – and now.'

'But madam, I cannot go and leave you here.'

'You can. You must. I am a mere woman, and neither Mellitus nor Balbus will take account of me – at least for now. I will send a message to your house. Through Cilla, whom you know you can trust. In the meantime I will find out what I can. Between us we will find some way to set my husband free. Listen. I can hear footsteps in the house. Go – go now. May all the gods protect us.'

Junio murmured in my ear. 'Don't go through the front part of the villa. Come through the rear gate – the way I came. I'll show you the way. Quickly, master, I can see their lights.'

So could I. There was already a glimmer in the passage-ways. I bent to kiss the lady Julia's hand and then, still tugged at by my slave, disappeared as silently as possible into the darkness towards the outer wall. It was extremely difficult to see our way, and we made the little gate beside the shrine only a moment before the search party of guards came clattering out into the court.

V

It is not easy to walk across an unfamiliar farm in misty darkness, especially hampered by a toga and without a light, but that is what I was now obliged to do. Marcus's villa, like most Roman country homes, backed on to the farmland and woods which made up his estate, and the little gate of the new wing gave out on to the orchard, thence to a muddy field and only then into the woods beyond. Mercifully the extension to the house was fairly new, so the orchard had just been fully walled and the guard geese were not yet in place. We did stumble over an ill-tempered sleeping pig, and disturbed a mangy and marauding fox, but there was no cacophony to alert the house and no one came shouting after us.

At last, after what seemed like several hours of slithering and sliding over our sandal-tops in mud, we stumbled into the welcoming shadows of the wood. It was cold and slippery and wet, and twigs and bracken snatched at us as we passed, but very soon there was at least a path. We struggled on – the detour had taken us miles out of our way – until we reached the road, and finally, muddy, wet and exhausted, we saw the roundhouse looming through the murk, the smoke from its welcoming fire seeping through the roof. There was the glimmer of a tallow taper too, and it was no surprise to find that even at this hour my wife Gwellia was up, awaiting my return.

'Libertus, husband!' she exclaimed, as soon as I had stooped to pass under the thatched entrance and into the house. 'Where have you been? And what has happened to your toga and your shoes? Kurso' – she motioned to the kitchen slave – 'bring your poor master water and a stool. You'll find both in the dye-house, where I was dyeing cloth.'

Kurso, whom I had acquired by accident some months before, gave me one of his worried looks and hurried off. He was still so nervous that he hardly spoke – at least to me, although I've seen him chatter happily to Junio, and Gwellia finds him indispensable. He had been savagely mistreated by an owner once, and had learned to move backwards more quickly than forwards from an early age.

I watched him go scuttling out into the night, towards the dye-house that my wife had spoken of – another woven wattle hut nearby, in the same enclosure and much like the one we were in, even to the central hearth, except that it was on a smaller scale. It housed Gwellia's spindles, fleece and looms, and – as I was well aware – an iron vat of some evil-smelling dye. My wife was adept at the ancient crafts, and even now was weaving me a cloak in the traditional Celtic plaid of our old tribe, but I had insisted that the dyes be kept elsewhere and ordered that the dye-house should be built. Much as I love our little home I have spent too long in fine Roman buildings, with windows and partitions everywhere, to sleep in comfort in the same room as a smelly steaming vat of decaying vegetation and hot wool.

Fortunately, once the materials are cut, a skilled group can weave a small hut in a day, and Kurso had shown an unexpected aptitude for mixing daub and waterproofing walls. Within our fenced enclosure Gwellia had a small thatched henhouse now, as well, so we had eggs, and plans for some beehives and raised foodstores too, instead of the holly-pits we used at present. A proper little Celtic dwelling place.

After the events of the past few hours, it seemed a haven of relief, and I was contemplating all this with a smile and allowing Junio to unlace my soggy sandals when Kurso reappeared – without the stool and water – and uncharacteristically burst into speech at once.

'Master! Mistress! There is somebody there!'

I looked at Junio, who was kneeling at my feet and now glanced up in alarm. He said, before I could frame the words, 'The guards?'

Gwellia said, 'What guards?' but Kurso shook his head.

'Not guards. It seems to be a boy – a slave. He's terrified. He's hiding in there by the fire, and won't come out. He wants to talk to you.'

'Golbo!' I said – a fraction ahead of Junio this time. 'Leave my sandals, Junio. I had better go and speak to him.'

Gwellia was looking from me to Junio and back again. 'Husband, you have only just come in. You are cold and wet and tired, and your toga's torn. I don't know who this slave is, or what he wants – coming here in the middle of the night – but surely you can at least command him to attend you here!'

I went to her, put my hands on her shoulders and looked into her eyes. 'Gwellia, my dear, there's been a dreadful episode. Trouble at the villa – Junio will explain. I must go and talk to Golbo. He may have seen something significant. Give me a brand.'

Kurso picked up a piece of pitch-tipped wood and dipped it in the fire obediently.

'Did Golbo say why he wanted me?' I asked, as I took the smoking torch. But Kurso had exhausted his conversational capacities and he simply shook his head.

I gave up and went out into the night and into the smelly darkness of the hut. At first I could see nothing but the cauldron of dye, still sitting on its stones over the embers of the fire. Then as my torch burned brighter and my eyes grew more accustomed to the gloom I made out the dim shape of Gwellia's loom-beam hanging by the wall – the weight-stones almost reaching to the floor – and there beside it the huddled figure of the slave.

It was Golbo, a cold and frightened Golbo, almost too terrified to speak. He had asked to see me, but as I approached he backed away, keeping the fire between himself and me. I stopped.

'Golbo – I believe that is your name – my house slave informed me that you wanted me. I cannot chase you round this hut all night. If you have something to tell me, do it now.'

'Citizen Libertus?' His voice was no more than a strangled squeak. 'You are a friend of my master's, I believe?'

'Marcus Aurelius Septimus is my patron, certainly.' I said it softly, but I chose my words with care. A pavement-maker – even if he is a citizen – should not presume to claim friendship with a man of rank. 'I have been of service to him sometimes in the past.'

Golbo nodded. 'I have heard him speak of you. That is why I came to you tonight. I – I did not know where else to go, after what had happened in the colonnade.'

A tide of relief flowed over me. Perhaps this affair would be easy to resolve. Golbo quite clearly knew too much, and that's why he had fled. Whoever murdered an important

48

man like Praxus would not think twice about silencing a slave. But if I could get Golbo to tell me what he knew, I could hide him overnight and go to a magistrate tomorrow to explain the truth. Marcus would be instantly released, and Golbo would be safe.

I was smiling as I said, 'And what did happen in the colonnade? Somebody sent you for water, was that it? That is what your mistress said to me. She thought it was your master, but perhaps it was not him? Was it someone else perhaps, someone who murdered Praxus while you were away? Who was it, Golbo? I know you are afraid – your testimony could convict the man – but you can confide in me.'

Golbo stared unhappily at the floor and said nothing.

'By telling me you will protect yourself,' I said. 'Once your testimony is known to the magistrates, there would be no point in killing you – that would only make the murderer's guilt more evident. You would have another witness, too – in me – so nobody could claim you were coerced into making false accusations. And you need not fear revenge. Once Marcus is released he will make sure of that. So speak up, boy. Who sent you to the spring?'

Golbo looked at me in misery. 'That's just the trouble, citizen. My owner sent me to the spring himself.'

I stared. 'Marcus?'

'Well, not in person, naturally – he was at the banquet with his guests. But he sent the message all the same. It was quite precise. I was to go at once and fill the pail, because the banquet was drawing to a close, and guests might wish to use the vomitorium before the litters took them jogging home. It's not an unusual request. He does the same thing each time there's a feast – except that tonight it was a little earlier, and he was displeased with me, it seems. I don't know why. I tried to keep the room as clean as it usually is.'

'But you didn't question the order when it came?'

Golbo looked more wretched than before. 'In any case I wouldn't question it. And the message was brought by one of Marcus's own slaves.'

'One of his own slaves? You are quite sure of that?' My mind was racing now. Of course, there is always the possibility of treachery, but in general the loyalty of Marcus's household is beyond doubt, and his servants would defend him to the death. We had seen that demonstrated that very night.

He nodded. 'I am quite sure of that. There *were* slaves in the villa who had come in from my master's town apartment in Glevum especially to help to cook and serve the feast – I might have been mistaken about them. But this wasn't one of them. This was a villa slave, called Umbris. I know the man. I was there when Marcus first acquired him – a present from a wealthy visitor.'

I nodded, though it was not a name I knew. Marcus has a multitude of slaves but I would have remembered that one, I was sure. Obviously one of Marcus's little jokes. The name derives from shadow, and is not a lucky one – except for a household slave perhaps, where silence and unobtrusiveness are desirable. Marcus had a sense of humour sometimes, when it came to naming slaves.

'So Umbris was . . .' I was going to say 'a bribe', but altered it, '. . . a gift?'

Golbo nodded. 'One among many, citizen. Many of us were.'

Of course, that was likely to be true. A man in Marcus's position scarcely needed to go out and purchase slaves from the shifty dealers in the town. The villa was no doubt full of similar 'donations', living and inert. There were always people trying to climb up the social scale who were only too eager to offer His Excellency anything he sought – in hopes of some little favour in return. I returned to a more profitable line of questioning.

'What kind of man is he?'

'My master thinks very well of him. He works hard and drives others hard: I cannot tell you more about his character than that.' Golbo gave a rueful laugh. 'Citizen, he is a senior slave. He works the dining room and I'm a bucket-boy – he's never deigned to address a word to me, except to give me orders, like tonight. But I could point him out to you. He's . . .'

'Husband!' Gwellia's voice from behind me cut across his words. 'I beg you, leave this till the morning now. You are soaked through to the skin. You must remember you're no longer young.' I turned. She was standing in the doorway of the hut. 'You'll be no help to your patron if you're ill in bed.'

I nodded. It was true that I was chilled and shivering. 'Very well, Gwellia, my dear. No doubt you're right. But what about the boy?' My plans of sheltering him overnight and producing him triumphantly in the courts were all in ruins now. This testimony would seal Marcus's fate.

'He'll have to find somewhere else to go.'

'My dear wife . . .' I protested. It was not like Gwellia to be hard-hearted in this way.

She softened a little, as I knew she would. 'Or he can stay here by the fire if you insist. But not inside the house. He is a runaway, Libertus, and I refuse to have him under my roof.' She saw my look and added urgently, 'Husband, it is you I'm thinking of. Junio has been telling me what happened at the villa earlier – and I'm concerned. It seems to me that, with your patron in the cells, the guards would be only too happy to press charges against you. If they find you harbouring a runaway, they will have all the evidence they need – and what will happen to this household then?'

She could hardly have mustered a stronger argument, but I still demurred. 'But if Golbo stays out here . . .?'

'You can say that he came in here to hide without your knowing it – which after all is no more than the truth. That might be some kind of defence. If he's in the roundhouse, there will be no possible excuse. Oh, Libertus, please do come inside. There is obviously something serious afoot. If anyone comes searching here tonight, it's better that they find us in our beds.'

This was so manifestly true that I complied. 'You are right, of course. Very well, I'll come with you now. Golbo, you can stay here by the fire, where at least you can be warm and dry tonight. There's clean water in the big bowl by the door, and a pile of fleece. Lie on it and pull some over you. Tomorrow we must think where you can go.' And what we should do about your testimony too, I thought, although I didn't speak the words aloud.

And then, at last, I did submit to Gwellia's urgings and went back into the house, where I allowed my weary slaves to undress me, sponge down my muddy clothes and legs, and help me to my welcome bed of reeds. Then they wrapped me in a woollen blanket and tiptoed away, leaving me to Gwellia and my thoughts.

I couldn't sleep. Gwellia invited me to talk, but the more I turned the events of the evening over in my head, the less sense any of it made to me. It was Gwellia, in the end, who voiced the thought that I could not allow myself to think.

'Husband,' she whispered, when I had rehearsed the same

thing for the twentieth time, 'has it occurred to you that Mellitus could be right? Perhaps it was your patron who pushed Praxus in the bowl. What other explanation can there be?'

'I don't know!' I exclaimed. 'Yet surely there must be one. I don't believe for an instant that Marcus murdered him.' But when I came to consider all the mounting evidence I had to admit the possibility, though I couldn't bear to contemplate it for long. That is why I didn't sleep all night, and why – as soon as the first light of chilly dawn broke through the sullen clouds – I slipped away from my still sleeping wife, pulled on my sandals and a woollen cloak, and went out to find Golbo in the hut.

But I was too late. Golbo wasn't there.

VI

I searched the whole enclosure – behind the woodpile, in the chicken-house, even under the holly branches in the grain pit – but there was no sign of him. I went out to the steep rocky lane which ran past the house, but there was nothing to be seen, only the hazy outlines of the trees looming at me through the misty murk. No trace of footprints, either, on the frosty earth.

I was still there, gazing intently at the road, when a voice hissed, 'Citizen?' startlingly close to me. I whirled round to see a cloaked figure detach itself from the white-grey haze of the woods.

'Golbo?' I said, but it was not the boy. In the dim half-light I recognised the lumpy maidservant who had fetched Junio to me the night before.

'It's Cilla, master,' the girl said, still whispering. 'Golbo has not been found.' She came up close beside me and went on, 'Be careful, citizen, we may be overheard. There might still be searchers on the roads. The lady Julia, my mistress, sent me to find you here, as soon as it was starting to be light. She says to tell you that the guards took ten slaves – the ones who were holding torches – as hostages last night. They marched them off into the town for questioning, along with Marcus and the doorkeeper.'

My heart, which was already lower than my still damp

sandal-straps, sank even more at this. Marcus was an important man, with wealth and influence: he would be locked up in the garrison – probably in the commander's house, in case he proved to be innocent in the end. But everyone knew what such 'questioning' would mean for all the rest. The servants would be tortured until they 'remembered' something significant – who had sent the orders to the colonnade, for example, or where Golbo had gone – whether or not the events they confessed had ever actually occurred. Over the years I have attempted to dissuade Marcus from employing such techniques, since I was once a slave myself with no civic rights of any kind.

However, it was Marcus who was now under arrest, and lesser magistrates – presumably Balbus in particular, since he was now the most senior of those left – would be looking for the 'truth' as quickly and ruthlessly as possible, to minimise their own political embarrassment. The routine and perfectly legal torture of a few slaves was hardly likely to trouble them.

Now I had a moral problem on my hands. If I found Golbo, should I take him to the authorities? Or should I give them his testimony in any case and hope to save ten other innocent slaves from hours of agony – at the end of which, one could be almost sure, somebody would break down under the anguish and invent evidence against Marcus.

I was debating this when Cilla spoke again. 'That is not the only reason why I've come. My mistress sent me to warn you, citizen. One of the serving girls overheard a conversation in the court. Balbus was arguing that they should send guards for you – he says you were the first to leave the banquet hall, and you probably helped my master in his task, because

Praxus was too big for one man alone to overcome. He said he saw you standing by the corpse, holding a heavy brass pot in your hand, and that you'd almost certainly used it to hit Praxus on the head so that Marcus could more easily hold him down.'

I felt a chill run down my back, colder than the freezing morning air. It was true, I had been holding such a pot, and there would be half a dozen witnesses to that. Of course, I had not hit Praxus, I'd simply used it to retrieve the wreath, as any of the torch-bearers would testify – but if Cilla was to be believed these were the very slaves who were at this moment being flogged and questioned at the jail. When the Romans scourge you, you are inclined to remember anything they wish.

'Balbus wanted me arrested by the guards?' I repeated foolishly. 'But surely only Mellitus could sanction that?' Praxus's bodyguard, like that of any military commander of high rank, would have been personally hand-picked from the legions under his control, responsible for his safety and answerable to him alone. These men had come with Praxus a few days ago, when he arrived from Gaul, and until alternative orders came they were not officially attached to anyone. A high-ranking official of the Empire, such as Mellitus, might co-opt them for some official role, but a mere local decurion like Balbus would need agreement from the ordo first, and probably the co-operation of the garrison as well, however many high-ranking brothers he might have in Gaul.

Cilla nodded. 'I think he hoped that Mellitus *would* sanction it, and perhaps he will, if the master does not confess. I don't suppose my owner will do that, citizen. Not when he is innocent of the crime.'

57

I rounded on her sharply. 'You know that? That he is innocent?'

The plump plain face puckered. 'Well, I thought . . . naturally. . .' She was gazing at me in disbelief. 'Surely, citizen, you do not suppose . . .? My master would never dream of such a thing.'

'Of course not,' I said hurriedly. 'I only hoped that you might have had some proof, so that I could declare it to the magistrates and have him freed. Supposing that anyone would listen to my plea.' It occurred to me that without my patron's influence that might be difficult to bring about.

She looked at me. 'The new high priest of Jupiter might help you there, perhaps. He's had no time to get involved in local politics, but he has dined at the villa once or twice. He has a theory that Governor Pertinax will be the future Emperor of Rome. Said he had read it in the stars. My mistress was very entertained. But if he believes that, surely he would help?'

I smiled wryly. If the high priest sincerely thought that Marcus might be an Imperial favourite one day, no doubt he would be anxious to assist – once he was certain that Marcus would be freed. It is always useful to have friends at court. However, remembering that self-important little man, I could not see him risking a confrontation with real-life authorities without the most compelling evidence – whatever omens he purported to believe.

I said gently, 'If we could show Marcus to be innocent, perhaps. Unfortunately, although we think he didn't do it, it will be hard to prove. All the outward circumstances seem to point to him.'

She nodded thoughtfully. 'Almost as if it was *designed* to look as if my master murdered him.'

'Indeed,' I said – although, on reflection, that was not entirely true. If anything, it had been designed to look like an accident, until an idiotic pavement-maker had opened his big mouth and suggested otherwise.

'I will go into the garrison,' I said, 'and see if I can have a word with Marcus, privately. The garrison commander is a friend of his, and I've had dealings with him in the past. I doubt if I'm in any danger yet and Marcus may know something which will help to prove the truth. If I discover anything, I'll come to the villa and tell Julia at once.'

Cilla shook her head. 'Until my master is at liberty, it may not be as easy as all that. Better to meet me secretly tonight and I'll take word. The house is under guard. There are fresh soldiers posted at the front gate now – that's why I feared there might yet be another search for Golbo by and by.'

'But you got out?' I was thinking about Julia and her slaves, virtually helpless prisoners in the house.

'I told them I was going to fetch some oils for my mistress, and they let me go. The soldiers are not interested in women's purchases. There is an old woman in a hut not far away who makes such remedies. My mistress buys one from her now and then: they are far cheaper than the ones in Glevum market – and just as good, she says.'

I nodded. I knew the poor wizened crone myself. Her husband had been a prosperous miller, till he crushed his hand, but now they were forced to scrape a living where they could, sleeping in a makeshift hut among the trees. She made her 'remedies' from berries, roots and herbs, while he bundled twigs for firewood and sold them in the town. Gwellia and I had sometimes bought some kindling ourselves, simply out of pity for their plight.

'But how will you get back past the guards?' I said.

She produced a small perfume jar from beneath her cloak. 'I will show them this. I really mean to go and buy some oils. Lavender, my mistress says, to soothe her shattered nerves.' She saw my concerned look, and grinned. 'Don't worry, citizen. She persuaded the captain of the guard that she was faint and ill, but it was her idea to furnish this excuse! But, if you will pardon me, I must go and do it now. I am already in danger of being gone too long. The guards will be suspicious otherwise. I will come again tonight at sundown and meet you here, to see if you have any news for us. I'll find some excuse to get past the gate – or if that's impossible I'll come through the orchard and across the farm, the way you came last night. The soldiers are guarding the main gates, front and back, but they have not yet discovered there's another way.' She nodded at me cheerfully, wrapped her grey cloak more firmly around her and set off quickly down the track.

I watched her till she was swallowed up in mist, and then I went thoughtfully back to the roundhouse.

By this time the little household was awake and bustling. Kurso was fetching water from the stream, Gwellia was clearing the ashes from round the baking pot, and taking out the hot fresh oatcakes which had cooked perfectly amongst the warm embers overnight. Junio was busy too, attempting to brush the dried mud from my toga hems.

He looked up as I came in. 'Here is Libertus, mistress, safe and well.'

I should have known that she would fear for me, but I had not thought of it. We had spent too many years apart: I had only recently found her again and I was not yet accustomed to her care. I gave her an apologetic smile. 'Golbo was not in the dyeing hut. I went to look for him.'

She did not reply. She simply gave me a reproachful look which tore my heart.

When I began to outline what Cilla had said to me about the guards, however, her manner changed. When I had finished, she said urgently, 'Husband, you are right in what you told the girl. You must go into the garrison, and see what your patron has to say. If he is guilty, persuade him to confess – confront him with all the evidence – otherwise you will end up before the courts yourself. And it won't be comfortable exile for you. If you are found guilty of complicity in a thing like this – murdering a high-ranking legionary commander – you will be lucky if they let you choose your death.'

And then what would become of us? There was no need to speak the words. If I was condemned and 'privileged to choose' – which meant hemlock and a comparatively quick, dignified and painless death – or even if I was merely exiled with my patron, life would not be easy for my wife. Next winter it could be Gwellia out there in the woods, with only rags for warmth, trying to keep starvation from the door with pathetic little decoctions of wild flowers and leaves.

'I shall go as soon as I have eaten,' I declared. 'This business is dangerous for all of us.' But in fact, although Gwellia's oatcakes smelt ambrosial, I could scarcely bring myself to take a single bite. It was all I could do to swallow the beaker of water which my slave had set for me.

Gwellia noted my distress, and assumed a wifely role. 'Well, if you are going to see the garrison you'd better wear your toga,' she said, patting my shoulder as she passed. 'Your pavements will have to wait another day.'

I sighed. That was a further worry in all this. Mosaics do not make themselves, and by moving to live here, outside the city walls, I had already limited my working hours. Now it looked as if another day was lost. I sighed again.

Kurso came in with the pail and I permitted him to pour some water into a wooden bowl for me. I splashed my face and hands in that while Junio rubbed my freezing feet with a linen cloth and a scoop of Gwellia's less caustic lye-and-ashes soap. (These days I reserved my Roman oil and strigil for the baths.) Then after the boys had eaten – their oatcakes and my own – Junio draped my toga, disguising the muddy bits as best he could, and he and I set off for the town, leaving Kurso to help Gwellia in the house.

Usually Kurso came to the town with me as well, to help cut tiles and to mind the shop, and went home in the afternoon when business was inevitably slack, but today I did not want to leave Gwellia in the roundhouse on her own. She had been asking for a female slave, I thought guiltily, but I had demurred, saying there were few good slaves available at this time of year. There hadn't been captives from the borderlands for months, and slave-ships from other provinces didn't often put to sea in winter storms. Besides, having been a slave myself, I didn't care much for buying servants – but now I was beginning to wish I'd got one, all the same.

It was a long walk into Glevum, several miles, and the lane – though shorter than the military road – was always treacherous. Now, when last night's rain had turned to ice, and the puddles and ruts were frozen underfoot, it was not only steep and rocky but slippery as well. Recent tracks showed where some intrepid horse and cart had passed, but we saw no sign of human life until we joined the major road, not far outside the city walls.

My business lay with the garrison, so I hurried to

the nearest man on guard. 'I wish to speak to your commander, urgently.' I outlined who I was and what I wanted there.

He looked me up and down, and for a moment I thought I would be turned away, but ultimately my toga won respect. 'I'll see what I can do for you, citizen, but I'm afraid your slave may have to wait outside.'

'I could go to the workshop, master, and await you there,' Junio said.

'A good suggestion,' I agreed, and Junio trotted off.

It seemed a long time before anybody came, but finally an escort was found for me, and I was shown to the commander's house. There I was ushered into his private waiting room, which, as in all such military establishments, was handsomely proportioned but uncomfortable and chill. After another lengthy wait – I suppose that is what waiting rooms are for – I was attended by a military secretary with a nervous tic. I explained my errand once again.

'I have come to ask permission for an audience with my patron, His Excellence Marcus Aurelius Septimus, whom your commander is holding under guard. There will be no objection to that, I am sure. Even prisoners in the common jail are sometimes permitted visitors, and Marcus is a personal friend of his.'

'Wait here, citizen. I'll see what I can do,' the fellow said, and disappeared again.

This time the wait was so extremely long that I was beginning to become concerned. I remembered that Balbus had wanted my arrest, and for a moment I feared that I had walked into a trap. I was seriously contemplating walking out and attempting to make a run for it when the fellow with the nervous tic came back.

'Your pardon, citizen, your request has been denied. Commander Protheus has instructed me to tell you that your patron Marcus is detained in comfort in the house, and that the commander will see that he is well treated. However, there is a question of a plot against the state, and in those circumstances a prisoner is not permitted visitors.'

'A plot against the state?' I forgot myself sufficiently to stand up and raise my voice. 'But . . .'

'Those are the standing orders of the Emperor,' the secretary said, taking a step backwards as though I'd threatened him. 'It's not my decision, citizen. Guard,' he called to a soldier beside the outer door, 'kindly escort the citizen outside.'

'But . . .' I protested, in genuine dismay. 'There must be some mistake. My patron is a very powerful man, of noble birth. He is related to the Emperor . . .' That last point was not, in fact, entirely proved. There are hundreds of Aurelians in the Empire, and not all of them are of Imperial blood. But rumour had always said that Marcus was, and, since he had never denied it, it seemed worth mentioning. As a lever, I had never known it fail.

It failed now.

'You heard him, citizen.' The guard from outside had come in by this time, and to my alarm had drawn his sword. 'Out. Now. With me. And no argument, or you'll find you're locked up in here yourself. Then you can talk to your precious patron all you like.'

'I'm sorry, citizen,' the secretary bleated. His cheek was twitching really badly now.

'Now, are you going to move?' the soldier said. 'Or am I going to have to make you move? And don't think for a moment that I won't. You haven't got a fancy patron to protect you now.'

It was then that I realised just what deep trouble we were in. Marcus's name, which up to now had always opened every official door and afforded me protection in all kinds of ways, had lost its power overnight. Even his friend the commander was refusing help, though he was obviously attempting to look after Marcus as best he dared.

I was marched at sword-point out into the street.

VII

Not only marched at sword-point but thrust into the road with such a heavy hand against my back that I almost stumbled to the ground. If I was not so obviously a citizen, I believe I would have had a kick to help me on my way. Even a passing turnip-seller stopped to stare.

I recovered myself, straightened my toga, and walked off into the drizzle with as much dignity as I could muster, trying to decide what to do. I had been so sure of meeting Marcus, and discussing things with him, that I really had no other plan. I am accustomed to working on his authority, but from here on I was clearly on my own.

As if to illustrate my gloomy thoughts the drizzling rain turned suddenly to a determined shower. There was a little temple to the local river god nearby: not a large place, but it had a portico, and I hurried – together with the turnip-seller and a half a dozen other passers-by – under the shelter of its columns. I huddled up against a plinth and tried to think.

There was one obvious strategy to try, except that I sadly lacked the wherewithal. The purse that I carried at my belt, although containing all the money I possessed, was woefully light. My few miserable silver coins might have been enough to purchase information from a tavern-keeper, or buy a few extra moments with Marcus from a willing guard (which was why I had taken the precaution of bringing them) but I would need a good deal more than that for any serious attempt at bribery. Official doors were closed behind me now, and it would take a very wealthy man to prise them open even a crack.

But I had to do something for my patron if I could. The charge of murdering Praxus had been bad enough, but this new twist was more serious again. Suspected of a plot against the state! I could not, for the moment, see how Praxus's death could be conceived of in this way, but I am not an expert in the law. Perhaps because his new appointment was an Imperial one, or simply because he was commander of the local force? Balbus would presumably know: not only was he schooled in civil law, but he must be familiar with military law as well – after all he had a brother who was a senior officer in Gaul and a candidate for senatorial rank in Rome. So there must be some legal foundation for the charge, or Balbus would never have permitted it. The cost of failure was too terrible – Marcus was an influential man.

If the case held, on the other hand, there were great rewards. A plot against the state was effectively three crimes at once, and any informant bringing a successful case was entitled to a share of the guilty party's estate. I could see why Balbus would resort to it – or Mellitus, or anybody else.

As well as straightforward treachery, there was *maiestas* – offence against the Emperor's majesty – one of the most effective tools for bringing any senior figure down. Also, since Commodus had officially declared himself a god, there was sacrilege as well. Any one of those crimes might carry the penalty of death, even for a man of high birth like my patron – or at the very least exile to a waterless island, which often came to the same thing. And our beloved Emperor was not noted for his clemency, especially towards those whom he suspected of plots against himself.

And it was all my fault. Why, oh why, had I opened my big mouth? If it had not been for my 'perceptive observations' the death of Praxus would surely have passed as an unhappy accident. Unfortunate for Marcus, as the host – acutely politically embarrassing – but nothing like as dangerous as what had happened now. And for the life of me I could not see how anyone but Marcus had had an opportunity to kill Praxus at the feast.

I was so wrapped in my own thoughts that I paid scant attention to the cloaked figure on the pavement opposite, not even when he stepped down from the kerb and headed towards our little group huddling underneath the portico. There was really no room for anybody else but still he came, picking his way fastidiously across the paving of the road, where the rain was already splashing up around his hems, and elbowed his way into what little space there was. There was a general murmuring but that was a military cloak and no one was disposed to make a fuss. I too kept my head down and shuffled up a bit, and it was not until he dropped his hood that I looked up in earnest and his eyes met mine.

It was the little secretary I had seen earlier.

I half opened my mouth to speak to him, but before I could utter a word he gaped at me, looked away, pulled his cloak-hood up again and was hastening away into the rain with the tic in his face twitching like a newly landed fish.

After a startled moment, I went after him. He was so keen to get away that I was sure he knew something he didn't want to tell. He was a younger man than I was, and he was hurrying, so he had reached the Apollo fountain outside the fish market before I managed to catch up with him.

'Officer!' I panted, as I reached his side. He did not deserve the title, but a little courtesy never went amiss.

He stopped. I thought for a moment he would hurry off again, but he simply stood there in the rain and refused to meet my eyes. 'What do you want? Why are you following me about?' he said.

I did not manage an answer straight away – I was out of breath – but he scarcely gave me time in any case before he was saying with a righteous air, 'If it is about your patron, there is nothing I can do. I told you what the garrison commander said.'

I looked at him. It was a risk, of course, and might easily result in my own arrest, but I had noticed his manner at the garrison. This was a nervous and unhappy man. I decided it was worth a try. I moved closer to him, slipped my hand beneath my toga-folds, and took out a *denarius* from my purse.

'Nothing?' I held up the coin.

He looked at it contemptuously – at it, I noticed, not at me. 'Nothing.'

I added a second coin to the first. 'Not even a message to His Excellency?' I said. Another risk. It is never a good idea to increase a bribe – it only makes the price go up again – and even if it succeeded this time there might be other men to pay.

'Don't you understand plain Latin, citizen? There's nothing I can do. Now, will you go away? I have an official errand to complete, and interfering with it is an offence against the law.'

But he was weakening. I could see it in his face.

'Perhaps there is just one thing I could say . . .' He tried to keep his face expressionless, but his eyes were on the coins.

I hesitated. This could be a trap. 'And that is?' I took out another coin and placed it, with the others, on the side of the water trough as if in sacrifice towards the god. Such offerings are not entirely unknown, and that way it was not officially a bribe. The secretary looked from me to them, balanced invitingly on the wide stone edge, and ran his tongue around his lips. He took a step towards me, and as he did so the corner of his cloak sent one of the coins rolling in the trough.

That did it. He stooped and snatched the others in his hand. 'Go away,' he hissed. 'Right away if you know what's good for you.' He looked at me, his little sly eyes bright. 'Now, that's all I've got to say. It's dangerous for me to talk to you. Leave me alone before I call for help, and have you taken into custody.' And with that, he turned and trotted off in the direction of the centre of the town.

And there was nothing for it but to let him go! Three precious denarii wasted and I had got myself soaked through to no avail. I dared not even fish into the fountain for the missing coin. The rain had eased and people were coming back into the street. Bribery was clearly not among my skills. Junio would have made a better job of it.

Junio! I must go to him. He must be wondering where I was by this time, or even whether – with Marcus under lock and key – I had succeeded in getting myself arrested too. Well, I would go and find him at the workshop and then we would go home and consider what to do. I pulled up my toga-folds to form a hood, turned towards the centre of the town, and hurried on, past the forum and basilica, and out of the north gate on the farther side.

My little shop was there, beyond the walls, in the straggling suburb which had grown up on the marshy river margins to the north-west of the colonia in the last hundred years: a swarming assortment of muddy narrow lanes lined with ramshackle buildings, many let out as poky rooms and workshops such as mine. In fact mine was more tumbledown than most, since rioters had recently set fire to it and attempted to burn the building down. Fortunately my expensive contribution to the fire watch had brought buckets and beaters quickly to the scene, and most of the lower floor was saved, though it was a different matter in the upper room which had once been my sleeping quarters. The beams up there were badly charred, the roof had fallen in, and the access ladder had entirely gone. It was almost impossible to live there now, even without the imminent danger of collapse: that was one reason why my wife and I had been so glad to have the roundhouse to rebuild, and why we'd moved out of town.

None of the damage to the shop had made any difference to the rent, of course, despite my representations to the landlord. He was a wealthy man, who'd had several of these tenements thrown up; a city magistrate, so there was no point in taking him to court. A contract was a contract, he declared: I had agreed to rent 'from ground to sky' – and that was exactly what I had possession of, even if the 'sky' began a little closer now. Nor would he make any repairs, although he did agree that I could have some done. Entirely at my own expense, naturally.

I was thinking rather bitterly about all this as I turned into the lane where the workshop stood, sandwiched between a candle-maker's and a tannery. It was a narrow thoroughfare, always full – as now – of slaves and tradespeople: men with donkeys, boys bent double under piles of smelly skins, and blowzy women touting hot greasy pies from trays. The gutters streamed with mud and all the effluvium of trade. Not an area where citizens in togas often came – I usually wore a humble tunic here myself. Already I was attracting curious stares.

I ignored them and was walking swiftly to my door when suddenly I saw a sight which stopped me dead. Someone was standing in the entrance to the shop, frowning down at my stockpiled heaps of marble chips and stones. It wasn't Junio. It was a stocky figure in military dress.

Bullface. I would have recognised that profile anywhere.

Almost without conscious thought I turned on my heel and began to walk even more swiftly back the way I'd come. I managed (with an effort) to control myself and neither looked back nor broke into a run, although the temptation to do both was very strong. I expected at every instant to hear a cry or the clanking of armour in pursuit, but I reached the end of the lane without incident.

Even then I did not pause, but turned into an even narrower alleyway, another and then another, till I reached an area I did not know, a world away from the familiar streets of the colonia or from the fine tombs along the Londinium road.

I was in a passage between two disused shops, which was used as little more than a refuse heap. The meaner streets of town are full of middens of this kind, the waste allowed to rot and wash away, or sometimes collected by the enterprising poor to sell as fertiliser on the great estates. No one had collected in this alleyway for years.

The winter sun had not penetrated here and the ground was wet and slippery with frost. I was sure that Bullface would not come looking for me here. But I was taking no chances. I slithered over noisome mounds of rotting kitchen waste – bones, chicken-heads, cabbage-stalks and worse –

and only then did I lean against the wall to catch my breath and try to make some sense of what I'd seen.

What was Bullface doing at my premises? It was no social visit, that was clear. Yet I had come more or less directly from the garrison and no one had attempted to detain me there, so there was presumably no official warrant out yet for my arrest. But there was something about the presence of Praxus's bodyguard which alarmed me very much – more than an ordinary member of the town watch would have done.

I recalled, with a cold tingle on my neck, what that slave-girl of Julia's had overheard. Balbus had wanted me arrested yesterday, but had lacked official backing at the time. Suppose that, instead of waiting for the proper authority, he had bribed the guard to go ahead and haul me in for private questioning, with the intention of bringing public charges later on?

With Marcus gone, Balbus was the senior magistrate in the area, and the courts would blink an eye at such un-authorised arrest. Though I was a citizen, and therefore technically protected from such things, it was unlikely that my rank was going to help me now. It did not take much imagination to see what Balbus hoped to gain. A witnessed statement by a citizen who was Marcus's erstwhile friend would seal the case, with no troublesome reprisals for the arresting magistrate. And if I could not be forced to sign such a statement of my own accord, as the price of my freedom and release, I could probably be coerced into doing so by force. Twenty-four hours of the kind of questioning I would be subjected to and even a strong man will swear to anything, I had no illusions about that. No doubt all this had been tacitly agreed while I was twiddling my thumbs outside the jail.

I sent up a mental apology to my secretarial friend. 'Get right away!' he'd said. Perhaps he had known the guard were after me, and had attempted to warn me that something was afoot.

The more I thought about it, the more likely this explanation seemed. If the murder of Praxus could somehow be interpreted as a plot against the state and Marcus was proved guilty of the crime, there would be a senior position to be filled, and Balbus himself would be a candidate – especially with part of the traitor's fortune in his purse. The Emperor rewards loyal vigilance. Balbus would bear watching if I escaped from this.

And if I were arrested but did not co-operate? The idea sent shivers down my spine. Who, that mattered in the town, would notice the absence of an ageing tradesman like myself? It would simply be assumed I'd run away, especially now my patron was in jail, and my absence would lend credence to his guilt.

Well, if that was Balbus's idea, I thought grimly, he would have to catch me first.

I only hoped Junio was safe. It was possible that they were already holding him prisoner at the workshop. That was a disturbing thought. For a moment I was almost tempted to go back, but I forced myself to stay still and let reason rule my head. Junio was relatively safe as long as I was free – the only point in holding him would be to threaten me. My best course was to get myself away, and make my plans when I was safe. But I was not safe here. Perhaps Bullface wouldn't find me, here outside the walls, but there were other threats.

This area of neglected back lanes on the fringe of town is quite notorious. There are reasons why white-robers don't venture there alone, at least not without the protection of a slave. Could I try to make a dash for it, and get back to the road? I edged to the end of the alleyway and peered out. An old man with a load of firewood on his back paused to give me a peculiar look.

I was still contemplating what to do, when a hand fell on my shoulder from behind.

VIII

'Hush, master!' Junio's voice was in my ear. 'Don't cry out like that. You will alert them that we're here. There are people trying to arrest you. You've seen that there's a guard outside the shop?'

I was so weak with relief that I snapped at him. 'Of course I did. And they will have no need of an arrest if you contrive to frighten me to death!' As he tugged me back into the passageway, I collected my thoughts sufficiently to ask, 'How did you know I was here? And how did you get here, in any case?'

'There's another entrance to this lane, down by the dyer's shop, and this alley runs right down to the docks. I come this way for water – if you don't need it clean. It saves queuing at the public fountains and good water is a waste when you only want it to mix mortar with. And I've got your fish-heads down here, once or twice, when there were none going cheap at the fish market.'

I nodded. I sometimes use fish-heads to boil up into glue. I need it to stick small mosaics on to backing cloth, so they can be laid as one single piece and then soaked off again. It is a technique which saves a huge amount of time – the fish-head glue soaks off quite readily – though I do not advertise the fact among my customers, who are often delighted by my speed of work.

Junio was anxious to show me how much he knew. 'There is a quick way through as well – this lane links up with a pathway further on, not towards the colonia and the docks, but upstream of that, the uncommercial part. I'll take you that way now. It isn't very pleasant, I'm afraid, but you had better not go back towards the town.'

The uncommercial part. I knew the area he meant. Not the main river with its bustling quays, but the turgid half-silted channel that wound upstream of the dock, its murky waters full of eels and makeshift water craft. There had been a sort of suburb there some time ago, built up over time as this loop of the river slowly silted up, but that had been mostly abandoned a few years ago after a period when the Sabrina burst its banks each spring and flooded the whole area waist-high. Recently, I was aware, a few hardier souls had crept back to the waterfront again and set up new homes and businesses among the remnants of the old.

I knew the place by reputation only. An area of brothels, taverns and shacks, where shadowy men eked out a living on the fringes of the river-trade and often on the fringes of the law, while those who wished to become invisible flitted between the ruins like living ghosts. People spoke of the 'Ghosts of Glevum' with a laugh, touching an amulet to dispel bad luck. It didn't seem a laughing matter now.

Not a place I care to visit, given half a choice. 'I suppose we must?' I said unwillingly. But I was already following Junio. No fancy Roman drains or fine pavements here – just a muddy passageway between high walls – but pretty soon we found the path he'd spoken of. I didn't like the look of it at all. It wound remorselessly away from the civilisation of the town down to a shady reach of swampy ground, where broken walls were interspersed with encroaching clumps of marsh-grass and reeds. Even the path itself seemed treacherous, threatening to sink at every step.

I felt like a condemned man forced at sword-point out towards the beasts – urged into certain danger by a greater threat. Suddenly it seemed that nowhere was safe, though I reminded myself that I was lucky to be here, especially with Junio at my side.

'I'm glad you managed to escape that guard,' I said.

Junio threw me a sardonic glance over his shoulder. 'There wasn't one guard, master. There were three.' He led me over another pile of bones and building waste. 'I found them at the house when I arrived. They asked for you, and I told them you had business in the town – I said I thought you were intending to visit the barber's shop after you'd seen Marcus at the garrison, and two of them set off to find you straight away.'

'But they let you go?' I was surprised at that. Holding my slave under duress would have been a useful way of securing me.

He turned and grinned at me. 'I volunteered to show them where the barber's was – they were from Praxus's bodyguard, they said, so they'd just come from Gaul and didn't know the town. I took them there, all right, but when we reached the door I stood back to let them in, then took to my heels. They were so busy looking in the shop for you, they didn't notice I was gone – at least I suppose they did, but by then it was too late. Watch your feet here, master, the ground is slippery.'

I negotiated the patch of marshy ground. 'So how did you know where to find me?'

'I didn't. I knew you were coming from the garrison – you clearly hadn't been arrested there – but I had no idea which route you'd take. I just prayed to all the gods that the soldiers didn't meet you on the way. I came back towards the workshop and lingered in the lanes nearby, hoping to catch you before you reached the house – I daren't keep watch for you openly. When I saw you turn the corner, I thought all was lost, but then I saw you double back, so I nipped round to meet you by coming through the alley the other way. Ah, here's the path I'm looking for. You see, it cuts straight down right to the waterside.' He gestured to an even narrower path that crossed our own.

'Where they sell fish-heads?'

He gave another grin. 'Indeed. And if you carried water from the river as often as I do, master, you would know all the short cuts too.' He led the way on to the smaller path, hardly wide enough to let us pass. It squelched with ooze. I could see the gleam of water at the further end and the ripe smell of river was reaching my nostrils already.

Yet at the water's edge there was clearly commerce. There were noises in the tumbled shacks on either side – somewhere I could hear the creaking of a pulley-wheel and the dull thud of a hammer striking wood – and ahead there was a pile of rubbish heaped beside the path. From the water came a distant hum of voices and the splash of oars.

I was a little reassured by this evidence of industry, despite the reputation of the place. If Junio had passed this way unmolested, perhaps I could do the same. 'Then what are we waiting for?' I said. 'Lead on.'

But Junio put out a restraining hand. He said, in a low voice, 'We should be safe enough for a minute here, it's true. It's daylight, and there's nobody about. But then, master, what are you going to do? You can't stay here. Thieves and beggars use these pathways after dark. And you can't go back to the roundhouse, either, if the search is serious. Everyone knows where to find you there.'

That was true, I realised. Even my drunken tablemate the night before had known where I lived, and it would not take long for a group of Roman guards to track me down. Equally, as Junio pointed out, I could not stay here. The afternoon was drawing on. No doubt by this time Bullface had been offering bribes for news of me. Someone was sure to spot me soon, and in my toga I was more conspicuous on these fetid paths than a Vestal virgin in a troupe of dancing bears. And I was still carrying that purse.

What had been a pittance at the garrison was more than enough to get my throat cut here. The drawstring pouch was still suspended from my belt, and though it was hidden underneath my toga-folds a determined thief would find it instantly. I knew that could easily spell death. (There is a capital penalty for theft on thoroughfares, intended to protect the course of trade, but sometimes it has the opposite effect. It is often safer to kill the man you rob – a dead victim can't tell tales to the authorities.)

As if to give substance to my darkest thoughts a fat, bearded man in a filthy slave-tunic staggered round the bottom corner of the path with an amphora full of something in his arms. He made directly for the rubbish pile and was in the act of tipping something over it – rancid fish-oil by the smell of it – when he looked up and saw us lurking there. His jaw dropped, and his jar almost did the same. His face took on a calculating look, and he stared at us for a long moment before he scurried off, taking his evil-smelling cargo with him.

That settled it. I turned to Junio. 'I don't like the look of this. That man would sell his mother for a *quadrans*, and cut her throat for two. He'll be back, with friends, if I am any judge, and they'll either rob me or they'll hand me in. If Bullface has been asking questions here, I'm lost. We'd better separate.'

Junio shook his head reluctantly, but I walked away from him towards the stinking pile. I saw that this one was made up of wood and rags – washed up from the river by the look of it. 'That way at least if they catch up with me, you can take word back to Gwellia,' I said, trying to sound masterful and firm. 'Go on – you go back the way we've come. I'm attracting more attention here than an arena full of beasts. Even if Bullface hasn't been this way, I might as well have put a label round my neck saying, "I am on the run, but I have money. Come and rob me now." Go and take the message while you can.'

I'd given Junio an order, but he did not obey. Instead he came up and whispered urgently, 'Then, master, why don't you take your toga off? You've got a tunic underneath.'

It was such an obvious idea that I don't know why it had not occurred to me. A man in a smart tunic in these parts might raise an eyebrow here and there but that was nothing compared to the stir my formal badge of citizenship would cause. Besides, Bullface and his men were looking for a man in Roman dress.

I nodded ungraciously, and raised my arms while Junio unwound the woollen length, and bundled it into his arms. 'But what about the purse?' I said, catching sight of myself as I looked down. The pouch, which had been hidden in the folds, now dangled invitingly from my belt.

'Why don't you hang that underneath your tunic, round your neck?'

My powers of reason, which had been paralysed by fear, came slowly to my aid. 'Better still, why don't you?' I said, undoing it. 'There's enough money here for a few nights' lodging, more or less. Take it to Gwellia, and tell her that if I don't come home tonight, she is to take a cart and get you all to Corinium as quickly as she can. Explain that Marcus has another villa there that used to be his wife's and that I'm sure the servants there will let you in. You've been before. You go with her and show her the way. I'll try to join you there as soon as possible.' As I spoke I hung the purse round his neck.

His tunic-top appeared to bulge a bit, but he hitched the toga-bundle up to cover it.

'This toga's very damp, master, and your tunic too. Are you all right?'

'I stopped to talk to someone in the rain. But that hardly matters now. The question is, what are we going to do with it?' I said. 'We can hardly just carry it around.'

Junio gave me his engaging grin. 'Of course we can,' he said. 'You are not thinking like a slave. Your toga's wet and muddy and it needs a clean – obviously I'm taking it to the fuller's shop, if anybody asks.'

'There isn't one here, surely? Any fuller who used the river water hereabouts would have the clothes come out of his treading vats dirtier than they went in.'

'There's a fuller's shop inside the walls, beside the docks – that gives us every reason to be here. We go back up the way we've come, slip inside the city walls from there, and try to get back through the southern gate at dusk. But we should move – that fellow with the oil will be back.'

It was such a simple plan it made me laugh, but all the same I had to shake my head. 'A good scheme, Junio, but you'll have to go alone. It doesn't take two slaves to take the laundry in. Anyway, I am too well known at those gates, in a toga or out of it, and no doubt if there is a warrant out for my arrest the town guards will be looking for me now. They will know that I have come into the town. I'll have to skirt the walls and go the long way round. Don't argue, Junio . . .' (he was showing signs of it) '. . . I am your master, after all. Better that one of us is safe, at least. Just keep out of the way of Bullface and his men, and as long as you're not seen with me you should be all right.'

I hoped that what I said was true. It should have been. Even if Balbus had given instructions to arrest me on sight, they would not usually extend to my slave as well. Yet there was so much that was inexplicable – someone had allowed me to escape from the garrison unchecked, for instance, when guards were waiting for me at my former home – I could not be sure of anything. But there was no time to think it through just now, and on balance I thought Junio was safe.

I said, 'Go now, and tell your mistress what I said. I'll try to get home as soon as possible.'

'And if the guards arrive at the roundhouse before you do . . .?'

'You'll just have to leave a signal, if you can. I don't know what. Leave something at the gate. Something unusual. But go – go now! It may be too late otherwise. Every instant counts.'

He was reluctant, but he went at last. I watched him set off back the way we'd come, with his burden tucked underneath his arm. He was whistling, the very picture of a carefree slave taking his master's robe for laundering. I, on the other hand, looked completely out of place.

For one thing, I thought, I was far too clean. I picked up a handful of mud from beside the rubbish pile and streaked my face and hair with it. It went against every instinct I possessed, but I was in the act of rubbing my backside – and therefore my best tunic – against the grimy wall when the fat bearded ruffian came back.

He was alone, rather to my surprise, and for a moment we stood eyeing each other up. He seemed as uneasy at this encounter as I was myself, and I saw his huge hands clench into fists. My hand went instinctively towards my belt, but of course I had not brought my knife with me. It is strictly an offence to carry weapons within the city walls, and though a dining knife is usually ignored, I had been visiting the garrison. I had taken no chances with the letter of the law. All I was carrying at my waist, now my purse was gone, was one of those fiddling Roman spoons – a present from Marcus at the banquet yesterday. It did have a spike at one end to open oysters with, but it was a small and decorative thing and precious little use in an emergency. For all practical purposes, I was unarmed.

Fatbeard took a step towards me. It was not a friendly step.

I gulped. I tried to remind myself that Junio had often been this way, unharmed. There was just a chance I could talk my way out of this. 'Is something wrong?' I said, using my native Celtic tongue. The man was unlikely to be of Latin blood.

He was chewing something, probably dried fish, but the rhythmic motion of his jaws stopped suddenly. It made him seem more menacing, if possible. He spat his mouthful out on to the pile and spoke. Latin – coarse and ill educated, but Latin none the less. 'I don't speak whatever tongue that is. We're Roman-minded here. And who are you?' His eyes looked me up and down, and came to rest on my best leather shoes, now ankle-deep in mire. His own lower legs were wrapped in bits of sack. 'Runaway slave, I'd place a bet on it! That's what you are, aren't you, fancy-feet?' You could almost see the promise of reward dancing in front of his greedy little eyes.

'Freed-man,' I said, matching my Latin form to his. I made to pull down the neck of my tunic so he could see the brand. It had been removed long since and the puckered injury was clearly old.

I saw his eyes narrow, but he let it go. 'Never mind all that. Seen a white-rober down here, with his slave, have you?'

I looked up and down the alley, and tried to feign surprise. 'Only me here,' I said unhelpfully. I half expected him to ask again what I was doing here, so I bent over and began to pick through the rubbish heap, as I have sometimes seen the beggars do.

He grunted. 'Fallen on bad times, have we?'

I shrugged and hung my head. 'You know how it is. The chariots . . .' It was the best I could think of at the time, but it was not impossible. More than one man has met his ruin by betting too much money on a losing horse.

He swaggered close to me. 'Bet on the reds, did we? Well, let me tell you something, friend. This rubbish heap's already spoken for. It's taken my pals a month to put together a decent pile of rags and wood, and for me to get hold of a pot of oil to douse them with. And then you come along and try to help yourself. Well just forget it, friend. You want a fire, you pay, like anybody else. And one more thing. You tell anyone you've seen me here, and I'll set a torch to you, as well. Especially that white-rober who was snooping round. You understand?'

Of course. I should have understood before. No one eking out a living in these parts could afford to throw away a jar of oil, however stinking and rancid it might be. Fatbeard had obviously stolen it – from his master probably. That was why he had retreated from a toga in alarm – ironically, he had been afraid of *me*. Now that he thought I was penniless, his swaggering manner had returned.

'I understand,' I said, 'I'm off. Looking for fish-heads, that was all. I understand there's a market for them in the town.' For a moment I forgot my role. My Latin was too good. I backed away, in the direction Junio had gone.

He scowled after me, then his fat face screwed into a puzzled frown. 'Here, wait a minute . . .' he began. 'Those shoes. That voice. You're no mere runaway. It was you dressed up in that toga. Course it was.' He gave an ugly little smile. 'So either you're a nasty little spy, sent by the market police, or you were impersonating a citizen, and that's a capital offence. I think you and me have a lot to talk about. Come here!'

But the rubbish heap was still between us. I reached out and toppled it across the path, and then I turned and ran.

I half heard him lumbering after me, but I did not stop. I was old but he was fat, and I was still sprightlier than he was, especially now that I was not impeded by a toga at every step. I had no idea where I was going, but when I saw a proper alleyway I took it. I panted down a narrow little path between two tenements and out into a crowded thoroughfare.

Straight into Bullface and his men.

I was trapped like an eel in a basket. There was no escaping them.

The three guards were only yards away, brutal as only private soldiery can be. They were coming towards me as I turned into the street, their faces black as thunder, marching like an execution squad and banging their shields with their daggers as they came. People were melting away to let them pass.

There was no way to avoid them. I leaned up against a friendly wall and shut my eyes.

IX

I felt, rather than saw, Bullface raise his arm, and a moment later a harsh backhanded blow sent me sprawling to the floor.

I waited, huddled on the ground, expecting a dagger in the ribs. None came. I opened one eye – just in time for Bullface to aim a spiteful kick at me, and then the group walked on without another glance.

I did not move again until they had moved round the corner out of sight. Then I raised myself gingerly on to one elbow, and felt myself all over to make sure I was alive. I was. Blood was streaming from a cut above my ear, my arms and legs were bruised and scratched from contact with the ground, and my ribs ached where Bullface's hobnailed foot had thudded into them. Otherwise – if there was an otherwise – I seemed to be more or less intact. I rolled over on to my knees and clambered painfully upright by leaning on the wall.

I stood there for a moment to collect myself. I could still hardly credit that I'd escaped again. I realised I had Junio to thank. Stripping out of my toga had been a good idea. Bullface was looking for a citizen – dressed as I had been at the banquet yesterday and again this morning at the garrison – so by becoming a dirt-streaked nobody in a tunic I had rendered myself effectively invisible. Of course it did not help my throbbing arm and ribs, but the attack had not been personal, merely an outburst of military impatience with an ageing non-citizen who got in his way. I sent up a mental prayer of thanks to whatever gods there were, and promised them a sacrifice or two, but I knew I was running out of miracles. No one can be that lucky for very long.

And I was not out of danger yet. I was not far from where my workshop was, and Bullface and his men were still in the area. Suddenly this suburb, where I'd lived and worked for years, had become a very dangerous place to be. I was beginning to wonder if I'd ever feel secure again.

Working on the old adage that the best hiding place is where the searcher has already looked, I told myself that my best course was to set off in the direction Bullface and company had just come from, and to do it as fast as I could limp. I was shaken, sore and bruised, but I thought that I could manage if I held on to the wall.

I had taken perhaps half a dozen painful steps before I realised that even this was not to be. Fatbeard had materialised from the passageway and was in front of me. He had armed himself now with a rough piece of timber from a rubble heap, and was holding it before him like a kind of club.

I looked wildly about, but I couldn't run, and anyway there was nowhere I could hide. Between Bullface's men and this ruffian, I was truly in a trap. Without my patron I was nobody, and though I was not very far from home there was no one I could look to for support.

Fatbeard reached my side in two long strides and seized me so roughly by the shoulder that I winced. I had already bruised it in my fall.

'All right, fancy-feet,' he said, thrusting his fat hairy face into my own. His breath stank of bad teeth and rotten fish. 'Let's have the truth. I thought at first you were some sort of spy, but you were hiding from those troops, weren't you?' He shook me fiercely. 'That's right, isn't it? So what do they want you for? Impersonating a citizen, and what else? It can't be for stealing purses, like an ordinary thief – they wouldn't go to all this fuss for that. So what was it? Selling secrets? What?'

Tradesfolk were coming back on to the street – Bullface and his guard had cleared it faster than the rain. For a moment I thought of hollering for help, but it was patently no use. People who were anywhere near us hurried past, averting their eyes and trying to pretend they hadn't seen. I could hardly blame them. If there is an altercation in the street, it is usually safer not to get involved, and my assailant was not a figure to be meddled with.

Fatbeard must have sensed the way my thoughts had run. He gave a nasty smile and inched me back into the alleyway, prodding me roughly in the stomach with his makeshift club. It was a large and ugly piece of wood, big enough to support half a roof, but he handled it as if it were a twig. It was enough to ensure that I did not resist.

'Well?' he said again, when we were safely out of sight of passers-by.

I could not have answered coherently if I'd tried. I wondered faintly whether a beating from that club would be better or worse than a systematic questioning by Bullface's men. On any logical reckoning, Bullface won. There was just a chance my rank of Roman citizen would help me if I were officially arrested. Here, a claim of rank was only likely to make matters worse: and if Fatbeard did thrash a confession out of me, he would presumably march me triumphantly away, hand me over and pocket the reward, in which case Bullface's men would get me anyway.

But instinct won. Something told me that Fatbeard did not love authority, and that being on the run from men in uniform might just be an advantage in his company. It was worth a try. I gave a helpless nod. 'I was trying to hide from those men, it's true. They've just got here from Gaul. They're not the regular garrison.' I don't know why I added that – it didn't help.

Fatbeard looked singularly unimpressed. 'If they come from Gaul, what do they want you for? And don't lie to me!' He gave me a warning clout around the shoulder blades, not quite hard enough to knock me down.

I wondered how long it would take to die, and how long it would take the news of my fate to reach Gwellia. What would become of her, if I was conveniently set upon and killed here in the street, thereby relieving the civic authorities of the necessity?

Perhaps it was the thought of that which helped me find my tongue enough to say, 'Listen – I am a poor pavement-maker by trade . . .'

Fatbeard interrupted with a sneer. 'A pavement-maker, is it? What about that toga, fancy-feet?'

I hesitated, fearing that the truth would shatter any fragile hopes I had. 'That slave you saw me with – I know him well. It is his master's robe – he's taking it to the fuller's to be cleaned – and he helped me to use it to disguise myself.' All of which was perfectly true, I told myself. I simply hadn't mentioned that the slave and toga were my own. 'I am a mosaic-maker, as I said. I have a little workshop on the northern edge of town. I try to ply my trade and mind my own business, in the ordinary way, but the commander of the force from Gaul is dead, and one of my customers – my patron – is accused of it. He was arrested last night by those men you saw – they were the dead man's bodyguard – and now they're after me. I found them on guard outside my workshop this afternoon. I didn't stop to ask questions – I just ran away.'

Fatbeard spat. 'You expect me to believe all this?'

'Ask anyone who was in the Street of the Tannery today. Or at the citadel last night. Ask anyone at all. I'm sure the story will be all round the streets by now.' I was safe in that. The forum wits say that a rich man cannot belch in Glevum without everyone's hearing of it within an hour or two, and for once I was glad of the rumour-whisperers. The story of Marcus's arrest must be the subject of the whole town's gossip now.

My questioner looked scornful. 'I *shall* ask people, fancy-feet, make no mistake. And if what you are telling me is lies, I'll make you sorry you were ever born. In the meantime, you come along with me, until I decide what's to be done with you.' He had me backed up against the wall, but now he stepped back and gave me a sharp prod with his club, urging me to walk in front of him.

I was still battered from my fall and from the guard's kick, so I could do nothing but shuffle on ahead. I lacked the strength or speed now to run away again, and there was no chance of giving Fatbeard the slip. Whenever I glanced backwards he was watching me – his little glittering eyes fixed on me as if attached with fish-head glue. In fact I soon learned not to glance at all. Each time I turned my head he jabbed hard at my spine with his piece of jagged wood.

We walked in silence down the muddy path. I was cold and I was hungry – I had eaten and drunk nothing since I left the roundhouse shortly after dawn – and with my bleeding face and bruised limbs I felt like misery itself. By now it was becoming dark, and though the rain had ceased a dank river-mist was rising. However, from what loomed up through the gloom, it was evident that we were going back the way I'd come, and I expected at any minute to find myself back at the rags-and-rubbish pile. But before we had arrived at it my captor stopped and pushed me roughly to one side, and through a gap where a portion of the wall had fallen in.

'You get in there,' he said, and thrust me forward into a kind of hut: a rough stone shed with no windows in the wall. It had the remnants of a roof, and from the general smell that rose from the earth floor it might once have been a shelter for a pig. The door, such as it was, hung lopsidedly, but even as he pushed me inside the hut I saw that Fatbeard was moving into place a huge flat stone to wedge the door, securing me inside more effectively than with any Roman barrel-lock and key.

'Wait here,' he said, as if I had a choice. 'I'm going to talk to a friend or two of mine, and then we'll decide what's to become of you. I think that you're probably worth something, handed in alive – but whether they'll think it's worth the risk, I'm not so sure. We aren't so very keen on soldiers and the law round here.' He was still heaving at the heavy wedge to close the door.

I tried to interpose my foot into the last thumb's-breadth or two of gap, but he was stronger than I was and I had to draw it back before he crushed my bones. 'Then we are of one mind,' I said. 'By all the gods, I swear . . .'

'Forget the gods,' he said. 'I've got my sources – ears and eyes across the town. We'll soon see if you're telling me the truth or not.' The last words were muffled as the door fell to and he let the huge rock topple into place.

'You can't . . .' I began, but it was too late. He had. I fancied I could hear his footsteps squelch back to the path. Then there was silence.

I tried to strain my ears for any noise, but if there was human life nearby, all evidence was swallowed by the thickening mist.

I have a horror of small places in the dark – born of a time when I was captured as a slave and kept chained and bound for days in a heaving stinking hold, seasick and desperate. To allay my rising panic I attempted to explore the inside of the hut, but it was already much too dark to see. Only the faintest sliver of grey light crept in through the crack above the door, and there was another lighter patch which resolved itself – when I became accustomed to the gloom – into a small hole in the collapsing roof. I stood beneath it, gulping in the air, and discovered that the hole also admitted water in a steady dismal drip, although the rain had ceased some time before.

I reached out a hand. Nothing but the cold, damp stone and an uneven muddy floor. Even if I had been young and fit, I could not have scaled those walls – and I was hurt and feeling every moment of my age.

There was nothing for it but to wait. The realisation left me almost paralysed with misery. Tired almost to exhaustion, too, but there was nowhere I could rest – any contact with the walls or floor was bone-searchingly damp, and the thin tunic was all the covering I had.

In the end I settled uncomfortably on my haunches and wrapped my arms round myself for warmth, occasionally catching the drips to moisten my parched tongue. What a contrast with the night before! Then I had been a guest in an expensive house, warmed with all the best food and drink a wealthy man could buy. Amazing to think it was such a short time ago.

I tried to beguile the endless wait by mentally running through events again. Praxus, one moment eating and drinking with the rest of us, the next staggering off into the ante-room to die. Face down in the vomitorium, but too big by far to push there unless he was already weak – even that red weal round his neck could not have been inflicted if he'd had his health and strength.

Try as I would I could see nothing that would explain all this unless there was something in his food or drink: and that had been supplied by Marcus from the start, cooked in Marcus's kitchen and served by Marcus's slaves. So had someone else got in and tampered with the food? It seemed impossible – Praxus's own bodyguard was at the gate, as well as the normal doorkeeper. And how could anyone make sure that Praxus alone would eat the poisoned dish?

Furthermore, I realised with increasing chill, when Praxus had not very soon returned, Marcus himself had gone out after him. Marcus, who would not reach out a hand to lift a glass if there was a slave nearby to hand it to him. There were no witnesses to what happened next. Even Golbo the little bucket-boy had been conveniently sent away, and he had told me himself that the instruction had come from Marcus personally, via a trusted slave. Then when – according to his own version of events – Marcus came upon the corpse of his most senior guest, far from raising a general alarm, he had sent for me.

The more I reasoned through all this, the more sinister it looked. Marcus thought Praxus was a violent and intemperate boor, and – in the temporary absence of the provincial governor – one who had been about to assume a great deal more power than was good for him in the running of the Republica Glevensis. I could imagine that, for the good of the colonia, my patron might feel the man was better dead, especially since he had designs on Julia as well. What I could not believe was that Marcus would perpetrate a deed like this and then permit his servants to be tortured ten by ten. He was a patrician, so a confession would not be extorted from him, at least until he came to Rome, but surely he was too humane . . .

I stopped. Supposing he had, after all, confessed? That might explain why everyone was after me, when I had been permitted to leave the garrison unchallenged so short a time before.

I shook my head. That was not an explanation, after all; if the authorities had *his* free confession there was no point in their arresting me. Unless they had decided, for reasons of their own, that I was somehow implicated too. I shivered. A Roman jail is not a pleasant place.

Though few things, I thought, could be worse than this. Apart from my throbbing bruises I was damp, and as cold and hungry as I'd been for years. I was getting stiffer by the moment, too. I struggled to my feet, and slapped my arms about to bring some warmth into my limbs, then sank into a huddle once again.

It seemed to me that I was there for hours, shifting my weight from haunch to painful haunch, listening for the tiny plash of that persistent drip, and watching the tiny strip of grey light above the door fade into darkness as the night closed in.

X

The first hint that I was about to be released was a faint illumination in the sky, following by a scuffling at the door and the smell of burning tallow in the air. Someone with a smoky torch was obviously moving back the stone.

I braced myself against the inner wall, ready for Fatbeard and his makeshift club, but when – with a final grunt and heave – the rock was moved away and the door tumbled sideways on its hinges once again, there was no sign of his massive frame. Nor of Bullface and his men, which was my second thought. Indeed, for an instant I thought that nobody was there.

Then from somewhere behind the pile of stones someone raised the torch, if it deserved that name: it was obviously a simple branch of wood dipped into tallow fat and set alight. It was a poor enough thing, but the flame seemed so bright as it approached after the darkness of the hut that at first I stood blinking in the light, unable to make sense of what I saw. I focused my eyes a little lower down, and saw two forms outlined against the misty dark.

Nightmare figures. Small, distorted and grotesque, like something conjured from a drunken dream.

The one who held the light, I now saw, was thin – the arm which held the torch aloft seemed to be thinner than the torch itself, and the face was no more than a wild-eyed skull under a mane of straggling white hair. Yet the bony hand which suddenly shot out and pulled me from the hut moved with the strength and speed of youth. He did not speak. There was something dreadful in this sinewed ghost.

He was no giant, but the second figure – though adult – was smaller still: barely more than half my height. I recognised the man. It was a club-footed beggar, known as Sosso, who sometimes haunted the tombs outside the gates. A successful beggar, too, largely because he terrified the passers-by. Apart from that misshapen foot, he had a twisted frame, and moved lopsided, like an animal. Though so extremely short he had shoulders like an ox, but no discernible forehead or neck, all of which gave him a general air of ugly malevolence. He was known to lurch up to lone people at the tombs, holding out his hand with threatening grunts. People with business in the area even equipped themselves with amulets sometimes to keep his dwarfish, loping form at bay.

I'd thrown him a brass coin myself once or twice – less out of pity for his undoubted plight than from a selfish instinct for self-preservation. He had shrewd and calculating eyes, and always looked like the sort of beggar who might remember one, and creep up one dark night to take revenge.

Now it looked as if that night had come.

Sosso was wielding a sort of knife, a piece of broken blade lashed to a stick and painstakingly polished and sharpened to a point. In his hands it seemed a more unpleasant weapon than any expensive dagger could have been.

'Come!' he grunted. Sosso, as I was to learn, could speak but he was not a man of many words.

I shuffled forward painfully. My fall, combined with that

long chilly wait, had stiffened all my joints. 'Come where?' I said.

'You'll see soon enough,' the skinny one replied. His voice was unexpectedly low-pitched and resonant, as if an oracle had spoken in a cave. He looked as if a breeze would blow him down but the vice-like grip on my arm had dreadful strength. The wraith had sinews like a vine. That, with his ghastly appearance, made him sinister.

'But . . .' I began, and was rewarded by the point of Sosso's blade against my ribs. 'Walk!' Sosso told me, and I silently obeyed.

The path, which had been difficult by day, was doubly treacherous in the dark. Apart from the threat of unseen obstacles, the night was close to freezing, and the mud sucked at my feet with ghastly tentacles of cold.

Our destination was not far away, I found.

First there was the acrid smell of smoke, then a reddish glow appeared through the gloom, and we found ourselves back at the rubbish pile which I had pulled over at Fatbeard's feet earlier that day. It had been assembled once again and, by some means, set alight and coaxed into a sullen fire. It now smoked and spat and sizzled intermittently but still gave off a faint reluctant heat.

Around it, crouched and huddled in the smoke, was the most wretched collection of humanity that I had ever seen. A haggard mother with a scabrous infant; a wretched, limping, pock-marked girl, perhaps fifteen years of age, from whom all bloom of youth had fled; a crone; a one-legged man; a man with half a hand; and another whom again I recognised. His whole face and body was a scar where – as I knew from his begging in the streets – he'd fallen in a boiling vat before his master turned him on the street. And behind all these, lurking in the shadows even here, a thin, sharp-faced man with tattered clothes and a youth with glittering and disturbing eyes.

I remembered what Fatbeard had said earlier: 'If you want a fire, you pay for it, like anybody else,' and wondered what the pathetic 'owners' of this fire could possibly possess that might be considered payment for the privilege. Perhaps they simply stole, or, in the women's case, frequented the darker passages behind the docks and sold the only commodity they had. If so, I thought suddenly, I began to understand. In circumstances like theirs 'possession' of a fire might mean the difference between life and death.

I saw for the first time what it was to be really poor. The misty damp seeped through my tunic-cloth, and I was shivering. Lack of food gnawed at my entrails, but compared to these people I was like a king. I have known what it is to be a slave, to sleep in draughty sheds with not enough to eat, and to possess nothing of my own, but – even when I was legally a mere thing myself – I had never faced this kind of cold and want. Even in the very worst of times, it is in a master's interests to see that his possessions have sufficient warmth and food to keep them strong enough to work. I had never been as these people were, without the prospect of a meal or even a proper shelter for the night.

Not until now, that is.

It was one thing, however, for me to feel some sympathy for them: there was clearly little sympathy for me. Sosso prodded me forward with his blade, while his companion kept a firm hold on my arm, but as I made my way towards the blaze I was aware of mutterings and discontent as I was forced to come between people and the fire.

The wraith aimed a kick at the ragged woman with the

child. 'Stop that grumbling, or this'll be the last time you get food and fire from us. This is the runaway man we were told of. Grossus said that we're to take look at him, and decide what's to be done. Now, mind your feet and let us get him to the fire, where we can see him better in the light.'

The woman cursed, but she moved her feet a bit – poor bleeding bundles wrapped in bits of sack – and we stepped over them into the dim glow given out by the fire. My skinny captor raised his tallow torch again, and held it so that they could see my face.

'Well' – clearly he had appointed himself spokesman for the group – 'you've heard what Grossus said. Found him lurking in a toga, spying on our pile – then picked him up a moment later, running from the guard. He claims to be a tradesman whose patron is in jail. What do we think about it, Grossus wants to know.'

There was some whispering at this, as some of them raised apathetic heads to look. The woman who'd been forced to move her feet gathered her ragged cloak around her child and spat. 'Why don't we just knock him on the head, and throw his body in the river? That tunic would fit any one of us, and there's good leather in those shoes and belt. They would fetch something in the market place.'

'Worth more as a ransom,' said the man with half a hand. 'If the authorities are really after him, the chances are they'll pay.'

There was a murmur of assent, but the woman snapped, 'That's all very well, but which of you is going to hand him in? You, Cornovacus?' She turned to the two men in the shadows as she spoke. 'The town guard has been seeking you for years. Or perhaps you'd like to do it, Lercius, and hope your master has forgotten that you ran away?'

The man with half a hand seemed unconvinced. 'There's some of us could do it. One or two amongst us are freemen born, and not all of us are thieves. Seems a pity to turn down a handsome sum.'

'Mightn't be a handsome sum,' the woman said. 'We've only got this blighter's word for it. More likely Grossus was right at the start, and he's a spy – down here working for the market police.'

The man in the shadows grunted. 'She's right. If we hand him in, Dis knows what the consequence might be. What if this idiot really has a patron, as he claims, and someone starts taking an interest later on? Do we want them asking questions about who it was who sold him to the guard? Besides, the wretched fellow's seen us now. Do the simple thing. Rob him, stick him in the river, and have done with it – that's what I say.'

I had attempted to interrupt several times, but a warning prod from Sosso's dagger somewhere in the region of my entrails had so far prevented me. However, matters were desperate now. I croaked out, 'What I said is true. I'm a pavement-maker from the town. My patron is Marcus Septimus . . .' I stopped, as Sosso prodded me again.

None the less, to my amazement, my words had some effect. The one-legged man looked up from the fire, then swung himself over, leaning on a crutch. He stared at me a moment, silently. 'I think I've seen this fellow in the forum once or twice,' he said at last. 'And Marcus what's-his-name was arrested yesterday. That much is certain. So it's possible the rest of it is true. What do you think, Sosso? Have you ever seen this man before? You must have done, if he is who he says.'

Sosso frowned. He lowered his makeshift blade an inch and pushed his filthy face up as close as possible to mine. He peered up at me as if he was learning to decipher writing, and I was a difficult inscription that he was struggling to read.

'Think so.' It was less an observation than a grunt. Then he shrugged and raised his knife again. 'Don't know. Might be wrong. Probably. Usually am.'

I wished devoutly that I had managed to make myself more memorable. If I'd only tossed either of these men a larger coin the last time we met, they might have recognised me now and that could have been enough to save my life.

'Well.' Now it was the ragged crone who spoke, through toothless gums. 'It's no good asking me. I can't see well enough to tell – but if that Marcus Whatsit is the same one I've heard about, it seems to me that we have problems here. Isn't that Marcus a friend of the governor's? And an important magistrate as well? That must make him the richest man for miles.'

'Meaning that our friend here might be valuable?' The wraith smiled, and his bony hand tightened disagreeably on my arm.

The crone gave a mirthless laugh. 'Meaning that he might be trouble, fool. If we dispose of him, there will be questions asked.'

There was a general rustle around the fire at this. Everyone seemed to have a point of view.

'Well, we can't just let him go – not when he can identify us all . . .'

'Better to hand him over to the authorities. There might be a reward . . .'

'For a freed-man when his patron is in jail? Not much, I shouldn't think. At least, not to the likes of us. Besides, it's always safer to keep away from guards . . .'

'But supposing his patron is released? There'd be worse trouble then. That Marcus person is a magistrate. We'd all end up before the courts – and probably before the beasts as well.'

'Wait a minute,' the pock-marked girl said. 'I've heard about this, now I come to think of it. One of the soldiers told me earlier, when I had some business near the garrison.' She did not mention what her 'business' was. She really didn't need to. All eyes were turned to her, and she stepped closer to the fire – clearly enjoying a little attention for a change – before she went on. 'They've got the most senior magistrate for miles locked up, because he killed some really important military man. Didn't want to do what the Emperor had said and share the local power with him, they say.'

Sosso's knife did not move an inch, but his indrawn breath sounded like a hiss. 'Great Jove! You're sure?'

She shrugged. 'That's what I heard, though one of my soldier friends – a prison guard – said there was more to it than that. The military fellow was a brute, in any case, he said – had his eye on everybody's wife and a whole history of rivals who just disappeared or turned up lying somewhere in a ditch. Kept a formidable bodyguard, it seems. It could be that this Marcus simply got in first. But they can't persuade him to confess to any crime, and his servants won't say anything at all, though the interrogators have had them half the day.'

It was my turn to draw in my breath, this time in sympathy. I wondered which of the servants had 'confessed' to Praxus's advance to Julia.

The girl was continuing her tale. 'But anyway the law's the law, and you know what the judges always say. *Cui bono?* Who benefits? If you look at it like that, this Marcus is obviously as guilty as can be. Besides, it all happened at his house and no one else had the opportunity.'

Sosso was shaking his head. 'Political? Don't like it.'

The wraith nodded agreement. 'Never want to get mixed up in politics. We'll all of us end up in jail, or worse. And this patron obviously has friends in high places. Suppose he does get out – where does that leave us then?'

'What do you think, Sosso?' somebody enquired. 'Do we hand him in? Or throw him in the river here and now? Probably safer to get rid of him.'

They were discussing my murder animatedly, as if I wasn't there. I opened my mouth to defend myself, but Sosso was looking at me thoughtfully, his blade still fixed at my stomach. I closed my mouth again.

'It's Grossus's fault,' the older woman said. 'He got us into this. Where is he anyway? When he came down with a brand to light the fire, he promised some of his mistress's soup tonight. Get down there, Parva. Stop your gossiping and see what's happening.' She gave the girl a shove, so that she moved away reluctantly and drifted off into the mist.

The others took no notice, and she went on grumbling. 'Trust Grossus to leave us with this mess. If he wanted the man robbed and killed, he should have done it himself while he had the chance.'

'We ought to do it, and do it now, and weight the body down. That way the authorities need never know. We'd take his belt and shoes, of course. One of us could sell them in another town,' Cornovacus put in.

The wild-eyed youth they had called Lercius came towards me. He had a piece of jagged timber in his hand. He raised it like a club, then jabbed it like a spear, and then tapped it lovingly against his palm. He smiled. 'Can't I just . . .'

That made up my mind. Sosso or no Sosso, I was going to speak. 'Listen!' I said loudly.

Lercius reacted instantly. The jagged wood jerked upwards at my vital parts. If Sosso's hand had not closed over his it might have been the end. Another inch and he would have disembowelled me.

'What was that for?' Lercius said, nursing his hand: Sosso was obviously very strong. 'He's not worth anything.'

I said bitterly, 'You're right, of course. With my patron locked away in jail, my life is of little value to anyone but me. It must be tempting to get rid of me. But there's another way. Help me, and my patron will be grateful when he's freed – which he will be, when I can reach the proper authorities. You heard what he said: I'm sure he can prove his innocence.' (I had my doubts about this, inwardly, but I wasn't going to voice them now.) 'You get me out of here, and I'll ensure that you get a good reward without any interference from the guards. And the same thing goes for . . .' I was going to say 'Fatbeard' but corrected just in time, 'the big fellow with the beard,' I finished.

If Grossus Fatbeard held these people in his power, as I deduced he did – extorting a proportion of what little they obtained in return for fire and a smattering of food – it was important that my promise covered him. It was a gamble, of course, and I had not the slightest notion of how the promise was going to be fulfilled, but it was enough to make them think.

There was a startled hush, and then the woman said, 'Well, you heard what Parva said. If he's sure that they'll release him in the end . . . it might be safest in the long run, I suppose . . .'

'I don't believe it,' Cornovacus said. 'This son of a dog is lying.'

'I still think I should . . .' Lercius brandished his pointed stick again. 'I'll get the truth from him.'

'Not now, Lercius!' somebody exclaimed and the crone said, 'Perhaps we should wait and see what Grossus thinks.'

I had them wavering at least, but it was Sosso who had the final word. Despite his unpromising appearance and grunting speech, he seemed capable of sharp intelligence and the others obviously deferred to him.

Now he was furrowing the place where his forehead should have been, and signalling to the rest to hold their tongues. Then, without lowering the knife, he turned to me. 'How much?'

I was startled into foolishness. 'How much for what?'

'Don't play games with us, pavement-maker, or we'll change our minds.' That was Cornovacus, coming suddenly to life and slamming me back against the wall so hard that I stood spluttering for breath. 'You know exactly what he means. How much to get you safely out of here?'

XI

As I struggled to regain my breath I tried to think. I had not expected such sudden capitulation, and the direct challenge caught me unawares. I realised I had no sensible reply to give.

I was suddenly horribly aware of how feeble my bargaining position was. I had no idea, in fact, what sort of 'good reward' Marcus was likely to agree to pay on my account, even supposing he was ever freed – and that looked far from certain, whatever I had said. Or he might be exiled – forbidden 'fire and water' within the Empire, as the formula required. In that case his goods would be forfeit to the state. It was even possible that, if he were suddenly released, he would pretend to regard the whole suggestion as a joke: Marcus was notoriously careful with every quadrans and of course I had no undertaking from him that he would pay anything at all.

It was a worry. No doubt these men would set the figure high, and I had no money of my own. Literally no money, now that Junio had my purse – not even at the roundhouse, if my instructions had been obeyed.

'We're waiting!' The wraith, who still had me in his grip, gave me a savage little shake. 'And no more lies about losing money on the chariots. We've asked. We know that you were never there last night!'

I had forgotten my pathetic little subterfuge, so this disconcerted me; and the suggestion that my story had been checked out like this made me more disturbed than ever. 'My patron knows how to show his gratitude,' I burbled, trying to avoid naming an outright sum. 'I'm sure that, when he's freed, he will surprise you with his generosity.'

I knew that it was weak. The man with half a hand obviously thought so too. He shook his head. 'Not good enough!' he said. 'We see money here and now, otherwise I vote we rob and kill him straight away. That way we're sure of something, anyway. Bury the body in the marsh; they'll never find it there.'

There was another murmur of agreement round the fire at this.

Lercius waved his jagged piece of wood again, his face in the sullen firelight wreathed in smiles. 'I'll find out if he has money, if you like. Or if you're going to push him in the river, let me have him first,' he pleaded.

There was something disquietingly infantile in his enthusiasm, and it dawned on me chillingly for the first time that he was not entirely sane. He was like a child who likes tormenting flies. The idea that I might become a human version of the fly was enough to send shudders down my spine. I tried to speak, but no words came out.

'Just a little bit?' he begged.

Sosso shook his head at him, but the wraith said warningly to me, 'He's right. You pay us something now, or there's no deal at all.'

I found my voice, but it was still unsteady as I said, 'I'll give you something when I reach the house. But I don't have my purse . . .'

At this Sosso gave a nod towards the man with the scars, who got up and shambled to my side. Then, almost before I knew what was afoot, a pair of expert hands were travelling over me, so quick and light that I scarcely felt them move.

'No purse,' the man reported, and melted back into the dark.

'He's got that fancy oyster spoon,' the woman said. 'That should be worth a *sestertius* or two. We'll have that for a start.'

'My spoon?' I hadn't thought of that. It was the one object of any value that I had with me, but it had hardly seemed adequate as a bribe. That was no problem. I would have given a thousand oyster spoons to be away from there. 'Very well,' I muttered hastily, eyeing Lercius, who was still loitering. 'The oyster spoon it is.' I started to unclip it from my belt, but Sosso intervened.

'Belt too!' he grunted, and there was nothing I could do but take that off as well.

'Now those.' He pointed to my shoes.

I did gulp a bit at this. I was almost freezing as it was. The idea of walking barefoot in cold ooze and mud, with who knew what lurking underneath the mire, sent physical shivers down my spine. Besides, once I had parted with my shoes, I had nothing left to barter with at all. Yet there was not really an alternative.

I made a last attempt. 'The spoon and belt now and the shoes when I get clear.'

'You heard. He asked you for the shoes! No arguments.' The wraith's iron grip tightened on my arm. 'You want us to let Lercius loose on you?'

I squatted on the ground and took off my shoes. It occurred to me that I was now entirely at the mercy of the gang. Why should I expect them to keep their word and help me? I couldn't run and they had everything I owned, except my tunic and my underpants. It would not surprise me now if they took those as well, and either left me here to freeze or trussed me up and tossed me into the Sabrina then and there. In fact I was half expecting it. I could see that it would give Lercius a thrill to undertake the job on their behalf.

Sosso had unexpectedly put down his knife and was sitting on the ground beside the fire, pulling off his own ancient, tattered buskins – if that is not too grand a name for them. They were foot-coverings of the crude old-fashioned type that land slaves sometimes wear: mere bags of uncured cowhide, stripped still bloody from the animal, bound around the foot, and worn until it has dried out to a kind of formless boot. Even in the dim light of the fire I could see that Sosso's were split and full of holes, and had rubbed raw patches on both his feet – the same feet which he was now trying to force into my soft leather shoes.

They were proper shoes, not sandals – the only ones I had – worn in honour of my visit to the garrison. They had been made specially for me by a shoemaker as part of my payment when I'd designed a pavement for him once, and they were made of soft goatskin, cut to fit my foot. They were designed to lace together like a sandal at the top, admittedly, but on Sosso's filthy and misshapen feet they looked ridiculous. Both of them were far too small for him, but the one into which he'd pushed his swollen foot scarcely stretched further than the sole, and he struggled to make the laces meet at all. Sosso, though, seemed pleased with the effect, pointing his feet and wiggling his toes like a Lydian dancing girl.

His delight in such a simple thing was so self-evident that, at any other time, I could have felt a pang of sympathy for him, but then I felt only resentment and despair. Acute discomfort, too. I now had no shoes myself and as soon as I stood up freezing slime oozed in between my toes while my soles sank into cold and gritty mud. Walking anywhere like this would be a misery. Though, I told myself, that was probably the very least of my concerns – I would be lucky to walk anywhere again.

Or see anything either, if Lercius had his way. He had crept forward while Sosso was preoccupied, and taken up my spoon. He was now holding it towards me and making little stabbing motions with the oyster-spike in the direction of my eyes. When he saw me flinch he giggled and gave it an unpleasant little twist. In his hands it was a weapon.

The wraith, who had been watching Sosso, turned to him. 'Put that down, Lercius. It is not for you. It's to trade for food,' he said firmly, and to my surprise Lercius gave a sulky shrug and did as he was told.

'Speaking of food,' grumbled the ragged woman, whose child had by now set up a thin, hungry wail, 'here's Parva with the soup. And none too soon. Grossus promised it to us hours ago.' She pointed down the alleyway, where the pock-faced girl was struggling towards us through the gloom, carrying a pail of something in both her hands.

Soup. At the very thought of it my stomach growled, and when the girl edged towards the fire – no reluctance to make way for her now! – and lifted off the lid, I thought that I should faint from hunger at the smell of it. No matter that it was the worst kind of soup the cheap hot-food shops sell: a thin and greasy brew in which fragments of fur and hoof are often visible and a bit of gristle is a tasty treat. No matter that it was the drainings of the pot. Tonight it might have been ambrosia.

I wondered how the waiting group would eat, since there were no bowls or spoons in evidence, but the girl unslung a sacking bag which she had been carrying, and opened it to reveal some broken loaves of bread. These she spread out on the upturned bucket-lid, while people clustered round impatiently. The bread was obviously hard and stale, but everyone fell on it at once, seizing a piece and dipping it into the soup, then sucking it voraciously. As if their lives depended on it – as perhaps they did.

Even Sosso had stopped admiring his shoes and sprang up from his muddy perch to take his place. I noticed that the others left him the biggest piece of bread. He impaled it on his knife blade and immersed it in the pail. He did not stop to savour it, as the others did, but gnawed at it hungrily at once, then dipped the remnants in the soup again and stuffed the whole thing in his mouth.

I had been watching all this hungrily, and was surprised at his restraint, but the reason for it soon became obvious. He speared another piece and gave it to the wraith, who was thus able to eat his meagre meal without for an instant letting go of me. Sosso took up his former station guarding me. The burned man produced a large dead eel from a sack, swiftly struck off its head with a sharp stone, stripped off its skin between his forefinger and thumb, then thrust a long stick down its throat and set it to cook across the fire. It was all done in a moment, and soon the smell of cooking eel arose. I have never cared for eel, but it smelt so good it almost made me faint.

'I need food,' I said uncertainly. 'Give me some. I'll pay.'

Sosso sneered. 'How? Your underpants?' The knife-blade flickered closer as he spoke.

Suddenly an inspiration dawned. 'I know where there's a denarius,' I said.

The knife withdrew perceptibly. 'Where?'

'In the fountain of Apollo, near the market place. I dropped it there myself. Or rather, I offered it to someone from the garrison, if he could get a message to my patron or give me some information at the least. But first of all he wasn't any help and then he accidentally knocked it in. It should still be there.'

'Not any more it's not.' The man they called Cornovacus stepped forward suddenly and I got my first proper look at him. He was tall and thin and scrawny, wrapped in filthy rags, and his face had the pointed features of a rat, but there was a certain darting sharpness in his eyes. He had a silver coin in his hand. 'This is the money, Sosso. I was going to give it to you for the common purse. By Dis, I think he's telling us the truth. He was at the fountain earlier – I saw him there. And he did put money on the water trough. Three whole denarii. I saw the wretch that he was talking to – a cursed fellow in a military cloak – stick out his greedy little hand and scoop the others up, may Jupiter turn his cursed blood to bile. But this one fell in.' He turned it in his hand. 'I got it out. I thought the Fates had smiled on me at last.'

'How could you know all that?' I was startled into speech. 'There was nobody about.'

Cornovacus laughed mirthlessly. 'That's what you think, my friend! We don't survive by being visible – especially not those of us who need to take a purse or two to live. I was there all right – in the shadows by the fish market. I saw you, as I say.'

That was a sobering idea, in itself, but now that he had

testified on my account I almost began to hope again. Then, suddenly, I saw the implications. If he had seen me, he had seen me in a toga, and in that case I was probably as good as dead.

His next words to Sosso confirmed my darkest fears. 'This scum on the wine of Bacchus may be what he claims. But that's not all he is. He put the coins on the corner of the trough. I saw him do it. But I didn't realise it was him. He didn't look much like a tradesman then.' The little rat eyes glittered as he looked at me. 'Dressed up in very fancy clothes, he was.'

There! It was out. I closed my eyes, and waited for Lercius and his piece of wood. But it was Sosso who whirled round to me. 'Where's your purse? Had money then.' His speech might be slow and jerky, I admitted to myself, but his thought was quicker than a flashing sword.

I am not prone to the sorts of oaths that Cornovacus used, but at that moment I almost cursed the Fates. If I had kept my purse I might have got away – or at least have eaten something warm before I died. 'I gave it to my slave to take home,' I said reluctantly, resigned to the truth now that I had nothing left to lose. 'Together with my toga. But I did have money earlier. Your friend is right.'

'Up to something with the soldiers, eh?' Sosso sneered. It was a long utterance for him.

'I keep telling you. I brought the money to try to bribe the guard. I wanted information, that's all. That's why I gave it to that man – he's a military secretary with the garrison. A nervous sort of fellow with a tic.'

Parva with the pock-marked face spoke up again. 'That's true, too. I know the man. He's the one I was . . .' She paused, then went on in a different tone of voice, 'The rat. He was carrying at least two denarii, and he only gave me three lousy quadrantes. Said it was all the coin he had.'

Sosso ignored her. He turned away and held a muttered conference with Cornovacus and the wraith, leaving me, for a moment, without a guard. Shoeless and helpless as I was, I contemplated making a bolt for it, but the sight of Lercius at my elbow dissuaded me. The others were still whispering, though I could not catch the words. I didn't like the look of it at all. What were they scheming now?

Suddenly Sosso came loping back to me, and the wraith resumed his firm grip on my arm. 'Agreed?' he asked the group.

'If he can afford to bribe the secretary, he can afford to pay to save his wretched skin,' the woman said. 'He's worth a denarius or two, by the look of him. Just the sort to have a wealthy patron, too. Let him promise, and make sure he pays.'

'If there is any problem, Lercius will soon take care of it,' the scarred man put in. 'Splinters under the fingernails and a heated brand or two. You know what these accursed white-robers are. He had a purse. It must be somewhere. I didn't lift it from him, that's all I know. He'll pay.'

Sosso nodded to Cornovacus. 'Very well. Get Tullio,' and the man slipped away, like the shadow that he almost was.

I wondered vaguely who Tullio might be and what further trouble he would bring. But there was little time to think of that. Sosso squared up to me – or at least up to my chest, which was about as far up me as he reached. 'One denarius for food. Two more to get you home. Tonight!'

It might have been a bargain in the normal scheme of things, but tonight he might as well have asked me for the Circus Maximus. Yet I was not in a position to object. I would have to agree and hope that I could barter later on – or perhaps find something in the roundhouse he could have. If Gwellia had not taken everything to Corinium, there was just a chance that I could produce enough to save my skin.

'Very well.' I found that I was shaking with relief.

Too quick! The crone said instantly. 'Make it four denarii. That's two for us at least. Grossus will want half, if he hears of it. Or maybe five.'

It was absurd, but I had to make a stand. The price could go on rising indefinitely. 'Three. You've already got my spoon and belt and shoes,' I said.

Sosso stood on tiptoe to leer at me. 'I know,' he said. 'Tough, isn't it? Four.'

I was shivering with cold. 'Very well,' I muttered. 'Four denarii. And not a quadrans more. And remember I can't pay you if I have died of cold before you get me home. Nor if I have starved to death. Where is this food you were promising?'

Sosso nodded. He left me to the mercy of the wraith, whose bony grip tightened on my arm, and walked purposefully to his discarded boots. He kicked them towards me. 'Fair exchange!'

They were split, spoiled, misshapen, but I pulled them on. There was no way to dry or clean my feet, freezing and muddy as they were, but the scant protection of those ill-fitting evil-smelling bags felt like a kind of paradise to me. I knew in that instant why, in this climate, shoes were such a prize and why Sosso had been so delighted to have mine.

Sosso hadn't finished. 'Sack,' he said, and someone fetched the one that had contained the eel. It stank and it was damp, but it was extra warmth, and I wrapped it round my shoulders like a cloak.

Sosso grunted with impatience, snatched it back and made three slashes in it with his knife. 'Like this,' he said, and pulled it over me, making a kind of ragged outer tunic of the thing. It was disgusting and uncomfortable, but I saw that he was right. The second layer gave me much more warmth than simply huddling it round me would have done. Then Sosso seized the smaller bread sack and arranged it round my head and shoulders like a sort of cape. I was still chattering with cold, but I was by now better dressed than some of the other members of the group.

'Food,' Sosso ordered, and someone handed me a piece of eel on a stick. Blackened on the outside and half cooked within, nevertheless it was hot and it was tasty. 'Another!' and I wolfed that down as well. Then someone was sent to put some extra water in the pail (I did not ask where from) and Sosso gave me that, and I found myself drinking the greasy remnants of the soup. Anything edible had been mopped up long before, but I sucked on the remaining bits of bone, and chewed the ear of something, till I felt a little better, and there was nothing left at all.

It was only then that I looked up. The rest were eating eel, though there was an altercation near the fire between the woman with the child and the pock-faced girl. I realised, with a pang of guilt, that I must have eaten someone else's share. I had been thinking resentfully of what a denarius would buy – honey cakes, hot pie, and a better class of soup – but I began to view my meal rather differently. It was possible these people had not seen food for days. What they had given me, though poor, was all they had – though naturally the weakest suffered most.

I felt better for it, too: not full or comfortable or warm, but

I was no longer in danger of a faint. I turned to Sosso since he seemed to be in charge.

'If you are going to get me out of here, when do we start? And don't play any tricks. If I turn up dead, they'll be looking for my shoes.' That wasn't true, but it was worth a try. The fire was burning low by now, and I noted with alarm that one or two had wrapped their rags round themselves and were curled up by the wall, as if they intended to be there all night. If I was expected to do that, I thought, I should be dead by dawn. 'What's the plan?'

Sosso said nothing.

'I mean it,' I said. 'What's the plan? Or don't you have a plan? Are you waiting to discuss it with your bearded friend? And what's your connection with him, anyway?'

Sosso bared his teeth in a sort of smile. His eyes and blade both glittered in the glow. 'Too many questions,' he said. He gestured to a place beside the fire. 'Sit down there and wait.'

'Wait for what?'

He smiled more broadly then. 'You'll see.'

XII

Sosso had instructed me to wait and see. I waited. I seemed to have been a long time waiting, but there was little I could see. The night was getting colder all the time and the fire was reduced to embers now. Those who had not brushed away the ashes at the edge and settled themselves where the ground was warm had slipped away into the dark.

Sosso and the wraith remained immovable. I was still huddled against the wall where I'd been put. At last through the muffled mist I heard a sound. A dull plash of oars came from the waterside and a muttered conversation reached my ears. Then a figure materialised through the gloom, and the man with the burned face was standing there.

'Tullio's here,' he said to Sosso. 'Down with Cornovacus on the bank.'

'He'll do it?'

'For the price.'

Sosso gestured to the wraith to raise me to my feet. 'Come on,' he said to me. He had his knife aimed somewhere near my heart.

'Come where?' I rubbed my arm. Where the wraith had gripped it, it was bruised and sore, and all my other injuries ached too.

'You'll see!' Sosso said again, and urged me forward with his blade.

I stumbled down the lane, my shapeless boots making me seem slower and more clumsy even than I was. We reached the waterfront. We had no torch, and at first I could make out nothing in the mist, but then I detected movement, and at last I saw.

Cornovacus was standing by the shore holding something on a length of rope. It seemed to be a sort of giant snail. As I moved closer I realised what it was.

It was a bent man with a boat upon his back. Scarcely a boat at all – more of a shell, a soft wood frame covered with the skin of animals, and painted with a kind of home-made pitch. I'd seen such things before: the river folk of the Dobunni tribe use them for catching eels and fish, and occasionally for ferrying goods across when the Sabrina isn't running very fast. They'd always looked as fragile as a leaf.

As I watched the man rolled his burden free and launched it silently into the stream. Then, as Cornovacus held it by the rope, the boatman stepped aboard, holding a single paddle in one hand. He looked like a river god himself, outlined against the sky – long hair, long beard, long robe, bare feet: that was all of him that I could see.

There seemed scarcely room for him to sit and the little craft was rocking crazily, though he remained standing and seemed unperturbed, holding himself upright with his oar. A terrible premonition came to me that all this was part of Sosso's plan, and that another such boat might be found for me. I hate boats. I have always hated boats, ever since I was chained aboard that ship – and I have never handled one. I knew that if I attempted to do it now, I'd drown.

I turned to Sosso. 'You don't expect me to row in one of these?' I was whispering, but the sound seemed very loud. Something rustled in a clump of reeds nearby.

'Of course not. It's Tullio's boat. He steers.' I was sure that Sosso's ugly face was grinning in the dark.

That so alarmed me that I almost squawked. 'Surely you don't mean that I'm to get in there as well? There isn't space. I'd tip it over, getting in.'

'Don't think so,' Sosso said. He took the rope from Cornovacus and pulled the boat in close against the shore, then bent and steadied it with his other hand.

'But . . .' I began. Cornovacus caught me from the rear, and clamped a firm hand across my mouth.

'By all the powers in Dis,' he muttered in my ear, 'keep your confounded voice down, or you'll have half Glevum coming for a look. Now, do you want to get out of here or not? You know what's happening. They're looking for you in the town, there are guards on all the gates, and no doubt there'll be a lookout on the roads by now. That leaves the river. How else are you gong to elude the guards?'

He was right, of course, Glevum is a fine colonia but it isn't Rome – they say there are close on a million people living there, and it is easy for a man to hide in such a crowd. Here it was different. Without a home, a patron, friends or family to shelter me, it was only a matter of time till I was found. But in that flimsy little flat-bottomed craft?

Cornovacus had no patience with my doubts. He put his weight behind me and steered me forcibly to the waterside; half carried me, in fact, with his hand still firmly round my face so that I could not protest. Even so, when we reached the very edge and I looked down into that tiny craft, I baulked.

Who knows how long I might have hesitated there, but the boatman said briskly, 'Get him in, before I change my mind. We haven't got all night.'

He put the paddle on the shore, and, steadying himself on one of the wooden posts which had been driven in along the river bank, he reached up with his free hand and seized me round the knees. Cornovacus caught me at the same time from behind and between them they tumbled me into the centre of the boat. I lay there, paralysed with fright as it tipped wildly from side to side, but, with Sosso firmly holding it, it did not overturn as I was sure it would.

I was just beginning to believe that the Sabrina would not swallow me that night after all, and was preparing to raise my head a little and look round, when I heard a splash and realised that Tullio had the oar and Sosso had let go the rope. We were adrift on the river in this cockleshell.

'Keep down and in the very middle of the boat,' the boatman said, and I tried hard to comply. 'Further,' he muttered, 'or I'll have to sit on you.' I crammed my nose against the woven frame, with my knees drawn up against my chest. My nose was pressed against a strake which reeked sickeningly of eels and pitch and something I did not care to think about, which he'd obviously been baiting his woven eel-traps with. The boat had begun to rock again, and I was certain that this time we would drown, but Tullio insinuated himself somehow into the space, and sat down by sitting over me, folding his legs in and over mine as if I were a kind of cushion for his knees. Thus wedged he pulled the paddle in – he had been using it to steady us, with one end forced against the bank – and began to ply it slowly to and fro, using it as a kind of rudder at the rear. The crazy pitching stopped and the boat took up a steady rolling rock.

I tried to move to ease my aching back. It was impossible. The slightest movement rocked the boat, and anyway there was no room to stir an inch.

'Sit still!' hissed Tullio. 'You'll have us overboard. Keep down. It's dark and there's still a bit of mist, but there's a light wind getting up so it won't last for long. We won't be the only boat that's out tonight. Besides, we'll soon be passing near the dock. There may be torches on the quay and we can't have you seen. Keep still, don't make a noise and – here – put this over you.'

He raised one buttock as he spoke, and – at the risk of oversetting us – extracted what was obviously another sack and draped it over my face and feet so that I was swathed in sacking from head to toe. I was momentarily grateful for the extra warmth – I was by this time almost numb with cold – but like everything else aboard the boat, including the boatman and my outer tunic, the sack smelt horribly of eels. That, combined with the movement of the boat, was almost too much for me. I retched.

'You be sick in my boat, and I'll pitch you overboard,' Tullio muttered fiercely.

The power of necessity is an amazing thing. I was cold, cramped, and seasick, but somehow I managed to survive the whole long aching while – it seemed like hours – until we had travelled safely past the town. Our passage was not wholly without incident. Several times I heard the splash of oars, and once there was a sudden jolt and then a glow of light. I couldn't see any more than that from underneath my sack.

'Who's there?' A whisper.

'It's Tullio and his eel-traps,' Tullio whispered back.

'Ah – I can see you now. Catch anything tonight?'

'Not much. Found a sack of something in the marsh and picked it up.' Through the sacking I felt Tullio's hearty slap around my thigh, as though he were demonstrating his find.

If I had not been so tightly wedged I might have jumped. 'Probably useless, but I'll dry it out and see. You?'

'Nothing much about, this time of year. What are you doing now?'

'Thought I'd try downstream a bit.'

A grunt. Then, 'Well, more fool you. I'm giving up. I think it's going to rain. Mind how you go past the quay, there's a wine boat in from Gaul. Night, Tullio. Don't get swallowed by the river gods.'

'I won't.' Then the muffled splash again, and silence as we wallowed in the wake. Only the swish and creak of our own passage then. Time passed more slowly than an undertaker's cart. After a bit it did begin to rain, softly but persistently, and creeping damp was added to my miseries.

Then all at once the sack round my head was lifted back and Tullio leaned forward to peer into my face. 'Are you still alive?'

I grunted something.

'We should be out of danger now. We're past the town. You can sit up a little if you like . . . Careful!' This as I moved and narrowly failed to capsize the boat.

I was still lying underneath his knees, but tried to edge myself a little more upright and discovered that the air was calm and fresh, despite the intermittent rain. Around us the river glimmered with greyish-silver light, and dark trees bowed leafless heads down to the waterside. I crawled up in the boat and propped myself with my head over the side, and was – at last – copiously and comfortingly sick. Then I plunged my hand into the river, scooped the chilly water up and rinsed my face.

I turned back. Tullio was watching me, unmoved.

'I'm not used to boats,' I whined.

'That's exactly why it was such a good idea. No one was going to look for you in this. Clever of your ugly friend to think of it.' He gave the oar a lazy twitch. 'Now, we'll go a little further on, and once we're safely past the *territorium*, I'll let you out on to the river bank.'

I nodded. The territorium was official land: the fertile area which bordered Glevum to the south and east. It had been annexed by the legions when the colonia was built, and originally apportioned to the founding veterans as part of their retirement settlement. Now, more than a hundred years later, it had become effectively an area of farmland, interspersed with semi-managed woods, and administered by the authorities to supply the garrison. It was crossed by the military road which was the quickest way to Marcus's estate, but much as I longed to be back on solid ground this was still official land, and it would be safer if I avoided it. Yet as we went downstream from here, we were getting further from my roundhouse all the time. Despite the threat that the guards would find me there, it seemed a refuge of delight. I only hoped that Gwellia was safe.

I tried not to think about the long walk through the night – possibly beset by wolves and bears – which would now lie in front of me. 'And you'll row back again?' I said, anxious to think of other things.

He laughed. 'Of course, it's possible to row,' he said, 'even when you don't flow with the stream. Across the narrows, certainly – I've ferried goods or people that way once or twice.'

'Oh!' That surprised me. I had supposed I was the first passenger ever to be crammed into his boat.

He ignored me. 'But upstream? Depends upon the tide.'

'Tide? I didn't know rivers had a tide.'

'Then you don't know much. All the way from the Hibernian sea, they say. That's why these boats are made the way they are – you can take them upriver, drop them in the stream, and travel with the current while you fish or bait your traps. Of course you can use the oar to steer and speed your way. Then, when you've finished, you can put the whole thing on your back, pick it up and take it home again. I carried it to you tonight – you were upstream of me.'

He made it sound simple, but the idea of walking several miles with the weight of that contraption on one's back seemed utterly impossible to me. No wonder Tullio had the strength and muscles of a god.

I was about to say something in reply when Tullio raised his hand. 'Hush!'

There was a gentle hooting, like an owl.

Like an owl, but not an owl at all. Tullio pulled on the oar again, applying real pressure to it now, and the little boat bobbed and circled to the bank. I saw at once why he had chosen to come here; it was clearly a spot known to fishermen. A long length of timber had been driven horizontally into the mud, presumably for hanging those long woven fish-traps from. The bank was flattened around it and a small path led away into the woods. Tullio caught an overhanging branch and pulled us in.

'Here!' said a voice. Tullio took up the rope that was affixed to one of the boat's cross-withies, which had been lying looped up on his lap. To my alarm I saw three figures detach themselves from the shadows on the shore. One took the line and secured a loop around the tree before handing the rope-end back to Tullio. Another reached out and pulled the coracle in hard against the mud.

My heart was thumping. Was I after all to be betrayed?

The third figure came down to the water's edge. He had an awkward, loping gait. 'Right. Out then.' He was outlined against the dark: small, squat, square and unmistakable, with no neck and one misshapen foot.

'Sosso! How did you get here?'

'Walked.' The youth who had been handling the line came scrambling round the tree, out of the shadows and down on to the bank where it was comparatively light. I saw with a shock that it was Lercius. 'We came the quick way, through the town and down the road. Nobody was looking out for *us*. No one tried to stop us. I'd have had their eyes out if they had.' Now that my status was agreed, he was suddenly talkative and willing to explain, as though he'd never threatened me at all.

The man holding the coracle looked up. It was Cornovacus. 'Don't look so startled, eel-eater. What did you expect? We weren't going to let you disappear. You haven't paid us yet.'

That was a problem yet to be resolved. I changed the subject. 'How did you get through the town gates? They would have been firmly closed just after dusk.'

'There are ways,' Sosso said.

'Sosso's clever. He got us in with a funeral procession returning from the pyre, and out underneath a military cart. He wouldn't let me . . .'

'Lercius, enough! Now are you getting out?' Cornovacus extended his free arm, and I struggled to my feet. It made the boat rock crazily again.

This time I did succeed in falling in.

XIII

For a moment my whole life flashed before my eyes, and I
floundered, spluttering. But I did not drown. For all my
frenzied splashing, I had merely fallen into the shallows and
the water was no higher than my thighs. Feeling rather foolish,
I struggled to my feet, but the ground was slippery and I
slithered in again. Strong arms seized my makeshift tunic, as
I came up for the second time, and Sosso and Lercius hoisted
me upright and dragged me up on to the bank.

Even in the misty moonlight I was a sorry sight, soaked
and streaked with mud from head to foot. One of my ungainly
boots had fallen off and sunk. It hardly mattered: I was so
tired and cold and shaken that I could not stand. I could do
nothing but lie exhausted and shuddering on a pile of sodden
leaves underneath the tree, convinced that I was going to die.
In fact, I decided I would welcome it, as a sort of numb
warmth spread slowly over me.

Sosso's voice seemed very faint. 'Great Jove! He's drifting.
Quickly! To that hut we saw!'

They must have lifted me and carried me for miles, but I
have no real memory of that. I found I was sliding into
shivering sleep. I dreamed.

In my dream my father had me on his back and was
running with me to the stone-built roundhouse that was my
childhood home. I wanted him to run. It would be warm

there by the central fire, and my mother would sing songs to me while I curled up on my bed of furs and slept. Then I seemed to be hanging upside down, suspended by my arms and legs, like a rabbit hung to cook above the fire. Then even that faint sensation dimmed and I surrendered entirely to unconsciousness.

I swam up into a half-waking world.

'You will be all right here,' my father said, and his voice was very odd and deep. My mother rubbed my aching limbs with balm and lifted a bowl of hot broth to my lips.

'Drink this,' she crooned.

The brew was hot and bitter. I felt the warmth course through me like a flood. I forced my eyelids open, expecting to gaze into my mother's eyes, but the beloved features melted and dissolved and I was looking instead at a wrinkled, toothless face surrounded by wispy tufts of thin grey hair.

Yet I knew I'd seen the face before. And some of my imaginings were true. There was the fire, and I was lying on a bed, though not my own. It was dark, except for the firelight, but there were some things I could discern. I was lying on a simple pile of reeds with a patchwork coverlet made of pieces of fur skin – they might have been from weasels – draped over me. I did not recognise the tiny room in which I lay. I gave up trying to make sense of it and shut my eyes again.

More liquid was forced between my lips. 'Citizen Libertus, you must stay awake.'

I opened my eyes stupidly. The wizened face pressed very close to mine. 'Don't you recognise me, citizen? I knew you at once, despite that dreadful sack they'd draped you in.'

'Sack?' Fragments of memory were drifting back. I moved my hand beneath the covering of skins to find the sack, but under the furs I was as naked as the day I was born. Then my fingers, moving on my chest, touched something sticky, thick and warm. Blood? I snatched my hand out and gazed at it, though the flickering fire was all the light there was.

The old woman laughed. 'Goose-grease,' she said. 'Plenty of it too. Best thing there is for warding off the cold and for preventing tightness of the chest – though you'll be lucky to escape that altogether, chilled and soaked through as you were. Still, that hot remedy of mine should help. I sent the same thing to your patron once, when he had a fever and a nasty chill. Now, Citizen Libertus, drink the rest of this.'

This time, I recognised my name and I realised who and where I was. I was an old man on the run and this . . . 'You're the firewood-seller's wife,' I said. 'I am in your hut.'

She nodded. 'Lucky for you, citizen, that your friends brought you here. Another hour of that wet and cold, and I doubt if even I could have helped you.'

'My friends?' Apart from Junio – and Marcus, I suppose – I had no one to whom I could apply the term. A tradesman who has been first a nobleman and then a slave is not in a position to acquire 'friends'.

'The men who brought you here,' the woman said. She gestured to the door. There was a shadowy figure sitting there, which I recognised as Cornovacus. He seemed to be asleep, propped up against the wall, his knees drawn up underneath his chin and his head resting on his folded arms.

I stared. 'Where are the other two?'

'Gone to your roundhouse, to see what they can find. I told them the way.' She peered into my face, and added, 'I hope I did right. I thought you'd wish it, since they saved your life. In any case, I had little choice. They had a knife.'

This mention of my house made me struggle up. 'My wife . . .'

'You needn't worry, citizen. Your wife and slaves are safe.'

I sank back. 'Jupiter be praised!'

'My husband saw them on the road. They'd gone long before the soldiers came.'

'Soldiers! So Junio was right. They came.' Once more I tried to sit upright, but this time she pushed me gently down again.

'Lie back. There is nothing you can do tonight. Perhaps in a day or two, if you are strong enough . . .'

'But I have chickens, possessions, grain. Gwellia cannot have taken all of them. There will be beggars, thieves . . .'

'Citizen, try not to distress yourself. If there is anything of value there, no doubt Sosso will bring it back to us. He's gone to have a look.' She turned away and busied herself with something on the fire. 'For now, try to get some rest.'

To see if there was anything to loot, no doubt, but by now I was too worn to care. Gwellia and Junio were safe, and so was I. That was the most important thing. The rest would have to wait until the dawn.

All the same I found I couldn't rest. A hundred questions tumbled through my brain. I wondered where the firewood-seller was now, since it was long past the middle of the night. He must have visited his home since he saw Gwellia, since he had managed to tell his wife all this. Where had Tullio and his boat gone, and what had happened to Sosso and Lercius? Where could I find the money to pay Sosso now? Above all, was Marcus innocent or guilty – and how, in the present situation, was I ever to find out?

That last thought vexed my tired brain, and I veered away from it. I seized on another little mystery instead.

'Sosso!' I said suddenly, as if this were the most pressing matter in the world. 'You called him by his name. You knew him before? Or did he tell you tonight what he was called?'

She was unhooking an iron pot from the fire, and mixing something into it from a clay bowl which she had nearby. She looked at me sharply, but – as if she was content with what she saw – she answered gently enough. 'Both. I had heard of him, and when he came I recognised the man. It is hardly a description you'd mistake. I said, "Are you Sosso?" and he said, "I am." I'm not ashamed to tell you, citizen, my husband has talked once or twice, when times have been particularly hard, of going to the tombs and joining him ourselves.'

'Joining him?' I made no sense of this.

'Sosso has a little band of men – and women – in the town. The Ghosts of Glevum, folks call them. You have heard of them?' She did not wait for a reply. 'They would starve without him. He has some arrangement with a slave who works in a hot-soup kitchen near the docks.'

'A big fat fellow with a beard?' I asked.

'I don't know exactly. All I know is that the owner of the *thermopolium* has a wife who is a member of that peculiar sect. You know the one. Believe in all sorts of peculiar things – only one god and that crucified Jew who was supposed to have come back from the dead. Anyway, you know what they're like.'

I nodded. I'd had dealings with Christians before. They weren't popular with the Emperor, of course, since they refused to sacrifice to him, but they weren't dangerous to know – the sect wasn't forbidden, like the Druids. Generally, in fact, they were not disliked; they tended to be sincere and generous, even if their beliefs were rather odd. 'All prayer and penitence and giving to the poor,' I said.

She looked up from mixing her brew, which was beginning to smell dreadful as it warmed. 'Exactly. So when the shop closes for the night, she sends her slave out with the scrapings of the soup vat to give to the poor, and a bit of the makings for a fire. Of course, he's got more sense than to distribute it for free – he's looking to buy his freedom by and by – and Sosso's come to some arrangement with him. His group always get the soup, and the slave gets a cut of anything they make.'

'I see.' That was close to what I'd worked out for myself. I said, 'I understand that members of the group do little jobs for the slave as well?'

'Spying mostly, from what I understand. Collecting information, and that sort of thing. Which councillor is taking bribes, who's standing for election, and who is visiting whose wife – anything he can turn to money in the end. It's amazing how indiscreet some people are, when they think nobody's about – but who takes any notice of a beggar in the street?'

I shook my head. 'You thought of joining this pathetic crew?' It was still an effort to say anything and I realised how exhausted I'd become. I ached in every inch, but I could not relax. My future, if I had one, lay in Sosso's hands, and I wanted to know everything she had to tell.

She looked at me. 'Citizen, you don't know what it is to be desperate. These people stick together and they share what they have. They would perish individually, together they survive. Believe me, citizen, if you have no money and you cannot work – whether you are freeborn and sick, or injured in some way, or even if you are a slave who's been turned out on the streets because you are no further use – you go to Sosso, if you don't want to starve. All the unfortunates round here know that. Sosso will look after you, if he takes you on. He's shrewd and he's handy with a knife.'

This was a new view of the underworld: Grossus as a sort of Marcus of the poor – patron and protector of his own brand of *clientes*, and Sosso as perhaps the chief of these, the inferior with brains whom Grossus relied upon. I had formed a grudging admiration for the ugly little man, but now I saw a parallel with my own position too. I didn't care for the comparison. 'He welcomes thieves and runaways as well,' I muttered ungraciously.

She stopped stirring and poured some of the liquid back into the bowl. 'All right, so there are some thieves and vagabonds as well, but this isn't a market centre like Corinium. People like that aren't drawn to Glevum as a rule; there are too many soldiers here. And as for runaways, Sosso was a runaway himself. Originally freeborn, they say, but very poor. His parents would have sold him for a slave, but he was a freak and no one wanted him. They left him on the streets, but he was picked up by a trader who put him in a cage and took him round the markets as a show. Charged an *as* to see him, till he got too big and cost too much to feed, and then he arranged to have him given to the beasts as comic entertainment at the Games.'

I nodded. Such freak-shows were not unknown in Glevum, at the Games, although most children born with less than perfect limbs were simply left to die. I felt some sympathy for Sosso, all the same. 'But he got away?' I said.

'He had worked out how to undo the cage, and the night before they came to get take him off, he ran away. He walked for days and days until he found himself here among the tombs. Now, citizen, I made this for you.' She handed me the evil-smelling bowl. 'Drink this; it will help you sleep.'

It occurred to me that she needed sleep herself. I took the bowl and sipped. It tasted as dreadful as it smelled. 'And so he came to Glevum in the end. How long ago was this?'

'Not so many questions, citizen.' Cornovacus was awake again. 'And you, you toothless crone, keep your confounded gossip to yourself – if you don't want Lercius to cut out your tongue.' The interruption startled both of us. I wondered how much he'd overheard. 'Now shut up, the pair of you, and go to sleep before I lose my patience with you both.'

The poor woman cowered. She had been good to me. I decided I had nothing left to lose. 'I've been taken captive and locked into a shed and then obliged to promise money to escape. I think I am entitled to know who I am dealing with.' It is hard to be dignified when one is lying on the floor, covered in goose-grease and weasel-skins and not much else, but I did my best.

Cornovacus's answer soon put paid to that. 'As matters stand you are entitled to exactly nothing, friend.'

And that, I thought wearily, precisely summed it up. I did as I'd been told. I drank up my disgusting draught, shut up, lay down and allowed my eyes to close. The old woman's brew was an effective one. In spite of everything, I drifted almost instantly into a deep and dreamless sleep.

XIV

I awoke to thin winter sunshine streaming on to my face, and the chatter of excited voices somewhere nearby. At first I could not work out where I was, but as I moved my head – slowly, because my neck was very stiff – and took in my surroundings, the events of the night before came back to me.

The pathetic nature of the hut was much more evident in the light of day – the bunch of reeds and skins on which I lay, a few tools, a single stool, a pot, and the row of little clay bowls by the wall. There was a rough log serving as a bench, on which rested a jug of water, a few herbs, a crust of bread and two battered cups – that was the extent of the possessions here. And yet these people, with a roof and fire of their own, talked about days when 'times were hard' and knew that they were fortunate compared to some.

Cornovacus was still there, sitting at his post by the door, but when I looked for the old woman she was nowhere to be seen. It occurred to me to wonder where she'd slept since there was no sign of bedding anywhere, and then realised – as I should have done before – that she must simply have curled up in her cloak beside the fire. She'd given up the only bed to me.

What rich citizen, I asked myself, would have done as much?

As if she'd heard my thoughts she hobbled in, a dead hen dangling by its feet from either hand, and her wizened face lit in a toothless smile. 'Ah, Citizen Libertus, you are awake at last. Don't try to move. You have slept well but you still need to rest.' She shook the chickens at me. 'But see what Lercius has brought us from your house. A good broth of one of these and you'll soon be on the mend.'

'From my house!' The brazenness of it made me sit upright.

Or try to sit upright. The instant I moved, I fell back on the bedding with a groan. Instead of being a creature with mobile arms and limbs I seemed to be one solid throbbing ache, as stiff as if I had been thrashed from head to foot. I had endured some savage beatings when I was first a slave, but not even they had left me feeling as weak and battered as this. I could scarcely turn my head and, although I could hear someone else coming through the open door, I could not twist myself enough to see.

'I wrung their necks. You should have heard them squawk!' It was Lercius. He burst into my view, his face alight with frank, unholy glee. He had his right hand concealed behind his back, but now he had my attention he brought it out to display a bloodied bundle in a bag. 'This one's even better. I cut off its head. Crunch, I went. Sosso let me. I used your axe. And it went on running a bit even afterwards, when it had no head. Blood was pouring from its neck. This one is for us – we're going to cook it on the fire tonight.' He thrust his hand into the bag and brandished the unhappy, headless thing.

My first thought was outrage. That was my old cloth bag he was carrying and those were obviously my chickens he

142

had killed! It was outright robbery, and I was about to voice my anger when the old woman spoke.

'I'm glad you found something at the house to save.'

'To save?' By now I was propped up on my arm, bruises or not. 'You mean the soldiers may have looted it?'

She paused a moment, then turned back to me. 'Lie back, citizen, and try to rest. There is nothing you can do. Oh, Great Minerva! I had not meant to tell you this so soon. But I suppose you'll have to know. When the soldiers came, they waited for a while, but when it was clear that you weren't in the house they went inside . . .' She hesitated.

'And looted it?' I could imagine it only too well.

She shook her head. 'They went with torches. Claimed they were searching it, my husband says – though you can believe that if you like. At all events, the thatch caught fire and, quite simply, the house burned to the ground. They didn't make much effort to try to put it out.'

I did lie down then, as if someone had knocked me down. Of course I didn't believe the story of the search. Those men had put a torch to it, though since they knew I was a citizen no doubt they thought the lie expedient. The punishment for convicted arsonists is fierce. However, it would be hard to bring a charge, even in ordinary times. This was neither a warehouse nor inside the town, and anyway it is always difficult to make a case against the guard. And these were no ordinary times.

My roundhouse! The beloved little house that we'd rebuilt ourselves, using woven branches in the fashion of the local tribes. We and our slaves had woven osiers round the stakes, and daubed the walls with mud and dung to keep out the searching wind and rain. Gwellia had cut and tied the bundled straw that formed the roof, had flattened the earth floor with patient hands and laid the firestones for the central fire. It was more than just a dwelling, it was a work of love, a symbol of our new-found hope and life. All reduced to ashes by a Roman torch. I have never felt so bitter against our conquerors.

'All burned?' I said. I thought about my workshop in the town, similarly gutted and destroyed. Fires were common enough happenings, of course – inevitable when there's thatch and naked flame – but both of those conflagrations had been deliberate. The Fates seemed to have placed a peculiar curse on any building which I called my home.

She shook her head. 'I think so, citizen. Or so my husband says. One of the soldiers chased him off at first, but when they'd left at last he did go back again.'

'Left these though,' Lercius said happily, swinging the hapless corpse.

'Where did you find them?' I enquired. I moved with exaggerated care, so that I was able to lean up on one arm.

'The chickens? They were roosting in a tree. The coop had been pushed over and they'd escaped. But I got up and caught them!' Lercius laughed. 'Woosh – like that. I was too quick for them. They couldn't get away. After I'd killed them, I put them in the bag. I found that in the lane. It was hanging on a bush – there were some things in it. I brought them too. Sosso says they might be worth something in the market place.'

He reached into the bag again – it was an old one that I'd once used for tools but discarded because it was split and frayed around the seam – and produced a stained, patched cloth which had once been a cloak and a pair of sandals with a broken lace. I frowned.

'You say you found these hanging on a bush?'

But Lercius had lost interest, and it was the woman who replied. 'He's right. The bag was in the lane. I saw it there myself when I went out to see a customer before you came. It was just dangling from a tree. I almost picked it up myself, but I thought that someone must have dropped it on the road and would be back for it. You wouldn't think that anyone would simply toss it there because they'd no use for it any more. Imagine throwing things like that away – a useful piece of cloth like that, and sandals which would be nearly good as new if you could afford a visit to the shoemaker.'

'They're mine,' I said. I felt rebuked. I had put them on one side myself, admittedly to use as rags or scraps, but I had effectively discarded them. I'd stuffed them in the bag and hung them from a nail in Gwellia's dyeing-house. So how had they survived the fire, and what were they doing in the lane, hanging on a bush? Perhaps the soldiers had been looting things and thrown this away in disgust as useless junk. Unless . . .

Of course! Junio! I had told him to leave a signal near the gate. This must be it. That bag would have drawn my eye all right. But . . . I frowned again. He was to warn me if the guards were at the house – yet according to what I'd heard last night, my wife and slaves had gone before the soldiers came.

However, this was no time for mysteries. These had been garments once. They were not glamorous at best, and they had not been improved by recent contact with the bleeding chicken corpse, but – as the woman said – they could, in an emergency, be used again. And it had dawned on me that they seemed to be the only clothes I had. I had glanced around the hut and noted all the contents earlier, but –

surely? – I hadn't seen my tunic, or the sack, or even the leather underpants I'd had on when I arrived. I hitched myself painfully a little more upright and checked again. There was no sign of them.

'Let me have those things. They're mine. I can clothe myself at least.'

Lercius ignored me utterly. I looked towards the woman, but she was pouring water into a pot and setting it to heat up on the firestones. She did not look at me.

I sat up fully now, clutching the skins against my goose-greased chest. 'What's happened to the rest of my possessions from the roundhouse?' I enquired.

'Possessions, citizen?' said another voice. There was little room inside the hut by now, but by craning painfully around, I could see Sosso standing at the entrance. He had another bloodied bundle on his back, wrapped up in what looked like my sack of yesterday – the remainder of my chickens, probably. He tossed it down outside the door and loped over to squat down at my side. The ugly face was twisted in a leer. 'You've no possessions from the roundhouse, citizen. There's nothing left of it.'

It was clear, at least, where last night's clothes had gone. He was sporting, not only my now misshapen shoes, but my tunic too – stretching the seams across the chest and shoulders so that the stitching in some places had already given way. The arrogance of his words and manner had me spluttering and I wanted to stand up and confront him face to face. But he had me at a curious disadvantage. It is hard to seem imposing in an argument when you are the only one with nothing on.

I stayed lying where I was. 'Those are my things,' I repeated, aware that I sounded like a fretful child. 'My bag, my cloak, my sandals, and – for that matter – those are my chickens too!'

'Not any more.' The ugly face was twisted in a leer.' Citizen! I hear you *are* a citizen?'

I nodded, knowing that would not endear me to the gang.

'Then listen, citizen. You owe us four denarii.'

Another nod. I didn't trust my voice.

'Tunic and chickens – first part-payment – understood?'

'And you'll pay the rest, by Mercury.' Cornovacus had risen to his feet. 'You're an accursed white-rober – you'll have money somewhere. White-robers always do. You'll tell us where, or I'll squeeze it out of you.' He spat. He was not a big man – he was tall and thin – but in this small hut the effect was truly frightening. And I had no money anywhere of any kind. Ordinarily I would have applied to Marcus, but he was in the cells.

'But . . .' I began and stopped. It was useless to protest. I had agreed to pay in front of witnesses – they had a verbal contract under law. Even Roman justice was no longer on my side. Not that I thought Sosso would bother with the courts. No doubt he had his own methods of enforcing debts.

I was right.

'You'll pay, citizen. I'll leave Cornovacus with you till you do. And Lercius too.'

Lercius, who had been happily dismembering his chicken with his hands, looked up at me and grinned. 'Like this!' He twisted off a leg. It was not a pleasant image, and his simple pleasure in it made it worse. I'd no doubt he would do the same to me with just as much delight. I was beginning to wish that Bullface had caught me after all.

I looked at the old woman for support, but she was careful to avoid my eyes. She had plunged one of the chickens in the pot – just as it was – and now she plucked it out and sat down on the stool, her fingers busy as she pulled the feathers from the skin. She kept her head down and said nothing, although I noticed that she still glanced nervously at the men from time to time. She was as terrified as I was of the gang.

I thought aloud. 'I'm sure my patron's wife would help me if she could – but I suppose there's still a guard outside her house.'

The woman raised her head and looked at me through her wispy strands of hair, although her fingers never faltered in their task. 'There is indeed. They've closed the back route from the villa now, by all accounts, so nobody can get in or out at all. They did let that serving girl come here last night before you came, to buy some comfrey for her mistress, but I don't think they'll let her come again. They almost didn't let her last night. She had to plead with them for hours, she said, until they finally agreed to let her out.'

'Cilla!' I had completely forgotten her. I'd promised to meet her in the lane after my interview at the garrison, so that she could take news to Julia. Was that arrangement made only yesterday? After all the shocks and tribulations I'd endured since, that conversation seemed a half a life ago.

'Is she called Cilla?' The old face wrinkled in a frown. 'I don't think I ever heard her name. She often came here on her mistress's behalf. Plump and plain-faced as a little pig, but pleasant and with more sense than you'd think.'

That sounded like Cilla.

'I wonder what will become of her, poor thing,' the woman said. 'She told me the soldiers took another ten slaves away to question yesterday, and threatened to take another ten today. They'll take her master's slaves at first, of course, 'cause they were at the banquet, but it must be dreadful waiting there like that, not knowing when it's going to be your turn. And now she's made herself conspicuous. I don't know why her mistress made her come – she wasn't going to die for the want of a bit of comfrey, I'm sure.'

Poor Cilla. I knew why she'd taken such appalling risks. She'd kept her promise and talked her way past the guards to meet up with me. And I had missed her!

Together with my chance to send a message to the house. Julia would have been a good person to beg money from. I had no doubt that Marcus would have lent me four denarii if I asked – especially if I'd succeeded in obtaining his release – but he would certainly have deducted them from anything he paid me later on. He was more cautious with his money than a mother with her child. Julia, on the other hand, would probably have given them outright. That would, at least, have paid Sosso and his gang and left me to face the ruins of my life.

I was mentally bewailing my bad luck and deciding that I must have done something serious to offend the gods, when Sosso spoke. 'So, you spoke the truth? Your patron is in jail.' He turned to the firewood-seller's wife, who by now was halfway through her task. 'You know this Marcus?'

Little feathers had starting floating up and attaching themselves to her rags and face and hair. She had to rub her toothless mouth and wipe away one that was sticking to her lips before she answered, 'Of course I do. And so would you, if you knew anything at all about town government. The most important man for miles he was – related to the old Emperor, they say, and a friend of the departing governor. Not that it seems to have done him any good. They've still dragged him off and clapped him in the cells –

and put a guard upon his house so no one can get in or out of it.'

Sosso said nothing for a moment. He looked down at his misshapen feet and then at me. Then, as if he'd come to a decision, he said at last, 'We could.'

I didn't understand. I goggled at him. 'What?'

'Get in. Some of us are very good at it.'

'But there's an armed guard . . .'

That grin again. 'There's one outside the garrison. We get in there.'

And then at last my brain, which seemed to have rusted with the cold and damp, creaked into action. What had Grossus Fatbeard said to me? 'I have ears and eyes across the town.'

If I could offer more than Grossus did, perhaps Sosso and his men would do the same for me. I could not show my face in town, or even hereabouts. Yet I needed to have news of my patron and, if possible, discover the truth about exactly what had occurred at the banquet. I had no idea at this moment how or where or from whom this information could be gleaned, but if I had someone to spy on my account there was at least a glimmering of a chance. After all, as the old woman had observed, 'Who takes any notice of a beggar in the street?' And if they had managed to get into the garrison . . .

'The garrison?' I echoed.

He shrugged, as though there was nothing remarkable in that.

I hesitated. These were not the kind of men to trust. They were desperate and I guessed that they would sell their services to the highest bidder. They might yet betray me to Bullface and his men.

Then I looked around the hut. I was at their mercy now. I had nothing, not even any clothes to wear. If I did not do something, I would surely starve. My house was burned, my patron was in jail, and my wife and slaves were safely out of town. What had I to lose?

'In that case, I have a plan for you. You get into the villa with a message for his wife, and I'll have the four denarii for you. After that, I want "ears and eyes" around the town. If you bring me helpful news, I'll see you're paid.'

'No tricks. No *aediles*?' Sosso said, and I realised that he had worries of his own. Some of his associates were thieves. They could be betrayed to the authorities themselves.

'None,' I promised.

He looked at his shoes – my shoes – then at me again. He grunted his favourite question. 'How much?'

'I can't tell you that. I don't know how much I need to know, or how long this thing will take.'

Sosso stood his ground. 'No good, citizen. How much?'

I tried again. If I could contrive to pay them by results, I thought, perhaps that would minimise the risk. 'You find out what you can and come to me each day until the Ides. I'll see that you get food and a sestertius every time – more if the information helps to get him free.' It was the best solution I could think of at the time. I prayed that Julia would agree to it.

Sosso shook his head. 'Food and a sestertius – all right. You get him out – we get half the reward he gives to you. Agreed?'

What could I say? It was unlikely Marcus would be freed. I would be lucky to keep out of jail myself. This might be my only chance. 'Agreed,' I muttered.

Sosso spat on one grimy paw and extended it to me. I was still clutching my tattered fur covering to myself, but I freed a hand and grasped his hairy one. I gasped as his powerful fingers crushed my own.

'Partners!' Sosso grinned. He seemed to come to life. 'Lercius! His clothes.'

Lercius put down his bloodied plaything and brought me the bag. I took out my old cloak and looped it round myself like a sort of makeshift robe, then struggled from the covers and fastened on the broken sandals as best I might. I stood up shakily. I looked like a beggar myself, but I was so pleased to have even these tattered clothes that it was some moments before I glanced up at the three men and saw them watching me.

It struck me what strange confederates I had obtained. A rat-faced thief, a half-crazed child, and a lopsided dwarf! It seemed to please them, though. Lercius smiled and nodded cheerfully and even Cornovacus had allowed his face to break into a sort of doubtful grin. Sosso – in my tunic, belt and shoes – was beaming broadest of them all.

Only then did it occur to me that he had planned this outcome all along.

XV

Now that I was dressed – after a fashion anyway – I instantly felt more like myself again. I still moved as slowly and as awkwardly as a badly laden cart, my head ached and I was stiff in every limb, but at least I was on my feet.

I shuffled to the doorway of the hut and peered outside. The early sun had gone behind a cloud and the day was raw and cold. The forest looked unremittingly dark and grey. The hut stood, just as I'd remembered it, in a clearing on a tangled forest path, but in the distance, through the branches, I could glimpse the lane. I knew it well – not the paved thoroughfare which was the military road, but the ancient, rocky cart-track of a lane, vertiginous in parts, which wound its way from Glevum to some ancient settlement, passing the corner of Marcus's estate where my roundhouse was – or used to be.

I stood leaning on the doorpost for support while I strained my eyes towards the spot. It was a long way away across the trees so I don't know what I hoped to glimpse – a wisp of smoke perhaps – but there was nothing to be seen. Much nearer to me through the trees, however, a movement caught my eye. There was a figure on the lane. A soldier? For an instant I was seized with fear. I slipped back into the hut and flattened myself against the wall.

'There's someone in the lane,' I said.

The woman put down her task and came to look. She peered intently in the direction I had indicated, but then she relaxed. 'My husband,' she said with a laugh.

When I looked again, I realised she was right. The man was hunched and slow, and manoeuvring a little handcart over the ruts and stones.

'Bringing something on the handcart, by the look of him. Good thing we kept it when we lost the mill,' she said.

Of course, the kindling-seller had once had a reputable trade before he crushed his hand. I glanced around the tumbled shack again, suddenly aware that this – or worse – might be my fate as well, if things continued as they were. There is no trade without customers, and a man on the run has no workshop where he can exploit his skill. It was not a comfortable thought.

I looked back at the toiling figure in the lane and said, with genuine concern, 'Poor man. He must have been out in the cold all night – it occurs to me that I've been lying on his bed.' It came to me, though I did not voice the thought, that since he had been conversing with the soldiers at my house he was lucky not to have been arrested himself. He had not even the protection of being a citizen.

The woman smiled thinly. 'Don't worry about him, citizen. I'm sure he was warm and safe enough.'

Lercius had jumped up from his grisly task by now and joined us at the door. 'Of course he was. He spent the night with us.'

I glanced at him. It had not occurred to me to wonder where he and Sosso had been. I had simply taken it for granted that they were creatures of the night.

Lercius looked at my astonished face, and grinned. 'At your enclosure, round the ashes of the fire.'

It seemed a very callous thing to say, but Lercius was not given to finesse. Besides, there was a certain grim sense in it, after all. 'My poor little house,' I said bitterly. 'I'm glad at least its disappearance gave you both some warmth.'

Lercius gave his idiotic laugh. 'Not their fire, citizen. Your fire. The one in the little hut. It had been raked out but there was still some heat in it.'

My mind stirred into action. Of course. I should have worked it out before. Lercius had killed my chickens with my axe. He must have found it in the dyeing hut. There was a fire there, and though Junio would have doused it before the household left, presumably there was enough warmth left in the embers to take some of the night chill from the air. And the chicken coop had been upended, too, not set alight. Clearly not everything had been destroyed.

'The dyeing house, you mean?' I said, with sudden hope. It was not much, but it was shelter of a kind – more in any case than this pathetic shack. With a fire and food, I thought, it might be possible . . . 'It didn't burn?'

'Some of the roof has gone, but most of it is there. Your slave saved it, perhaps. He could have beaten out the flames and poured water on the walls. The firewood-seller insists he wasn't in there when the soldiers came. But I think he was. There was a water pot inside the door and it was already empty when we got there. He probably used that. This morning we had to fetch water from the stream to drink.'

'My slave?' I interrupted. I could make no sense of this. Kurso the kitchen boy, perhaps? Had he been left behind in case I came? Or perhaps Junio had disobeyed me and stayed to make sure that I was safe? That was possible, and it would explain the bag – the danger signal – hanging on the bush.

I turned to Sosso. 'You think my slave was there?'

Sosso merely grunted.

It was Lercius who said, 'He's still there now. We didn't realise that at first. Not until this morning when we first woke up and needed to find some food. I went outside and had a look around. That's when I found the chickens. And there were a few nuts and beans stored in a pit.' He looked at me, as if for confirmation of the fact.

I nodded. I had put them there myself, and lined the storage pit with holly leaves to keep the rats and predators away.

'Well, we ate those, but it wasn't much, between the three of us. There was a great cooking pot over the fire but the stuff in there smelt terrible, so I didn't think it was anything we could eat.'

'It wasn't food,' I said, moved to a reluctant smile by the thought. 'It's dyestuff. My wife was softening walnut shells, I think, ready to steep with lichen and make some dye for wool.'

'That's what the firewood man said. He wouldn't let me taste. He found a piece of cloth in it as well. It was an awful colour – greeny-brown.'

I frowned. Gwellia would have been dyeing unspun wool, not cloth. 'You think that might have been my slave's?' I asked. 'His cloak perhaps?'

But Lercius was pointing down the path. 'I don't know. They wouldn't let me near. But here's the firewood-seller now. Better if he tells you himself.'

I looked down the path, where he was gesturing. Sure enough, the shuffling master of this tiny hut was lumbering towards us now, accompanied by the creak of wheels and a grunt of breath. His hair was straggly, long and grey and his beard was much the same, but what I could see of the gaunt face was creased with the effort. The cart was clearly heavy, and even from here I saw that it was not piled high with wood, but with all sorts of things which I recognised as mine. From my dye-house, all of it. Three unwashed fleeces, I saw as he drew nearer to the hut, and on top of them hunks of unspun wool, held down by the weight-stones from the loom, while Gwellia's cracked bowls full of lichen and dried flowers, wooden wool-combs, and even one of her stone spindles were balanced haphazardly here and there. The whole load looked amazingly precarious, as if it might fall off at any time, yet he had struggled several miles with it across a track as rutted as a rough-ploughed field.

He paused now and dragged a grimy hand across his brow. He was panting and sweating though the day was chill, and he stood a moment rocking on his heels and looking from one to another of our little group.

'Where is the citizen Libertus?' he said uncertainly. 'I was told that he was here.'

'Come, husband,' the woman said, 'don't stare at us like that. Surely you recognise the citizen? He has bought firewood from you many times. And these other men you know.'

The firewood-seller looked at me closely, then gave a little nod. 'I'm sorry, citizen. I didn't recognise you in those clothes. My name is Molendinarius.'

Molendinarius, I thought. Still called 'miller' though there was nothing of a round-faced miller in the man who faced me now. He was thin to the point of looking starved, and, though he clearly retained a certain scrawny strength, recent exertion had made his breath come in dreadful rasps. His damaged hand, a pitiful stump dangling from the wrist, was bound up in a piece of sack, and the rest of his clothing was the merest rags. Beside him, my makeshift robe and broken sandals felt positively elegant.

'I hope I've been of service, citizen,' he said, with the fawning meekness of those who seek reward. 'I have saved most of what can be rescued from your huts.'

'Then why not leave it there?' I said, rather astringently. 'I could have made a kind of home with it.'

He shook his head. 'My guess is that the soldiers will be back. In any case there is a guard next door. They're posted all round the villa now, keeping a sharp lookout in the lane. They saw me come and go. They would discover you in no time at all.'

I took in the implications of this. 'So they permitted you to loot my house, in fact? Take care they don't arrest you for a thief.'

He smiled, a slow smile that showed his broken teeth. 'Oh, I took care of that. They saw me coming with an empty cart, and leaving with one too. I took these things away a little at a time, and hid them in the woods. Then when I'd passed the guards I slipped back into the trees and piled the cart again. But it will be more difficult next time. This stuff is light. There's still a big iron pot which was on the fire, and – among other things – a long piece of dyed cloth which we found inside it. I've left it there to dry.'

'Lercius told me you had found a cloth,' I said, 'though I can make little sense of that. My wife might have put in some unspun wool, but I cannot imagine what the cloth might be – unless' – inspiration struck me suddenly – 'it might have been my toga?'

Molendinarius looked surprised. 'It might have been a toga-length at that. It was about the right length and width for that – and now I come to think, there might have been one curving edge to it.'

It was ridiculous how pleased I felt at this. I could hardly wear it as a toga, certainly, but the idea that I possessed a length of woollen cloth, even a wet and dun-coloured piece of cloth, made me feel as if I'd won a fortune on the dice.

Molendinarius was frowning at me as he said, 'But why should anyone put that in the dye?'

'I think my slave put it there to hide it from the guard. Well thought of, Junio! Where is he anyway? Lercius said you'd found him at the house.'

He looked at me sharply, and his manner changed. 'We found traces of him, certainly. Lercius didn't tell you where?'

I was about to shake my head, when suddenly I knew. Lercius had been burbling about discovering my slave when he described how Molendinarius had found the piece of cloth 'as well'. As well as what? I felt a cold sickness in my stomach as I said, 'Not in the dye-pot?' Please don't tell me that, I begged inwardly. Not Junio. Not dead.

But the old firewood-seller was shaking his head regret-fully. 'I'm afraid so, citizen. Though . . .' he paused, 'not all of him.'

My legs, which had been shaky anyway, gave way entirely at this, and I found myself sitting abruptly on the ground. Junio! Dear, stupid, pigheaded, clever Junio! Why had I permitted him to leave me in the town and go back to the house alone? I might have guessed that he'd refuse to leave, and put himself in danger in the process. I tried in vain to tell myself that in waiting here he had disobeyed my explicit instructions to the contrary. Dead, and, from what Molendinarius said, dismembered too.

The Romans despise a man who weeps, but my voice was blurred by most unmanly tears as I said, 'One of the guard did this? I'll find out who – Sosso, you and your men must help. If I get out of this alive, I'll kill the man who did it with my own bare hands.'

I had raised my voice, and the old woman stooped to touch my arm. 'Citizen,' she murmured warningly, 'you'll bring the guard. Who knows who can hear?'

Lercius, though, was less restrained. 'I'll help you,' he piped up at once, his eyes burning with enthusiasm. 'You show me who it is and I'll make sure he has a long and lingering death. I'll tear his eyes out and his tongue, and I'll carve him up . . .' He began to demonstrate in dumb show what he had in mind, capering ecstatically around.

'Enough!' Sosso commanded, and Lercius fell silent. I felt some sympathy with his plans. I could gladly have done those things to the murderer myself.

The firewood-seller cut across my thoughts. 'It can't have been the soldiers,' he said. 'I saw them come, and go. They didn't go into the little hut. They peered in everywhere when they first arrived, and then they simply waited at the gate till it was getting dark and it was clear that you weren't going to come that night. They didn't even go inside to light the torches – one of them had flints and kindling cloth – though they did have one last search before they left. The leader made a great show of bending down as he came back through the door, but he made sure that he set the thatch alight. I was watching, hidden in the trees. I even spoke to them once or twice.'

'Part of the guard round Marcus's villa?' I enquired.

He shook his head. 'On the contrary,' he said. 'There even seemed to be ill-feeling when they met. That was what drew me to the spot. The ones who burned your house marched down the lane where the others were already standing guard. I heard raised voices and a lot of challenges. One lot were new to Glevum – somebody's private bodyguard, I gathered – but they took no notice of the local guard. "Orders," they said, and just marched on. Certainly they were unpleasant men – especially the big one who seemed to be in charge – but I don't see how they could have killed your slave. They didn't have the opportunity.'

I had been listening to this with only half my mind. Most of my thoughts were still with Junio. 'I'll find out,' I said. 'What have you done with him, my slave?'

He looked distressed. 'I've brought him. What we first found of him.' He went towards his handcart as he spoke. 'Prepare yourself, citizen; it's not a pleasant sight.' He took down the wool, whorls and stones and flung back the fleeces as he spoke. Underneath was something wrapped up in a sack.

'Show him!' Sosso and Cornovacus had come over to look.

Molendinarius nodded slowly, and moved the coverings. I gagged. I was looking at a head. A head dyed sickly greenish-brown – as Lercius had said – and staring at the sky with sightless eyes. Though hideously discoloured, the familiar features were still recognisable.

I would have know him anywhere. He had fled to me fearing for his life, but it had not saved him in the end. My heart went out to him. It was unreasonable that I should also feel relief.

'This is not my slave.'

XVI

Sosso exchanged glances with Molendinarius and then looked at me. 'Not convincing, citizen,' he said. 'You've got a slave. He was a slave. Saw the rest of him.'

'His body was lying in the pit. I found it,' Lercius interrupted eagerly. 'When I found the beans and nuts. There were just some branches pulled back over him.'

'Had there been a struggle? Were there other wounds?'

'Not a scratch,' Lercius replied. And then with a relish which I found difficult to tolerate, 'I had a good look. There was a lot of blood. It must have come spurting from his neck. We found where it was done, as well. Blood all over one end of the hut and some on the axe. I thought at first that what was on the blade was only chicken blood, but when we found the two bits of slave we realised . . .'

Sosso gave him a look that silenced him, and said, 'A slave. Slave brand, slave tunic, slave token round his neck.'

'A slave,' I hastened to explain, 'but not my own. He was my patron's bucket-boy. He was afraid he would be taken in for questioning.' I gave them a brief outline of how Golbo had run away to me, but did not mention that his testimony appeared to question Marcus's innocence. If these men were going to assist me to clear my patron's name, I reasoned, it was better if they had no cause for doubt. 'I left him sleeping by the dye-house fire,' I finished. 'When I came back in the morning, he was gone. I haven't seen him since.'

'He can't have gone far,' the woman put in unexpectedly. She had walked over to the cart and was inspecting its grisly burden with a kind of horrified curiosity, though she must have seen a severed head before. Those of rebellious tribesmen are still occasionally exhibited when there have been border skirmishes – though admittedly they are not usually dyed. 'Perhaps he was hiding in the thatch, and one of the soldiers found him and killed him after all.'

'Keep silence, wife!' The firewood-seller's voice was sharp. 'Haven't I told you I was watching them throughout? You think I would have missed it, if one of the guards had dragged a headless torso from the hut?'

She turned aside, subdued, and began moving the fleeces and other goods inside, but his words had given me to think. 'If it was not the soldiers,' I said hastily, 'who could it have been? You say you watched them leave? When did you leave yourself?'

Junio would have seen the implication of those words at once. I suspected that Molendinarius had gone to loot the house, so it was possible that – if disturbed in the attempt – he'd killed the slave himself. After all, he was skilful with an axe. However, the old man seemed not to have thought of that.

He answered in that croaking rasp which I was beginning to associate with him. 'When the soldiers left, I followed them down the road a bit, to make sure that they were safely gone, and when I came back I found the fire was out. The living hut was gone but the other one was hardly touched. That surprised me, I confess – I came straight back here to tell my wife.'

'And to pick up your handcart?' I suggested, suddenly understanding the answer to part of the mystery at least. 'You must have thought there were some things of value there.'

He was unabashed. 'Well, citizen, if they were out to arrest you with your patron, I didn't suppose that you were ever coming back. And the guards posted round the villa weren't watching out for thieves. I knew there would be something in the hut. Better we had it than somebody else, I thought.'

I raised an eyebrow. 'But you were prepared to share it with Sosso and his men?'

This time he did colour slightly as he said in his breathless rasp, 'It wasn't what I meant to do, but when I got back home to pick up the cart, I found them here with you. And – you never know – I might need Sosso and his men one day. I told them all about it. We decided there were far too many people for this hut, and anyway it wasn't safe to stay here in your company, in case the soldiers thought to search the place. So after I'd had a piece of bread and broth, the two of them came back to bed down there with me. You were so fast asleep you didn't stir. We left one man to keep an eye on you. It was a risk, but Cornovacus was certain that he could get away, even if the guard turned up, and let us know.'

I glanced towards the woman, who was stooping at that moment to pick up the heavy loom-weights from the ground, but she did not react in the least to this assumption that she and I were automatically dispensable. All she did was look up briefly and say, 'Anyway, you had no choice. Sosso had a knife.'

Her husband grunted at her to be silent and turned to me. 'We had no means of making fire, which was fortunate, or we might have boiled that head up again, and then we'd never have known whose head it was.' He nodded towards the gruesome thing on the cart. I wished he'd cover it, the more so as Lercius was edging up to it with a fascinated grin and extending a probing finger towards Golbo's eyes.

His eyes! Of course! If the eyes were still intact, no one could actually have boiled the head.

'Don't you see?' I said, aware of the impatience in my tone. (This was a little unfair of me, since I'd only just worked it out myself.) 'That head was never boiled – though that was probably the murderer's idea. It was put into the pot after the fire was doused. So it could not have been the soldiers, as you say.' I went on in a more conciliatory tone, 'So who killed the slave, and why?'

'One of the other accursed sons of Dis – those soldiers who were posted in the lane?' That was Cornovacus, who had been following the talk with interest. 'The woman says they're from the garrison. Those boys would chop the head off anyone.'

I shook my head. 'That would make no sense. They wanted to arrest Golbo, not kill him.' I sighed. It seemed I would have to explain this, after all. 'He was the last person in the colonnade when Praxus died. That was why he ran away. He feared his testimony would harm his master's case. If the guards had caught him, surely they would have captured him and taken him in to the garrison for questioning. Then they could have extorted the evidence they want.'

'Perhaps it was a warning,' Molendinarius said. 'That people should not get involved in this.'

'Then why move the body?' I returned. 'Put the head into the pot, perhaps – that is a kind of warning, I suppose – but why take the trouble to drag away the rest of it, and hide it in the pit? More effective, surely, to leave it where it was?'

'He's right, by Mithras,' Cornovacus said. 'Almost as if whoever did it didn't want it found. I've never known soldiers do anything like that. Those sons of rats and vermin haven't got the wit. If they'd found the boy, they'd either have killed him where he stood or dragged him off to torture him.'

I was following a different line of thought. 'I wonder why Golbo let himself be found? If he'd been hiding in the thatch, I suppose he might have come down when the other hut caught fire – but if so the soldiers would have caught him, or Molendinarius would know. More likely he was hiding in the trees nearby. So why come out?'

Lercius grinned. 'To save the hut. I told you somebody had doused it all. It didn't do itself.' He bent forward and grinned into the dead face. 'Why don't you tell him? Lost your tongue?' He would have opened up the mouth and peered inside, if Cornovacus had not prevented him.

I turned away revolted, but I had to concede the point. It did seem likely that Golbo had tried to save the dye-hut, otherwise the fire would have caught it too. It was too near the roundhouse to escape. 'Perhaps you're right,' I said, and Lercius preened. 'When he was sure that everyone had gone, he went inside and doused the fire. So Golbo was killed later, when the fire was out. But the axe was there. You used the thing yourself. Why didn't he use it to defend himself?'

It was the firewood-seller's turn to let impatience show. 'Who knows? Thought it was you, perhaps. Or maybe somebody crept up on him.'

That was a possibility, of course. Yet, remembering the evidence, I found it difficult to believe. When the slave had come to me he had been too frightened to remain there overnight, though then he was comparatively safe. If he had been in the hut alone last night, surely he would have been nervous and alert and kept that axe beside him all the time? Indeed, on past evidence, at the slightest noise he would have tried to run away unless his assailant overpowered him at once. Yet there was no evidence on that discoloured head of any kind of bruise or scratch that might suggest a struggle. No fear in the expression on the face. If anything, it wore a look of disbelief.

'Must have been somebody very strong,' Lercius put in admiringly. 'Took the head off with a single stroke. Neat as a scythe-blade through the corn.'

That aspect of things had not occurred to me, but when I turned unwillingly to look again, it was obvious that Lercius was right. The head had been chopped off as smoothly as though a butcher had cut through a slice of meat. My axe is sharp enough, but it is heavy. Whoever wielded that blow had been a man of considerable strength. That suggested Bullface and his men, despite what Molendinarius had said.

'That blow would be difficult to do,' Molendinarius said, with a sort of professional dispassion. 'Unless the boy had his head down on the floor. Or else his attacker towered over him. Have to get just the right angle to get it off like that.'

I looked at him again. He was, by his own account, the last person at the scene before Sosso arrived, and the one who had first found the head. Though he dealt chiefly in kindling wood he obviously had expertise with chopping instruments. Though he wheezed and grunted as he breathed and was as thin as bones, could he have done the deed if he had sufficient skill? I shook my head. He lacked the guile to be a murderer and talk so freely of how it was done.

Why should he kill Golbo anyway? For that matter, why should anyone? Just to loot the place? It seemed unlikely. Up to now, when faced with any sort of threat, Golbo's first thought had been to run away. 'Unless,' I thought suddenly, 'it was someone he recognised, and had no reason to be frightened of.' I was startled to find that I had said the words aloud.

The others stared at me in astonishment, but the woman had followed what I meant. 'Perhaps what my husband said was right. He did think it was you. Then he would not look to arm himself. Or if not you, then someone else he knew.'

I glanced at Molendinarius. Was that a possibility? Someone from the villa had arrived, instructed to silence Golbo at all costs, and so protect the master? That seemed even more improbable. There were guards posted up and down the lane expressly so that no one could go in or out. Except Cilla, I remembered guiltily. She was a big girl – was she strong enough to wield the axe? Supposing that she had been the one who called by at the hut? Would she have done it for Marcus. Or for Julia?

I could imagine it. Golbo in the shadows by the fire, looking up nervously as she came in. He had no reason to be afraid of her: he knew her, they had been slaves together in the villa, so he would not think to run away or reach for the axe. On the contrary, he might have smiled, asked her in, invited her to tell him what the news was from the house, even – perhaps – turned away and bent over the water bowl to offer her a drink. And she moving behind him, putting a hand out for the axe, and . . . It was an unpleasant picture, and I shut it out.

I turned to Sosso. 'Can we discover if anyone went down the lane last night?' I asked, without much confidence.

He thought a moment. 'Parva. Best one to find out. Go fetch her, Cornovacus.' This was delivered in a series of short grunts. Then he grinned at me. 'Got to get inside that villa, haven't we? Food and money first, work afterwards.'

It wasn't at all what we'd agreed, but I was ready to assent to anything. 'Then I can send a message to my patron's wife,' I said, looking round unavailingly for something to scratch a message on. The others watched me uncomprehendingly. In the end I snatched up a smoothish piece of wood from the woodpile beside the hut and roughly scrawled *I need four denarii urgently. Libertus* on it with a charred stick from the fire.

I gave it to Sosso. 'Give this to the lady Julia,' I said. 'She'll know it comes from me.'

'What is it?' He rubbed at it doubtfully.

'Don't do that,' I said. 'You'll smudge the writing out. How will you get your four denarii if she can't read my note?'

He looked at it again. 'It's writing?'

I nodded, and the others crowded round to look. It had not occurred to me, although it should have done, that none of them could read. Even the ex-miller came to see.

'I can do numbers,' he said proudly. Sosso gave him the piece of wood. He looked at it intently, upside down. Then he gave it back and shrugged. 'But not this fancy stuff.' He turned away.

Sosso looked at me. 'What does it say?'

I read it to him. He shook his head.

'Not good enough. We don't have anyone who can read – not even Parva, though she was slave-girl in a wealthy house until she caught the pox. How do we know you're not betraying us?'

'How do I know you're not betraying me?' I said. 'You could give this to the soldiers in the lane. I've got as much to lose as you, I think.'

He returned it gravely. 'True. All the same, can't take that. Too big. Not going through the gates, you know.' He permitted himself an ugly little grin. 'Not this time, anyway.'

I gazed at him in consternation. 'Then how can I send a message.'

He smiled again, showing his blackened broken stumps. 'We'll tell her. And four denarii is not enough. How you going to pay us from now on? Can't get into the villa every night.'

I was ashamed to realise I'd not thought of that, but I said in a lofty tone of voice, 'But surely, we must leave a note somehow, for her to find. You can't walk up to her and talk to her. For one thing you'll be seen, and for another you'll frighten her out of her mind – she's never heard of you, and won't believe I've sent you. Why should she? She probably thinks I'm in the jail by now. Or dead.' All that was true, I thought. This enterprise seemed more hopeless by the hour.

Sosso thought about that a moment. 'Is there something she'd recognise?' he grunted. 'A ring? A brooch? Got anything like that?'

'Not any more,' I said, with some asperity. 'I had an oyster spoon that would have served. Her husband gave it to me, but you demanded it.'

He frowned. 'Pity Cornovacus has already gone,' he said, and for the first time I realised that he had. One moment the man was standing at my side, the next he had simply disappeared. I had heard Sosso give him the command, but I had not registered movement or sound of any sort. No wonder the rat-faced man was a successful thief. 'Have to be this, after all.' He looked down at the stick again. He had been fondling it in his hand all this while and it was smudged past reading now.

I sighed, and was looking round for something else – even a thin piece of bark to strip – when the woman plucked softly at my arm. 'Citizen, I've got something here. That slave-girl left it yesterday. She swore me to secrecy, but it's possible that you could write something on it.'

She led the way into the hut, bent down on her creaking knees and rummaged painfully around under the loose reeds of the bed. 'I was to hide it well, and if anybody came and waited at one special place – she told me where – I was to give it to them. Her mistress would pay me handsomely if I did, she said. That's why my husband was loitering near the lane last night. But no one came. Only the soldiers who burned down your house, and a slave-messenger from the Glevum garrison. But none of them stopped where she had said.' She frowned, kneeled up, and then resumed her searching with the other hand. 'Ah, here it is. I don't know if it's any use. It might be. It's used for writing things, I think.'

She was holding a wax writing tablet in her hand.

XVII

I knew who the tablet belonged to from the elaborate ivory carving on the box, but in any case it was tied and sealed – with what I recognised as the impress of Julia's seal-ring on the wax.

'Cilla gave you this last night?' I asked, unable to believe that Julia had sent a message to me, and I had spent the night asleep on top of it.

The old woman nodded. Now that she had it in her hand, she seemed reluctant to part with it. 'Perhaps I should . . .'

'This was meant for me,' I said. 'I was to meet Cilla in the lane, and obviously her mistress meant that she should give me this.' The old woman was still looking doubtful but before she could protest I took it from her, slipped my finger underneath the tie and burst the seal. You could almost hear the silence in the room.

Julia's inimitable style – full of misspellings and a complete feminine disregard for the rules of Latin prose. The message, however, was disturbingly clear. *My friend if you receive this be warned they are looking for you too there is no hope for marcus though I have tried to buy him out they let him send one letter that is all they claim they have found a document sealed with his seal which shows that he was planning to dispose of praxus so that romnus could take over his command and lead a revolt against the emperor I don't believe this if its proved I'll take*

173

poison myself and kill the child. I sank down on the bedding with a groan.

'What is it, citizen? Bad news?'

I nodded. 'The worst.'

I meant it. Until now, despite what common sense might say, I had been trying to persuade myself of Marcus's innocence. However, if evidence like this existed, I would have to revise my views. Romnus was a name I vaguely knew – I was sure that I'd heard Marcus mention him, quite openly, though I could not now remember what the context was. I take little interest in military affairs. But if I had heard it, others would have heard it too, including several of the household slaves, and no doubt the torturers would soon learn of it. That would look black for Marcus at his trial. Certainly there would have to be a trial – something which up till now I'd half hoped to prevent, preferably by providing some explanation of how Praxus died and getting Mellitus to withdraw his murder charge.

But this changed everything. My informants at the garrison had been right. There *was* a charge of conspiracy against the state. It now seemed inevitable that the whole affair would be transferred to Rome. Of course, that had always been a possibility – Marcus was far too highly born to be tried by any local magistrate, and every Roman citizen had the right to appeal to the Emperor. But the crime of maiestas was particularly serious. Even if Governor Pertinax had still been in Britannia, a case like this would still have gone to the Imperial City for the Emperor himself to arbitrate.

And it was no use hoping for any clemency. Commodus had a high opinion of himself – as any man must do who thinks himself a god, and has renamed the months and even Rome itself in his own honour – and was commensurately ruthless with his enemies, or those he believed to be his enemies. There was no shortage of candidates. Commodus imagined there were plots against him everywhere, so if any real evidence of conspiracy was brought he always made an example of those responsible.

Nothing was likely to save my patron now, short of some supernatural intervention by Jupiter himself, as Julia's despairing letter clearly recognised. Marcus might be permitted – as a concession to his rank – to choose his mode of death, so that he could drink a draught of poison in his cell, or fall on his sword like a gentleman instead of having his head struck off by the executioner. On the other hand, Commodus might chose to make a public exhibition of his death: several of his former favourites had been hewed to death or dragged around the city on the hook. Or, if Marcus proved too popular with the crowds – which, given his lineage, might well be the case – he was likely to die of some mysterious illness, or be 'murdered by an outraged member of the populace' before the case was heard.

'Your patron?' Sosso was at my side, frowning at the tablet in concern.

I knew he couldn't read a word of it, and for a moment I was tempted not to tell him what it said. Once Sosso knew the facts, I thought, that could well be the end of any co-operation from the gang. If – or rather when – Marcus was found guilty of this crime, all his goods would be forfeit to the state. That would leave me penniless and Sosso was not a man to work without reward. However, I knew it was impossible to keep this to myself. Julia had already heard the news, and if it was official all Glevum would know of it by dawn.

I sighed and read the letter out to him.

As I did so, I tried to calculate. What would Julia and the child do now? Marcus's various estates, his forests and his farms, his luxurious apartment in the town, the villa and all his other worldly goods, would be forfeit to the Imperial purse. No doubt that was another reason why Commodus was so keen to prosecute his wealthy enemies.

Sosso listened in silence as I read. Out of deference to Julia I decided to omit her last remark about taking her own life. I put the tablet down. 'She says she does not believe it,' I concluded. I braced myself, expecting him to burst into a rage, now that my promise of money was unlikely to be met.

Sosso astonished me. 'We'll work fast, then.' I had been expecting him to refuse to help at all. My surprise must have been written on my face because he grinned, baring his blackened tooth-stumps again. 'Won't get our four denarii otherwise,' he said.

He was right, of course. Julia still had money. The property in Corinium was not under threat. That house and its estates belonged to Julia herself – she had inherited it in her own right from her previous husband and had brought it to this marriage as part of her dowry settlement. So Marcus had only the legal 'use and profit' of it, not the ownership, and it was exempt from seizure if he fell from grace. That meant that Gwellia and Junio were safe, for the moment anyway. The realisation almost gave me hope, and I began to think constructively again.

I got slowly to my feet. 'Wait!' I said – he was already halfway to the door. 'Give me a chance to answer this. If you can get into the villa, you can give her my reply.'

He nodded, frowned, then shrugged lopsidedly. 'Make haste, then. There's no time to lose.' He broke into his ungainly run and loped outside. I heard him calling, 'Lercius!'

I turned to the woman, 'Is there a *stylus* here?'

For a moment she looked mystified. 'You can use anything you see,' she said, stretching her toothless gums into a smile as if she wished to be of help.

I realised what a stupid question it had been. Of course there was no stylus in a house like this. I looked around for ways to improvise. There was a wooden stick the woman had used for mixing up her stew. The end was rounded and I used that as a flattening edge to erase the letters and smooth out the wax. Then, using a thin stick of kindling as a point, I made a mark. It worked. I could scratch a few words of reply.

I looked up. The woman was watching me with awe as though I were a conjurer doing tricks. 'Surely you've seen letters written before? You must have seen scribes in the market place?' There were usually a whole row of them squatting on the pavement by the wall: tattered and disagreeable old men who will read and write anything for a fee – not very accurately, from what I've seen of them, but I suppose that those who cannot read or write themselves are hardly in a position to complain. It did mean, however, that being literate was not usually regarded as something akin to sorcery.

'I've seen the men who do it, citizen, but I've never seen it done,' the old woman said, and moved herself to get a better view – so close that I could hardly write at all.

There is never a lot of room on a wax tablet, especially a decorative one like this, and it was intimidating writing under scrutiny, even by somebody who couldn't read. Nevertheless I outlined the position as succinctly as I could, including the embarrassing request for cash. Then I folded the two hinged frames of wax back together and tied the cord again. I even went to the length of making an impromptu seal of my own, by holding Julia's seal above the fire until the wax began to melt and then pressing my thumb into it across the knot. Then, leaving the old woman goggling, I went outside to find Sosso.

I found him standing with the kindling-man.

'Got to get rid of that,' Sosso was murmuring, gesturing towards the cart. I realised he was referring to poor Golbo's head, which to my great relief they'd covered up again.

'I suppose we could put it with the body in that pit,' Molendinarius suggested. 'Cover it up with branches or fill it in with earth.'

In the light of Sosso's previous haste, it seemed an odd time to be discussing funerals, but I was glad that somebody had thought of it. Golbo deserved that dignity at least. But I had views on how it should be done.

'A good idea,' I put in hurriedly. 'But let's do it decently. Wrap him up and make some offerings of bread and water, so that he's provided for on his journey to the underworld. Golbo was slave in a Roman house. He would have wanted that.'

He would have wanted a good deal more, in fact. Even slaves in Roman households worry about their funerals. Doubtless Golbo, like the rest of Marcus's servants, had paid his dues to the slaves' funeral guild so that even if his master died and failed to provide he would still be entitled to a proper pyre, with priests and sacrifice. Of course, if that happened, the ceremony would be shared with other slaves from Glevum who had died that day, and the ashes would be buried in a common tomb, but the appropriate sacrifice would be made and the spirits of the dead would rest.

Molendinarius looked at Sosso. Sosso shook his head. 'As he is. With the rest of him. In the pit.'

'I'll come and help you dig one a little further off,' I persisted. I am not superstitious about burial itself, but I didn't want it right beside the house. For Gwellia's sake, if not my own, I didn't welcome the idea of poor Golbo's ghost haunting my roundhouse for ever, looking for his missing skull.

Sosso shook his head again and drew a finger across his windpipe in a gesture that said more than any words.

The firewood-seller spelt out the message for me in his wheezing voice. 'He means it would be dangerous. You can't go to the house. Those guards won't have given up, just because they didn't find you yesterday. They'll be back – you can be sure of it. You go back there and start digging pits and you'll get yourself arrested, sure as Jupiter made thunderbolts. I'll take care of it . . .'

Sosso interrupted him. 'See to it.'

The man nodded. He took up a few rough armfuls of kindling from his pile, and stacked them on the handcart with his stump of a hand, so that the bag with its grisly contents was concealed. Then he set off lurching down the path again. I was surprised how easily he'd accepted Sosso's authority. He was clearly an obstreperous old man, but here he was obeying orders like a new legionary recruit.

Sosso grinned horribly at me. 'Promised him a share of our reward,' he said, as if to prove that – although he couldn't read a written word – he was adept at reading thoughts. 'Right, it's time! Lercius!' He gave a whistle and the boy came running up. Sosso turned to me. 'You coming?'

I nodded, though I really had no idea at all what lay in store. I opened my mouth to ask, but Sosso shook his head.

'No talking now. Too dangerous. Follow us. Keep close behind.' He set off, loping in the direction of the woods with Lercius scurrying at his heels.

In my still weakened state they were too fast for me, but I limped after them. I saw them, to my astonishment, abandon the little path and slip in among the trees. I hoped Sosso knew what he was doing. Perhaps Molendinarius had told him where to go. I hoped so. He was not familiar with the area, yet he was striking out with confidence towards the deepest stands of trees, as if all the local rumours of marauding wolves and bears had no more truth in them than the political scandal at the barber's shop. I followed him reluctantly. I have never encountered anything more violent in these woods than a shrew, but I'm still cautious when I am off the beaten track. At least, for once, I could smile at the idea that there were cut-throats and robbers about. I knew it was true: I had brought them with me.

As the thick trees closed around me, I heard the old woman call.

'Citizen!' she pleaded in a wavering tone. 'You have been ill. You should be resting.' It was true that I still ached in every limb, and I hesitated, almost tempted for an instant to go back.

Sosso paid no attention, either to her or to me, but simply went on walking deeper into the trees. He was limping grotesquely as he always did, but he chose his route with skill, moving so lightly that he barely bent the grass or left a footprint in the fallen leaves. Anyone attempting to follow him would have a hard task to pick up his trail. Lercius was swift and noiseless too, and I felt clumsy as a bull as I stumbled after them.

XVIII

Sosso and Lercius were moving so quickly through the woods that I was in danger of losing sight of them myself. There was little foliage to screen them at this time of year, but already the two men were half lost among the trees. I hurried after them, ploughing through the fallen leaves and dodging the bare branches that whipped at my face. I was panting hard when I caught up with them.

Despite his warning earlier, I had vaguely supposed that Sosso was going to lead the way towards my roundhouse and the pit where Golbo's body lay, simply avoiding the main paths where there might be guards. But as we struggled through drifts of rotting leaves and over rutted, muddy tracks I realised that this was not the case.

We came to a fallen tree a little bigger than the rest, and suddenly he veered sharply to the right, as if this was a marker on a predetermined course. He led us quickly to a place where the trees were decidedly less dense, and I saw that we were coming out on to the lane: not near the corner where my enclosure was, but some way short of that, where the old road skirted Marcus's estate, uncomfortably close to where I had yesterday failed to meet Cilla as arranged.

However, we did not take the track. Close to the outer limit of the trees, Sosso made a sudden sign that I should stand still and wait. I did.

He gestured to his right, and I saw what he had seen. A guard, chainmail and helmet glittering, was pacing up and down the lane not very far away. The forest-side border of the lane at this point was a grassy bank, with only a few trees dotted here and there – tall, so that all their branches were high up, and they provided little cover if one wished to hide. The outer wall of Marcus's land formed the other boundary of the lane. If we were spotted, there was nowhere much to run. I was uneasy, fearing that we'd walked into a trap.

I looked around for Lercius, but could see no sign of him. I tugged at Sosso's tunic, and mouthed urgently, 'What's happened to the boy?'

Sosso placed a finger to his ugly lips and signalled me to look into the trees, above the soldier's head. There, in the twisted branches of an oak, was Lercius. He had scaled it, swift and noiseless as a rat – though the lower branches had been lopped – and now he was hiding in a fork. I began to understand his value to the gang. Many a performing athlete could not have done so much.

Once I had seen him, however, he seemed hopelessly conspicuous. There was very little foliage on the tree. One glance in the wrong direction from the guard and the boy must inevitably be seen. I turned to Sosso, frowning.

Sosso smiled. Then, opening his hand, he showed me two stones that he'd picked up earlier. They were a fair weight – each perhaps half the size of my clenched fist, but he held them easily. Then, as I watched, he raised one arm and with a single smooth movement hurled one of the stones as far as possible. It flew as though it were a pebble, away from Lercius and the guard, and hit the wall at an angle, rebounded with a clatter, and bounced down the track. The soldier turned. One could almost see him furrowing his brow as he put one hand on his sword-hilt and took a few steps forward, peering down the lane.

What happened next was so quick that it seemed a blur. Sosso took aim with the second stone, and at the same instant seized my makeshift robe and thrust me back against a tree where I was out of view. I heard the impact as the missile hit the wall, and bounced in fragments on the stony path. From my hiding place I saw the soldier draw his sword.

'Stop in the name of Rome. Who's there?' He came a little further down the lane. By now he was within a pace or two of us.

My heart thudded, thinking we'd been seen, but he blundered past and went on in the direction of the sound. As he did so I saw Lercius shimmy out across a branch and drop, lightly as a cat, on to the top of Marcus's orchard wall. In another instant he was out of sight.

Relief almost betrayed me. I was ready to make a clumsy run for it, but Sosso had more sense. He touched my arm and motioned me urgently to stay where I was, and a moment later the guard came back again, shaking his head.

We waited for what seemed to me an age. The soldier took up his post and sheathed his sword again, but he was still peering suspiciously about. We lay where we were. I could hear my heart thudding, so loudly that I was sure the guard would hear, and my limbs ached with holding one position for so long. Even my breath came so hard that it seemed to drown out the gentle rustle of the wind in the trees and the coo of a pigeon, which were the only other sounds.

At last, when the soldier had relaxed and resumed his pacing up and down the lane, Sosso made his move. Choosing the moment when the guard's patrol routine took him the maximum distance from us up the lane, my companion beckoned me and led the way noiselessly back into the trees.

I lurched upright and stumbled after him but I did not have his skill and I was aware of every rustle and the creak my flapping sandal made. Then I stepped upon a branch and heard it crack. I looked round, fearing that the guard had heard it too.

He had. He had drawn his sword and started after us. 'In the name of Commodus Britannicus, Divine Emperor of Rome and all its provinces, come out and show yourself!'

I slowed, ready to obey, but Sosso flashed me his blackened ugly smile. 'Not you!' he murmured, and turned back himself, loping to the path with his lopsided gait. He purposely exaggerated the limp, and held his head on one side and his mouth ajar, with his arms held up by his sides.

'Urgh! Urgh! Alms!' I heard him croaking, 'Urgh! Jove's name! Urgh!'

That was a clever move. There is a widespread belief among worshippers of the Roman deities that among the crazed are those who have been touched by a supernatural hand and thus enjoy special protection from the gods. Soldiers are notoriously superstitious, of course and – since they are required to make oaths and sacrifices to Jupiter and Mars, whatever other religions they profess – Sosso was clearly assuming a kind of moral shield by calling on the name of the father of the gods and looking as lunatic as possible. If my life had not depended on the stratagem, it would have made me laugh.

It was successful, too. From where I was hiding in the woods, I could see the soldier backing off. 'Go on! Be off! Don't come close to me!' He held his sword up warningly.

'I've heard of you. You live the other side of Glevum, out among the tombs. What are you doing here?'

Sosso lurched closer to him. 'Birds! Eat!' he grunted, in a tone so horrible and slavering that even I shuddered, though I knew what the soldier could not guess – that this ugly, harmless little 'idiot' was in fact a natural leader capable of lightning thought and complex plans.

Indeed, I realised, I was witnessing one now. Allowing me to alert the guard had been no accident, and Sosso was talking to the man not merely to protect me, as I'd half supposed. Behind the soldier, on the orchard wall, I saw a hand appear, and then another, followed first by Lercius's face and shoulders and then – with a swift upward push – by his body too.

Sosso loped closer to the guard, leering horribly. 'Alms!' he said again, making as if to paw the soldier's arm.

The man stepped backwards. 'I ought to take you under arrest,' he muttered, but he dropped his sword. He was clearly nervous, though, and watching Sosso like a hawk. 'Go on, get out of here, before I change my mind.' Behind him Lercius ran along the wall and dropped to safety further up the path. I saw him scuttle silently across the lane and disappear into the woods on my side of the track.

Sosso must have seen him too. He gave one last, mock-despairing 'Urgh!' and then turned away. He loped towards me, turning off the path and ploughing through the moist brown undergrowth. This time he made no effort to be quiet. The guard watched him till he reached the shelter of the trees, then went back to pacing up and down the lane.

I must have made a bit of noise myself as I joined Sosso in retreat, but the soldier did not glance our way again. I had enough sense not to speak until we reached the fallen tree once more and were well out of earshot of the guard. Lercius was already there, sitting on the jagged stump and grinning like a frog.

Sosso nodded at him. 'Succeed?'

'It was easy, except for a pair of alarm geese that tried to hiss at me, but I managed to take care of them. I just dropped in among the bushes at the back and it was only a moment before a servant came along. It was a slave-girl, come to feed the geese.'

'She didn't scream?' I said, trying to imagine what the poor girl must have felt, unexpectedly accosted in her owner's private orchard by an unknown ragged man, who – knowing Lercius – most likely had an evil smile on his face, and a horribly dead goose in either hand.

Lercius grinned wider. 'She didn't get a chance. I came round behind her and covered up her mouth – then I showed her that wax writing tablet thing you gave to me. She didn't struggle after that, so I put it in her hand and let her go. I think she was the one who brought it out, and once she saw it she accepted me. I didn't even have to squeeze her very much,' he added, with a suspicion of regret. He looked at Sosso proudly. 'I told her what you said I was to say.'

'No soldiers?' Sosso said, ignoring this.

Lercius shook his head. 'There are only two soldiers in that whole new annexe part – or so the slave-girl said. There were more to start with but apparently the owner's wife made quite a fuss. Told the officer in charge that she didn't want soldiers leering at her as she walked about, and demanded to have the women's quarters to herself.'

I could scarcely suppress a smile at this. It was typical of Julia, I thought. It would be a strong man who could resist her pleas, if she looked demurely up at him under her beautiful brows as she smiled bravely and told him how distressed she was. I could imagine her deploying her considerable charms upon the centurion in charge. Julia was very skilled at obtaining her own way. 'So the officer agreed?' I said.

Lercius nodded. 'That's what comes of having looks and money, I suppose. For the lady they relaxed the guard. Inside that part of the house at least. Only those two guards posted at the exits now.'

Sosso had been listening closely. 'And the rest?'

'A dozen or so in the main part of the house, so the slave-girl says. When they come off duty, that is where they go. They've found the amphorae of wine that are sunk into the kitchen yard by now – judging by the noise they make, apparently. Otherwise, they're watching at the gates and patrolling round the walls, to stop people getting in and out.' He grinned again. 'They're not expecting trouble. The two that were in that women's area were strolling up and down, not taking any notice of what went on. I glimpsed them when I was struggling with the geese. I'd thought they would discover me for sure – one of the stupid things did flap and squawk just once before I silenced it. But they scarcely glanced my way – too busy talking to one another.' He winked. 'Complaining about how boring it was, I expect. They didn't even notice that there weren't any pigeons about, when I gave you the signal that I was coming back.'

So that was how Sosso had known when to make his move. I was impressed. I'd registered the sound myself, but it had seemed so natural that it had not occurred to me that anything but a bird was making it.

'And did you get the money?' I enquired.

Lercius looked at me in surprise. 'Money?'

'I asked Julia for those four denarii,' I said.

'She'll give you that herself, I expect,' Lercius said. 'When you go in.'

'When I . . .?' I looked at Sosso sharply. There was no way I could do what Lercius had done.

The dwarf just laughed, enjoying my obvious bewilderment. 'That's right. Give it to you then. More, if she's got any sense.' He was revelling in this, taunting me with hints, so it was clearly useless to ask anything outright. He gave another ugly little smile. 'Remember your promise. Money every day. Or . . .' He made that slitting gesture once again, and turned to Lercius. 'You told her?'

'I did. I said I did.' Lercius was indignant. 'Everything you told me, all about the cart, and bringing all the stuff in for the farm. At least I told the slave-girl. She said she'd tell her mistress and it would be arranged. I was lucky there. She knew this citizen.' He turned to me. 'You know the one. A chubby girl, with great big . . .' He made gleeful grasping motions with his hands.

'Enough!' Sosso interrupted him. 'But well done! Extra chicken stew for you. Come on.' He did not pause, but led the way into the trees again, and once more I found myself following him blindly, as if I were the stranger in these woods and he had walked the paths for years. He moved so quickly that there was no more time for talk, and I struggled after him until (rather to my surprise, I confess) we branched out of the trees again and found ourselves in the clearing where the firewood-seller had his hut.

XIX

There had been trouble at the hut, that much was obvious. The meagre possessions which I'd seen earlier had been dragged outside and strewn haphazardly on the ground, while the roof and woodpile had both been pulled apart – with unnecessary violence, by the look of it. The wool from my dye-house lay in sodden piles and there were shards of broken pottery everywhere. Even Gwellia's bowls of carefully sorted dyestuffs had been overturned. In the midst of all this chaos the old woman was scrabbling on her knees, trying to collect the pathetic objects together again as best she could.

She looked up wearily as we approached and I saw that her old eyes were filled with tears. 'The soldiers, citizen,' she murmured brokenly. 'They have been here, searching everything.'

'Soldiers? What were they doing here?'

Even as I framed the words, I knew what she would say. 'Looking for you, citizen. I'm sure of it, although they didn't say. When I asked questions, they just . . .' She raised one hand to her wrinkled cheek and I felt a burst of anger as I saw the dull bruise darkening.

'What kind of soldiers? Were they from the town? The garrison?'

She shrugged helplessly. 'They were soldiers, citizen. That is all I know. Soldiers with armour, swords and leather skirts.

Though, come to think of it, I'm sure they're not the ones I've seen down in the lane. Great ugly men, these were, like brutes – the leader in particular.'

'A brute with big shoulders and a face like an ox?' I said, and saw from her expression that I had guessed right. This was the work of Bullface and his men.

She caught her breath. 'You know the men?'

I nodded grimly. 'I've seen them, once or twice. I know they're after me. So they came here. I'm sorry. What happened then?'

'They asked me who was hiding in the hut, and I said nobody. I tried to plead with them, saying we were poor and there was nothing there.' She stifled a sob. 'But they wouldn't listen. They pushed past me – pushed me over – and went in. And then . . . did this. Turned the whole place upside down. Just picked up everything and threw it on the ground. Outside in the mud, of course. Scattered the woodpile, pulled down half the thatch. They even emptied out the water bowl, deliberately, all over that new wool and spoiled it. They threw away my remedies and ground them underfoot, although I begged them not to. The gods only know how I shall eke out a living now. But they wouldn't stop. Poked at the bedstraw with their swords and then pulled it to the fire and let it burn.'

'As well you'd given me the writing tablet, then,' I said. I intended only to encourage her, but to my dismay I saw the helpless tears begin again. Obviously she hadn't thought of that. If they'd discovered that, it would have meant the scourge for her at least.

'Thank all the gods that you went with Sosso, citizen. If you had been here . . .' She shivered.

If I had been there I would surely have been killed, and so

would she. That was what she meant, and it was self-evidently true. Yet it puzzled me, when I considered it. Who had sent Bullface here to look for me? Not the commander of the regular Glevum garrison, it seemed. He had troops stationed at the villa, certainly, but when Lercius was there this afternoon there was no sign of activity or particular alert, as there would certainly have been if official search parties were out. Lercius had been explicit on the point. Besides, the garrison commander was an old friend of Marcus's: even if he had been seeking my arrest – perhaps as an unwilling witness or co-conspirator – he would have wanted me brought back alive.

An unofficial party then? That was an uncomfortable thought. Up until now I had supposed that Bullface and his men, although seconded from the legionary ranks to serve as Praxus's private bodyguard, were still Imperial soldiers under arms and therefore subject to orders from above either from the garrison or some high-ranking individual. Specialist groups can be co-opted to civil tasks sometimes, while waiting for a posting to come through. That was how Mellitus had used them on the evening of the banquet, and I suspected that Balbus had attempted to do the same.

But was it simpler than that? Were they acting on their own account, determined to avenge their master's death, either for themselves or for someone else? That was the most unnerving possibility of all – a small marauding private unit, under Bullface's command, subject to no official scruples or restraint and operating outside the law. Did that explain why 'soldiers' had set fire to my hut – and why I had escaped the garrison in town, only to find Praxus's guard awaiting me?

I was still lost in this disturbing line of thought when Lercius interrupted me. He was examining the contents of the hut with an expression of ill-disguised dismay. 'What happened to our chicken stew?' he blurted suddenly. It seemed a callous question, in the circumstances, but I was ashamed to realise that I had some sympathy. I had not eaten since my share of roasted eel the night before, and already I was feeling hunger-pangs.

'The soldiers poured it all away. Most of the liquid seeped into the ground,' the woman said, picking up the battered cooking pot. 'But obviously I've rescued what I could.' To my amazement she whipped off the lid, and revealed a little pile of broken chicken flesh. 'Some of it got quite muddy, I'm afraid, and although I tried to clean it in the spring, until I get another water bowl I have no way to do it properly. But if you don't mind . . .'

Mind? I'd have eaten through more mud than that to get at sustenance! Lercius clearly felt the same: he had already plunged a hand into the pot and was chewing greedily on a piece of thigh. Even Sosso abandoned his prowling round the hut and came over to join us at our feast.

We ate with our fingers, since there were no bowls – apart from Sosso who still had his knife, and used it to spear the choicest morsels for himself. It tasted wonderful despite the flecks of dirt – as things do to a starving man – and we made short work of it. Even the woman had a piece or two. I was just considering the empty pot, and wondering what Molendinarius would say when he returned to find that we had eaten all the food, when I looked up and saw him toiling up the track.

He was pushing his handcart, by the look of it, now piled high with something and covered by a dingy green-brown cloth. Behind him were two other figures whom I did not recognise at first, but as they drew closer I realised that it was

Cornovacus and the pock-marked girl. At the same time I was aware of an unpleasant odour in the air, as if someone had been rolling in the drains.

'Ah,' Sosso grunted, wiping his ugly face on the hem of what had been my tunic. 'They've come. Time for you to go.'

'Go where?' I asked, trying to forget the puzzle of the smell. I was beginning to trust that Sosso had a plan, since he'd plotted everything successfully till now. A plan was needed, too. It was already clear to me that it was no longer safe for me to stay here in the hut – and clearly the round-house and my workshop were equally dangerous. Bullface and his men would not give up. They would certainly be back to search for me again, and I had few illusions now about what I could expect if they once managed to lay hands on me. 'Go where?' I said again.

Sosso grinned. 'Villa. Naturally. Need the money, don't we?'

I gaped. 'But I can't . . .' I made a despairing gesture. I tried for a moment to envisage myself shimmying up trees and leaping down from branches, as Lercius had done. I failed.

Sosso gave that throaty, mirthless laugh. 'Don't worry, citizen. No climbing walls. You get in through the gates.' He gestured towards the firewood-seller's cart. 'See, there.'

Molendinarius swept off the cloth in a dramatic gesture, and the full stench of what it had covered reached my nostrils. It was unmistakable – rotten meat and decaying vegetables, with a fair admixture of human excreta too, I guessed. It was so powerful it almost made me reel.

Cornovacus nodded cheerfully. 'Got it from the middens just outside the town,' he said proudly. 'Got all the members of our group on to it, worked them like a slavemaster, and –

193

by Pluto and all the powers of Dis – they managed to get this together in an afternoon.' He looked at me as if expecting to be complimented on this unlikely achievement.

'What's it for?' I said guardedly.

'It's for the farm, of course,' Molendinarius explained impatiently. 'Buy this sort of thing, landowners do. Always a bit of money to be made, if you can get your hands on it and you've got a handcart you can move it on. Only, you tend to have to fight for it – everybody's got the same idea.'

The idea of coming to blows over the contents of cesspits and rubbish heaps was new to me, but I was beginning to learn how the really poor and desperate could scratch a living from the most unexpected sources. Besides, I had other, more pressing, questions on my mind.

'And how is this going to get me through the gates?' If Sosso supposed that I would lie down on the cart and have that noisome mess spread over me, he would have to come up with some other plan. A man would choke to death in minutes from the smell.

Sosso bared his ugly tooth-stumps in a grin. 'Push it.'

This time I fairly gaped. 'Me? But I'll be recognised.'

He chuckled; it was not a pleasant sound. 'I doubt it, *citizen*.'

The pock-marked girl, who had been standing by, seemed to take courage at Sosso's mirth, and ventured timidly, 'Citizen, they're not expecting you and if they were they wouldn't know you now. No one ever looks at dungheap-men, in any case – they keep as far away as possible. Have you seen yourself?'

I had not, of course – there was nothing in the hut, not even a pail of clear water, that one could see one's reflection in – but I realised instantly that she must be right. Not only was I wrapped in makeshift clothes and sacks, but I knew my hair was matted and my face unshaved, and parts of me still bore faint streaks of mud. Also, there was a cut above my eye, and I could feel that it was swollen and my cheek was bruised. No one who knew the old Libertus would glance twice at me.

'Besides,' the girl went on, 'I shall be there to help.'

I was on the point of asking what help she would be, when Sosso said suddenly, 'Enough! Come on!' and there was nothing for it but to go.

XX

We trooped in silence down the little path back towards the lane. I had a hundred questions, but I was wheeling the lopsided cart and that took all of my concentration until we reached the wider track, and it was not a great deal easier even then. I am accustomed to handcarts – I have one of my own – but this one had a damaged wheel and the resultant lurch made manoeuvring it a misery. The stinking contents shifted at every bump and fissure in the road, and threatened to fall off and shower me. I marvelled how the one-handed miller had managed it. The smell was perfectly atrocious, too.

Nor did my companions offer any help. The old woman had remained behind, still collecting up the strewn possessions from the hut, and Parva had forged ahead of us somewhere. As soon as we reached the public road the other men withdrew into the trees, leaving me to wheel the thing alone.

I turned towards them to protest but they were gone. I was horrified. Suppose I was walking into a trap? Sosso had not fully explained his plan to me, or told me what I was supposed to do. It would have been very easy for Cornovacus to have called into the garrison and offered to betray me for a price. I did not like this feeling of being in other people's hands – especially a band of vagabonds and thieves.

I gave the handcart a bad-tempered push, with the result that it lurched into a deepish rut and stopped with a jerk that almost lost the load.

I thought unkind thoughts about the Fates and stooped to extricate the wheel from the hole. When I looked up there was a soldier on the road in front of me, stationed so that he would block my path. The Fates, I thought, had evidently heard. For a moment I contemplated abandoning the cart and bolting for the trees myself, but I had just sufficient self-restraint to see the idiocy of that.

If Sosso's plan was going to work at all, I could expect to meet a soldier at some stage. This encounter was the test of it. I was supposed to be delivering fertiliser to the villa from the town, and this was an appropriate route for doing it – not the main military road where a poor man would be obliged to take to the verges on the way, but this steep and bumpy lane where at least I could occupy the track until it joined up with the wide and gravelled road which led to the main entrance of the villa. Of course I could hardly turn up there like a visitor, but beside the front gate was another track that led round to the farm and to the inner gateway at the back. If the perimeter of the villa was patrolled, I would have to get used to passing the guards.

I ruffled my thinning hair as far as possible across my face, hunched my shoulders and lurched off towards the soldier down the lane.

It was the same man that we'd seen earlier, but this time there was no sign of an alarm. He didn't even draw his sword. He simply nodded at me as I approached, and asked me brusquely what my business was.

'Fertiliser from the streets,' I said, lifting up a corner of the cloth so that he could see, and also obtain the full benefit of the smell. 'They take it at the villa, to put round the plants.'

I had taken pains to disguise my voice as much as possible, and my heart was thudding so loudly that I thought he had to hear, but he didn't give me a second glance. 'Well go on then, get on with it.' He averted his head fastidiously. 'What a stench! Worse than a gladiator's armpit! Get it out of here!' And he actually stood back to let me pass.

My route took me past my roundhouse gate, but there were soldiers on the lane and in my present role I dared not stop to look. However, it seemed to be as Molendinarius had said. Only a pile of charred remains showed where the sleeping house had been, but the dye-house and the rest of the enclosure seemed more or less intact. That was all I could determine before I was challenged by another guard. My throat went dry and my heart thumped painfully but, again, once I showed him the nature of my load he lost interest in me and waved me through.

I was stopped once more before I reached the track to the farm, and had to pass a sentry at the outer gate. Every time the outcome was the same. I was beginning to feel a bit more confident.

Things were not so simple when I reached the inner gate. In place of Marcus's usual gatekeeper, who was elderly and always half asleep, there were two armed soldiers posted in the gatehouse there, and they were very much awake. From the way the younger one swaggered out and blocked my way, I was convinced that my whole lurching ordeal had been in vain.

'Well?' His tone was bullying. 'What do you want? You can't come in here.'

I went into my fertiliser speech again, but this time it did not have the same effect. He shook his head. 'No one is to come in or out, by order of the garrison. I have my instructions. Now go away. Go on, beat it, before I take my baton to you.' His colleague, who had been standing at the doorway of the gatekeeper's post, took a step towards me as if to prove the point.

'The other soldiers let me past,' I protested, but there is no point in arguing with a guard. I began to turn the cart round. That was far more difficult than simply pushing it.

They watched me struggling.

'Oh, come on!' Parva unexpectedly appeared from the little room, a sort of stone hut set into the wall. 'Make up your mind, you two. Who's interested in this stupid beggar and his cart of muck? You heard what he said. Let him in and let's get on with it. A quadrans each – I haven't got all day.'

The younger soldier still looked hesitant, but the other winked at him. 'She's right. Vital supplies, that is. You know our orders. We aren't to interfere with vital farm supplies and profitable trade. You know what the authorities are like. When this estate is taken into Imperial hands, they want it as lucrative as possible.' He jerked a thumb at me. 'Go on then. In there beside the inner wall. You dump it there, and mind you keep in sight, where we can keep an eye on you. No funny business either or I'll have both your ears.'

I straightened the cart before he changed his mind, and suddenly there I was inside the gates. It was so familiar – the piles of heaped wood for the furnaces, the beds of winter greens, the fruit trees neatly planted up against the wall – that it was hard to believe how much my life had changed. There was even a land slave sweeping up the leaves. It all looked strikingly peaceful and affluent after the wretched hovels where I'd spent the last two days.

However, there was no time to stand and stare about. The younger soldier was still scowling after me. His companion had already disappeared. Having no shovel or real idea of what was appropriate, I lifted the cloth and began to scrabble the muck on to the floor with my hands. The soldier grunted something which I could not hear, but he seemed satisfied, and after a moment he too turned in the direction of Parva and her raddled charms.

The land slave was less amenable. He put down his brush of bundled twigs and hurried across to me, his face a picture of incredulity.

'What are you doing, you old fool? You can't offload that here. Get out before I call my mistress. She will have you whipped.' His voice was so loud that I feared the guard had heard, but there was no sound from the gatehouse. Presumably they were otherwise engaged.

'Hush,' I murmured as soon as he was near enough to hear. I realised that I knew him slightly, had even spoken to him once or twice, but there was not a flicker of recognition on his face. 'Your mistress is expecting me, I think.' I certainly hoped that this was true. I guessed that when Lercius had gone across the wall, this was the message he had been told to give – though nobody had said as much to me. 'Tell her the ordure she required has come.' I dropped my voice. 'Tell her a pavement-maker has delivered it. Quickly, before those guards come back. Now, if you wish to save your master's life.'

He gave me a startled little nod, and darted through the door which led in the direction of the house. I went on shovelling with my hands, taking as long as I dared. It would take him some time to cross the inner garden and the court and find his mistress in the further wing. But I dared not stop altogether. The older of the guards had wandered back by now, adjusting his tunic, and was standing by the gate again, watching me in a desultory way.

I had almost finished pulling off the load when the land slave reappeared, followed by Julia herself, with Cilla at her side. She was as beautiful as ever, though she did look drawn, and the strain of the last few days was evident. Even the soldier at the gate was looking at her appreciatively.

'Lady!' I murmured deprecatingly. It suddenly occurred to me how odd this must look, the mistress of the house appearing in honour of an itinerant beggar with a load of rotting rubbish from the streets.

Julia ignored me and walked on to the gate. The soldier straightened up perceptibly, and held himself peculiarly upright, as if he was sucking his stomach in and trying to force his chest-armour out. Julia had that effect on many men. She had chosen a sombre dark grey *stola* this afternoon, in deference to her husband's plight, and had covered her hair and shoulders in a dun-coloured mantle too. It was almost funeral attire, and it made her look more than usually fragile and pale.

'I am sending a messenger to Corinium again,' she said, in a voice that was deliberately loud enough for me to hear. 'Please see that he is permitted to leave without delay. I intend to remove there, as you know, if things do not go well at my husband's trial, and obviously there is a great deal to be done if the house is to be prepared for me.'

The soldier shrugged, but his manner was respectful as he said, 'Lady, that's impossible. We've already been too lenient as it is, letting that messenger through yesterday.'

'I had your centurion's permission for that,' she replied, with dignity. 'Both to let him in and send him out again.'

'I know that, lady, but of course when that was first agreed the villa was only under guard. We hadn't had instructions then to seal it off. But now that your husband – begging your pardon, madam citizen – has been discovered in a plot, naturally the house is under scrutiny and private messengers are not allowed.'

'Not even if I send it through the guard? If I could get a message to the commander of the garrison, surely he could see that it reached Corinium? There are always messengers riding to and fro – and he could ensure that there was nothing treasonable in what I wrote. When my messenger came back from Corinium he brought me word that I have a visitor – a lady and her slaves – and naturally I am concerned that she is properly received. Of course there are servants at the house, but it is hardly civilised to leave her there alone.'

So Gwellia and Junio were safe. It was clever of Julia, I thought, to find a way of making sure that I discovered that, without addressing a single word to me. It was a huge relief to know. Indeed, I was so busy thinking about that, I stopped unloading the muck.

The soldier spoke again. 'Orders are orders, lady. It's not in my hands – or even in our centurion's any more. We're only doing what we're told.' He gave her what was obviously his official smile. 'Once the trial is over, you'll be free to go. I'm sure your visitors will understand. Your usual hospitality is legendary. Look at that banquet you gave the other night.'

Julia gave a ladylike but contemptuous snort. 'At which one of my two house-guests died – in the presence of the high priest of Jupiter as well – and the other was forced to leave the house and seek accommodation in an inn, because the household was put under guard?'

So Mellitus had been forced to put up at an inn? He would not have appreciated that. I chuckled inwardly. I had forgotten that he was a house-guest at the villa that night – and naturally he couldn't decently remain alone with Julia and an infant child, once Marcus had been taken into custody. Still, it was interesting news. Perhaps Sosso and his men could find out which inn it was and see if anything was to be learned from there, although by this time the procurator would certainly have left. He would either have gone back to his home town or, more likely, have become the house-guest of some other councillor in Glevum. There must still be administrative matters to resolve. After all, that was what he'd come to the colonia for.

Something else had become clear to me as well. This total ban on communication with the villa was recently imposed. I had half deduced that for myself, from the freedom which Cilla had earlier enjoyed and the fact that Julia had been permitted to receive that letter from Marcus. Indeed, even after the new charges were first laid – Marcus had mentioned them in his note – it seemed she had still been permitted to send messengers to the Corinium house and receive replies. Something since then had clearly changed. It could only be the production of clear evidence – either a statement extorted from one of the tortured household slaves confirming that Marcus had mentioned Romnus's name, or the production of the famous document. Or, more likely, both.

There was no time to think about that now. Julia was still talking to the guard, and it was evident that she intended me to hear.

'I have done my best to co-operate with you,' she said, 'letting you search my husband's study, and take that document and things away. Surely you can co-operate with me, in such a simple matter as a messenger? An important man like you?'

I couldn't see her face, but I knew that she had lowered her head and would be looking at him from under downcast lids. No wonder the commanding officer had listened to her pleas and reduced the guard in her wing of the house. It would not surprise me to learn that he now made a point of patrolling that area himself. Julia had no power at all in law, now that her husband-guardian was in jail – she would have been helpless to prevent the search and seizure of Marcus's things – but she knew how to wield the other powers she had.

The guard looked self-important, and I thought for a moment that he might weaken and agree, but the younger soldier sauntered out of the gatekeeper's room just then, and – thus observed – the senior took a different line.

'Lady, I have told you several times. There is nothing that we soldiers can do. If you have a complaint to make, make it to the commander of the garrison.'

'But how am I to contact him, since I cannot even send a messenger?' Julia said plaintively.

The soldier clearly could not answer that, since it was impeccably logical, and looked around for someone on whom he could vent his embarrassment and so reassert his authority. He saw me loitering by the cart, and I was the obvious candidate.

He bawled at me. 'You! Old man! Get a move on there – don't stand there idling, just because you think that no one's watching you. I know your type! You've got a job to do. Get on with it!'

'Ah!' Julia turned to me. 'Indeed. The fertiliser for my flower beds. I suppose the man needs paying. Cilla, see to it. Four quadrantes, I think that was agreed?'

Cilla came over to me, and ostentatiously dropped four quadrantes in my hand. I stared at her. Surely Julia would give me more than this?

'Say thank you, citizen, and try to look impressed,' the slave-girl murmured, moving so that she stood between me and the guard. 'My mistress has a plan. Beg for some clothes – it seems you need them, too. I wouldn't have recognised you dressed like that. What happened to your toga?' She glanced towards the cart.

She was right, of course. I don't know why I hadn't realised it before – the turmoil of the last few days seemed to have dulled my mind. But now I saw what Cilla had observed. The big sludge-coloured cloth that had been tucked around the cart had dropped to the ground and opened out. One long edge of it was visible, curved in the distinctive toga-shape. The truth was evident. This now-stinking piece of rag had been my proud mark of Roman status, until Junio had come home and hidden it in the dye.

I kicked the garment over with my foot, so that the shape of it was less conspicuous, and bowed my head obsequiously. 'Thank you, miss,' I said aloud, for the benefit of the soldiers, who still had their eyes on us. Behind them I saw Parva slip out of the gatehouse and away. I wheedled my voice into a pleading whine. 'I think I was promised a few rags, as well? Something to keep out the winter cold?'

'Ah, that slave's tunic that got torn and stained with wine last Janus's Feast! Of course. He's quite right, Cilla – Marcus promised him. You'll find it somewhere in the kitchen block, if someone hasn't torn it up for rags. And there's a loaf of bread that he can have, as well – left over from the banquet. People went home so suddenly that night, even the pigs can't keep up with the scraps.'

I was puzzled. This, obviously, was part of Julia's plan. A three-day-old loaf of bread was scarcely edible and besides – to my knowledge – the diners had all finished long before the unfortunate events that brought the banquet to a sudden close, and dined superbly too. Unless this somehow offered information as to the murderer, I could see no advantage in the gift. However, I clearly could say none of this aloud, so I cried, 'Jove and all the deities bless you, lady!' with what I hoped was an appropriately humble show of gratitude.

Julia acknowledged this with the curtest of short nods, as though I were the nobody I seemed. She turned back to the guards. 'I don't know what Governor Pertinax would say, if he knew how his personal representative was treated now he's gone!' she snapped, and went back through the inner door with Cilla at her side.

Her departure was followed by an awkward hush. The soldier was scowling at me again. There was nothing for it but to put down my coins and unload the last few stinking remnants of my load.

No one had offered me a spade at any point, but now that the cart was empty the kitchen slave came over with the broom and began ostentatiously to sweep around the pile, as if to tidy it as much as possible. I picked up my ex-toga – fwhaw, how it stank! – and wiped my hands on it, then bundled it back on to the cart, artlessly folded with the curved edge innermost. I tied my pitiful payment into the corner of my makeshift garment, as I have seen beggars do.

Cilla came back with an old blue tunic on her arm, and a loaf of bread which was as hard as bricks. She tossed them on the cart without a word and disappeared and I was left to wheel it away: past the gatehouse, down the farm track – unmolested – and out on to the lane.

XXI

I found that I was sweating with relief, despite the cold. The cart was much easier to manage, now that it was empty, and I made good speed back to the spot where I had last seen Sosso and his men, although it was beginning to get dark by now. Molendinarius was there in the deepening gloom, gathering fallen branches into piles, and collecting twigs as though for kindling. When he saw me, his face twisted into its customary scowl, but he straightened up and came to me at once. It was clear that he had been sent to wait for me.

'Well,' he demanded. 'You got what you went for, I presume? Now have you finished with my cart, or has a poor man got to go on lugging his means of livelihood around with him by hand?'

I scooped up my loaf and tunic (the toga stank so much that I abandoned it) and left the cart exactly where it stood. 'Don't worry, you'll be paid,' I said, thinking of those four quadrantes in my hem. How Sosso would be paid was something else, but I had confidence in Julia. I was looking forward to examining my gifts in detail – it would not have surprised me to find a message scratched into the bottom of the loaf, or cleverly concealed in the tunic-folds.

The firewood-seller sneered unpleasantly at me. 'Of course I shall be paid,' he said. 'I wouldn't have lent it to you otherwise.' He bent and began to load his brushwood on to the cart. 'You'd better go on up towards the hut. The others are waiting for you there – trying to decide what's to be done with you.' He spat. 'More trouble than you're worth, it seems to me.'

Once I would have felt sympathy for him, struggling to eke out a living with one damaged hand, but he was so unpleasant I was fleetingly tempted to regret my generosity in buying unwanted kindling from him in the past. Then I recalled that without his grudging hospitality, and his wife's care in particular, I would have been either dead or captured by this time. I nodded and went up towards the hut.

Even in the dusk it was possible to see that the area had been painstakingly cleared and swept, and everything restored to order once again. A warm glow emanated from within, and an enticing smell was beginning to emerge. Another of my chickens, I presumed. The woman was squatting near the hut, sifting a pile of herbs, and as I approached she looked at me, and smiled her toothless smile. 'Were you successful, citizen? Did you get the money from your patron's wife?'

I avoided the question. 'Not directly,' I admitted. 'I got this, though.' I had examined the bread from every angle as I walked, but in this light I could see no sign of messages on it. I had even tapped to see if it was hollow, but it was denser than a piece of stone. I gave it to her now.

Her face fell. 'Great Minerva! What's the use of that? You couldn't eat it if you soaked it for a week. What's in it, anyway? A lump of iron?'

And then, of course, I understood. 'I'll investigate,' I said, carefully removing the item from her grasp. I took it up, and slammed it with all my force on to a jagged piece of stone beside the path. The loaf cracked, and I saw that I was right. It was not ordinary dough but hard and powdery, like mortar, and the edge of a coin was clearly visible. A silver denarius, by the look of it, and there were clearly others in the loaf. What a cunning and resourceful woman Julia was!

'I shall need my axe or something to get into this,' I said, trying to keep emotion from my voice. No need to advertise my sudden wealth. Although Sosso and his men had proved themselves willing to help for a price, they were still beggars, vagabonds and thieves, and Molendinarius had looted my roundhouse, after all. I turned the loaf so that the coin was out of sight. 'Or perhaps that stone you use for grinding herbs.'

The woman nodded and I moved towards the hut. Sosso and Cornovacus were there, deep in conversation by the fire. They were squatting on the floor – which was devoid of bedding, I observed. The two of them looked up as I came in.

'I've got the money – or the means of getting it,' I said quickly, before Sosso could ask. 'And a lot of useful information too.'

Sosso got slowly to his feet.

'If you are going to work on my behalf,' I went on briskly, 'I've got some notion now of where to start. I need somebody to go into the town and see if they can find the inn where Procurator Mellitus stayed – and if possible discover where he is now. Also, and most important, if you can get into the garrison, I'd like to know what documents were found, and exactly what they are supposed to say. And Balbus should be watched, as well – and any other dignitary who was there that night, even the high priest of Jup . . .'

'Later, citizen.' Sosso's unlovely grin looked calculating in the shadows of the fire. 'First the money. Then we'll talk again.'

211

'All in good time. I need this dwelling to myself awhile,' I said. I did not want him to guess about the loaf, so I added quickly, 'My patron's wife has given me some clothes to change into, and suggested whom we could approach for help.' It was true, too, if I understood her right. She mentioned the high priest of Jupiter – my own words a moment earlier had reminded me – and judging by what Cilla had told me on the morning after Praxus's death, the high priest might be prepared to lend a sympathetic ear.

Sosso, though, was shaking his head. 'Not safe! You can't go into the town.'

'I have been thinking about that,' I said. 'I can't stay here, it's true, but if you smuggled me back inside the city walls – perhaps making use of the cart again – I could go to my workshop and hide there. If the guard are sure that I'm outside the town – and that seems to be the case, since they've been searching here – they'll hardly waste time looking for me there.'

Cornovacus had been getting to his feet. 'Think yourself clever, do you, citizen? Well, let me tell you something you don't know. I called at your wretched workshop yesterday, when I was in the town. There's been a guard seen twice outside your door, may Mars strike him dead! We've left a lookout on the street, so when the place is safe he'll send us word. You can't be keener to get back than we are to get rid of you. But obviously you can't go yet – unless you *want* to risk your scrawny neck?' He paused. I shook my head. 'In that case, you remember Tullio?'

How could I forget? I was still aching from my uncomfortable ride and the ignominious impromptu bathe. 'You want me to travel in that little boat again?' I couldn't keep the panic from my voice.

Cornovacus laughed scornfully. Sosso said, 'Simpler than that. He's got a wife and children. And a hut. He'll hide you, for a price.'

'It will be risky. His wife may not agree.' I was imagining what Gwellia would say if I suggested endangering us all by hiding a stranger who was wanted by the guard.

'She will, if she's paid enough,' Cornovacus said, with finality. 'It's hard to feed and clothe five children on what Tullio makes from catching eels. He's always desperate.'

Sosso nodded. 'So, where's the money?'

I was reluctant to reveal the secret of the loaf. I jangled the coins which were tied into my hem. 'I've got some here. And there'll be more. But first, as I said, I need a moment to myself – to think and put these clothes on, among other things.'

I did not suppose they would agree to this, but Sosso simply rolled his eyes at Cornovacus, and said, 'Don't be all night. It's late.'

He went, gesturing to his companion to follow him. Cornovacus didn't go at once. 'We shall be right outside the door,' he said, glaring at me suspiciously. 'And don't go helping yourself to the confounded soup till we've been paid, or by all the gods . . .' Sosso came back and jerked a thumb at him, and he went out, still grumbling.

I knelt down stiffly on the earthen floor. The loaf of bread was far too hard to break with my hands and I was obliged to hack it first, using the iron knife nearby. As I did so, more coins were revealed. I prised them out, and then began to grind the residue.

They were not all denarii, as I'd thought at first. There were a few of those, but there were a score of sestertii, as well, and a large number of copper coins – both quadrantes and *asses*. They were all stuck together in a lump – as if somebody had scooped up all the cash they had, and simply dropped the handful in the mix. As I riffled through the dust the pestle made, I discovered several more, but the most exciting find was in the crust. A single gold *aureus*. It made me gasp. I have rarely held an aureus in my hand. That coin alone repaid my debt to Sosso six times over, and left me cash to spare.

I was gazing at it in amazement and delight when I became aware of stealthy movement at the door. I glanced up and realised that Cornovacus had been watching me, He leapt back as I raised my head, obviously anxious to be unobserved, but I could see his shadow on the wall. I slid the aureus into my sandal – the one that laced up properly! – and untied the four quadrantes which I'd tied into the hem of my makeshift robe. I kept one of them concealed in my hand, until a moment later the silhouette was back, showing that Cornovacus had returned.

Pretending not to notice him, I slid out of my makeshift robe and put the pale blue slave's tunic on instead. Then, looking fearfully about, as if afraid that I was being watched, I made great play of tying up the quadrans coin, this time into the corner of my former cloak, which I then doubled up and wrapped around me with the hidden money on the inner side.

I saw the shadow stiffen on the wall and knew that Cornovacus had been watching me. I also knew that he was an accomplished thief. If he had spied me with the aureus, I thought, it would be interesting to see what happened to that hidden coin.

I had already taken the precaution of tearing a wide belt-strip from one long ragged edge of my former garment, and now I twisted one end of that to form a pouch, scooped the remaining coins into it, tied it round my waist and went outside. Cornovacus was leaning casually against the hut.

He greeted my appearance with a grudging nod. 'There you are! Dressed up in your finery, I see. Taken your confounded time about it, haven't you?'

I made no reply to this. The tunic was – as Julia had said – an ancient one, stained with red wine and tattered around the hem, and I had a damp, smelly apology for a cloak. I was, at best, attired like a slave, and I still had one sandal with a broken strap. Yet I felt extraordinarily comfortable, almost like a proper man again, except that I sadly needed a barber and a wash – if not oil and strigil at a Roman bath, at least a scoop of Gwellia's soap to remove the dirt, and clean water to rinse with afterwards. However, this dwelling offered no such luxuries. 'Where's Sosso?' I said.

'Gone on ahead to meet up with Tullio. Lercius went to fetch him earlier. I am to take you to them – when you've paid.' His voice was carefully neutral but his eyes flickered greedily towards my belt. I realised that I must be on my guard. That purse made me a potential target once again.

'My agreement was with Sosso,' I said, with more casual assurance than I felt. 'I'll give the four denarii to him. And I've got instructions for him, if he wants to earn some more.'

I thought for a moment there would be an argument – one which I would assuredly have lost – but eventually Cornovacus gave a grunt. 'Very well. I'll lead the way. Come on. And you'd better have that money, citizen, or I'll personally tear you limb from limb.' He made the very word 'citizen' sound like an insult.

I stood my ground. 'You promised me some soup.'

'Only if you pay for it,' he said.

'I'll pay the woman separately. I have the money now.' I patted the coins that were round my waist. 'As I think you know.'

He turned a sullen red at this, but all he said was, 'Very well!' He raised his voice. 'Woman! Bring the citizen some soup. And don't be all the accursed day about it, if you value that scrawny neck of yours.'

The woman disappeared inside and came back with a chipped bowl from somewhere, full of steaming soup. There seemed to be no spoon available, so I sipped it directly from the lip, aware of the dreadful odour which still lingered on my hands. The broth was from my chicken, and tasted wonderful. I prised open the knot around the coins and held out a sestertius to her. She looked at Cornovacus doubtfully, then without a smile or word of thanks she snatched it from me, hid it in her dress and scuttled off into the hut.

Bizarre, I thought, that I should pay so dearly for a watery soup made of my own stolen chickens. But the woman had been good to me, and now that I had coin, I did not begrudge her a part of it. I sipped the remainder of the soup while Cornovacus watched impatiently. I did not hurry, though the light was fading fast. This was the best meal I'd had since the banquet.

I have thought since that it might have been the soup that saved my life, because as I finished it, Sosso came loping lopsidedly up the path again, followed by Lercius and Tullio.

'Guards! On the lane!' he grunted as he panted up. 'We'll wait here till they are gone.' He cocked an enquiring eyebrow at Cornovacus. 'Got the money?'

The tall thief shook his head, but before he could say a word I intervened. 'My arrangement was with you,' I said. 'It's here. Four denarii, I think we said?'

'Five,' Sosso said at once. 'One more for Molendinarius. For your accommodation and the cart.'

Lercius was skipping up to us, his face alive with that malicious glee. 'Trouble?' he said, as one might seek a treat. 'Let me . . .'

'No trouble,' I said hastily, and untied the coins again. As Sosso watched I selected five denarii, and held them out to him.

Cornovacus was looking at the coins in my hand. 'Give us some smaller coins, for Pluto's sake,' he said. 'If I turn up in Glevum with a denarius the shopkeepers will think I've stolen it, and send for the market police instead of serving me.'

I could understand that. In the normal way, the chances were that he *would* have stolen it. But I counted twenty sestertii from my purse and put the silver back. Cornovacus nodded as though pleased with this and even patted my back approvingly.

Sosso flashed his blackened tooth-stumps at me, and took the coins. 'Easier to share this out, as well,' he said. He seemed genuinely delighted by the sum, although it suddenly struck me how trivial it was, divided among all the members of his group.

'More where that came from, if you'll work for me – being my "eyes and ears" as Grossus says.' I was aware of feeling in control again. 'Money is power,' Marcus always said, though I had never felt the force of it till now.

Cornovacus looked sharply at the dwarf. 'Grossus will want his share of that, of course? You'll have to go on paying that slimy toad each day. Otherwise we lose the soup and fuel – then Dis knows where we'll be when there's a frost. This "citizen" ' – he looked scornfully at me – 'won't be paying us for long, even if you agree to work for him. They'll send his wretched patron off to Rome – or else they won't. Either way, that is the end of it.'

I didn't care for his assessment of affairs, but Sosso jerked his head in what might have been a nod, if he'd possessed a neck. 'Grossus? Paid him already. Parva's gone. She had money from the guards. Up at the villa earlier.' He turned to me. 'Now – you want watchers? Where and who?'

I spelt it out for him: I wanted information about everyone. Anyone I could think of who was at the feast. Balbus, Bullface, Mellitus, all the guests – even Gaius and the high priest of Jupiter. I closed my eyes, attempting to recall the people at the scene, and who was sitting where. Loquex was spouting his appalling verse, and . . .

'Loquex!' I suddenly exclaimed. Why hadn't I thought of it before? He had left the dining room only a few moments before Praxus died. If nothing else, he must have seen who was in the corridor and court. And, come to think of it, I had not seen him afterwards. It would definitely be interesting to talk to him.

'Loquex?' Sosso looked puzzled. 'Never heard of him.'

'An ageing poet in the colonia. Ekes out a living writing dreadful verse and going around performing it at feasts. Has an apartment on the top floor of a building near the baths, I think. If you can find him, bring him here to me.'

Tullio, who had come up behind us, startled me. 'Not here, citizen. You're coming home with me. We'll have to avoid the main tracks on the way, and keep a sharp eye out for the guard. Sosso says they are already in the lane.'

'They were going down to your roundhouse by the look of it,' Lercius put in, as though this was the most cheerful news for weeks. 'Good thing that messenger has gone.'

I whirled on him. 'What messenger?' I looked round

to Sosso for support, but he and the others had already gone.

Lercius shrugged. 'Didn't I tell you? He turned up at the roundhouse earlier when I was back there looking for a pot. Said he was heading to the villa of Marcus Septimus, but he had a message for the owner of the roundhouse on the way. From someone in Corinium. A slave.'

'My slave?' I could hardly frame the words. 'From Junio?'

Lercius grinned. 'That's right.'

'What was the message?' I said, struggling with an impulse to seize him by the neck and shake the information out of him.

'Just that your wife and slaves were safe. Oh, and that somebody else was in Corinium. He did say the name, somebody beginning with an M, I can't remember now.'

'Not Marcus?' I said, hopeful suddenly.

He shook his head.

'Mellitus?' I suggested. His home was in Corinium after all.

Lercius brightened. 'Mellitus. That's right.'

'So Mellitus has gone back to Corinium? Already? You're sure that's what he said?'

'I think so. I wasn't listening very carefully.' Lercius looked at me sheepishly. 'When I turned round the messenger was gone. It was so dark and shadowy. I didn't see him go. I was thinking about the body in the pit, you see. Molendinarius let me bury it.'

Thinking about the body in the pit! I could imagine Lercius only too clearly, gloating over poor little Golbo's corpse and listening with only half an ear. Well, if Mellitus was home that was interesting news, but it was one less trail that Sosso could pursue. I could send to Corinium perhaps, but there was nothing to be done about it now. The night was cold and it would soon be dark.

For a moment some association flickered in my brain. Something that somebody had said. I couldn't place it.

'Well, if any message comes again, make sure you let me know.' I sighed. I was suddenly aware of how weary I'd become. 'I'll go with Tullio, before it gets too dark to see. If Sosso discovers anything, he'll know where to find me. Tell him I'll pay him as agreed – and don't forget to pass the message on this time!'

He nodded. I turned to Tullio. 'Lead on!'

XXII

It was getting really dark by now, though there was a misty moon, and we slunk along the margins of the lane, taking to the trees again whenever there was movement on the path. We kept well out of sight and saw no guards (although we heard them once or twice), just a tired donkey-cart or two and a drunken traveller reeling to an inn. We took care that none of them saw us.

We reached the bottom of the hill but then, instead of following the road towards the town, Tullio turned on to a less frequented route, a small rutted track that had once led to some forgotten farm. Then even that trail petered out and we seemed to walk for miles along neglected paths, now barely discernible and full of sharp stones and unexpected holes, while creatures rustled past us in the dark. The coin in my sandal rubbed my heel, and soon I was limping as badly as ever. And still we walked.

Suddenly Tullio stopped and placed a finger to his lips. 'Listen!' he said. I listened. Far away a lone wolf howled, but apart from that the night seemed empty, cold and still. I shivered. And then I did hear. Water, lapping at the banks.

He turned to me, and I could tell by his voice that he was smiling. 'The river. Can you hear it? We're nearly there.'

The last half-mile was marshy, difficult and slow, but at last we turned a corner and there, undoubtedly, was a house

– a little roundhouse not dissimilar to mine, except that this one was so low and small it scarcely stood above the level of the reeds. Already I could smell the smoke that rose up from the fire, and see the occasional spark against the dark. Tullio gave a piercing whistle to warn of his approach, and then led the way, picking his way across the reedy marsh, into a fenced enclosure made of plaited osiers, and so into the house.

It was even smaller and lower than it looked, built of osiers itself, and thatched with reeds. I had to bend half double to get in through the door, but inside it was welcoming and warm. A skinny woman started up from a bed of skins and rushes at our approach, disturbing a small child in a woven basket at her side who set up a disgruntled wail. In the firelight four other pairs of sleepy eyes regarded us from another pile of reeds against the further wall.

'Husband!' the woman said, clutching her garment to her, and regarding me with ill-disguised alarm.

'This is the man I told you of last night – the passenger I took downriver in the dark,' Tullio said, bluntly but with some rough affection in his voice. 'I promised Sosso we would take him in – he'll pay us for his keep.'

'But husband . . .' the poor woman wailed, looking around her tiny house despairingly. It was clear that she was wondering where I was to be put.

'No buts, wife,' Tullio said. 'The matter's settled. Now, fetch us a drink. Our guest is thirsty. We have been walking for a long time.'

The woman looked resentful, but she did as she was told. She went to the pot that was hanging on the fire, and a moment later I was holding a rough bowl of something warm. It smelled and tasted strongly of eel, but it would have been impossible to refuse. I swallowed it, feeling the liquid warmth seep through my bones.

Meanwhile the woman roused her children from their bed and divided their bedding-reeds into two unequal piles, of which the largest was assigned to me. Sensing that protest would only make things worse, I lay down gratefully, taking off my mantle to spread it over me.

As I did so I realised, with no real surprise, that the coin which I had tied into my hem was gone. I smiled ruefully – remembering how Cornovacus had clapped me on the back. One had to admire his skill, but it had taught me what I wished to know. I must be on my guard. Sosso's gang might be working for me now, but still they would lose no opportunity to rob me if they could.

I waited until Tullio and the woman were in bed before I removed my chafing sandals from my feet and slipped the aureus into my belt. Then, taking care to lie across my purse, I shut my eyes.

When I opened them again, broad daylight was streaming through the door. The beds were empty and Tullio was gone. His wife was sitting outside the doorway, gutting fish, while two of the children scrabbled at her feet, and the baby slept fitfully in the basket at her side. I got rather stiffly to my feet and, stooping as I passed the entranceway, went out to talk to her.

As soon as she saw me she paused in her task, and went to fetch me water in a cracked earthen cup, together with a hunk of ageing bread. It was not an appetising meal, but from the envious looks the children cast at me I understood that it was more breakfast than they'd had themselves. They watched me in grave silence as I ate.

I tried to have a conversation with the wife, but it was

well-nigh impossible. She seemed embarrassed by the presence of a man, and would only answer in a word or two if I asked her a direct question, and not always then. She was called Capria, I learned – the name means 'nanny-goat' so whether it was Tullio's half-affectionate sobriquet for her, or whether she was a land-child and called that from birth, it was difficult to guess. She had five children and had buried three more, all of cold and hunger in the bitter winter a year or two ago.

She answered my queries like a slave, obedient and polite, but blank. I wanted to discover more, so I continued to press for information long after normal politeness would have forced me desist. The older children were with Tullio, she said, collecting worms to go and fish for eels. There were few eels in the river at this time of year, but there were always some, and that was what the family chiefly ate. In spring especially, there were lots of fish: Tullio made traps for them, and sold them in the town to pay for cloth and grain and oil, and other necessities of life.

I could think of nothing else to ask, and she was volunteering nothing, that was clear. She had cause to be resentful, I realised suddenly. This little house was safe from those who did not know their way across the marsh, and I could see why Sosso had suggested it. All the same she was afraid – not just of me, as I had thought at first, but of the risk that I posed to her family by simply being here.

I made a last attempt at friendliness. I gestured to the fish that she was filleting. 'And sometimes there are fish to spare?'

For a moment the thin face was brightened by a smile. 'Sometimes, at some seasons of the year, there are so many fish you can walk out to the shallow pools left by the tide and catch the stranded salmon in your hands.' The smile faded.

'Then we might eat some of them ourselves. But mostly it is eels.' She lapsed into silence once again, and went on with her task.

So even the fish that she was gutting was on my account. I felt a rush of sympathy for her. 'Perhaps, if I am to stay here in the house, there is something that I can do to help? If your children are collecting worms, for instance? I don't know much about it, but I could do that too, perhaps.'

'Perhaps.' She did not look at me.

I said with sudden inspiration, 'If any soldiers come this way, that would be a good disguise. They won't be looking for a fisherman.'

She looked at me without curiosity. 'When my husband returns, he can show you how. Until then, better wait inside the hut.'

It seemed a very long time until Tullio came back. I watched the wintry sun move halfway round the sky. Then I sat down on the bedding pile to think, wondering where Sosso and his men were now, and whether they could possibly discover anything that would help my cause.

I doubted it. The case against Marcus looked very dark indeed. First there was the death of Praxus – and, much as I wanted to believe in my patron's innocence, I could not see who else could possibly have managed that.

Then that treasonable document had been discovered in Marcus's house. Of course it was always possible that someone else had put it there after Marcus was arrested, knowing there would be a search – but again, it was hard to see how it was done. Not only was the villa under constant guard once the death of Praxus had occurred, but the incriminating letter was sealed with Marcus's own seal. Yet Marcus wore his seal-ring on his finger all the time. He was wearing it on the evening of the feast – I'd noticed it – so no one could have forged the letter later on because the ring had gone with him to jail. I sighed. If I was Emperor Commodus, I thought, I would have found Marcus guilty straight away.

And yet, and yet . . . Someone had killed Golbo too. The authorities weren't interested in the mere murder of a slave, but surely it had to be significant? Marcus didn't do it – he was locked up at the time – although it was just possible that he had ordered it. But now someone was having me consistently pursued – not through the usual legal channels, but by Bullface and his men – and I was quite sure that Marcus wasn't responsible for that.

I sighed. It was physically alarming, but a comfort mentally – it convinced me that there was someone else involved and that I was not a fool to go on questioning.

'Citizen?' Tullio's gruff voice from the doorway made me start. I scrabbled to my feet. 'I believe you offered to help us with the eels?'

I nodded.

'Then come now, and I'll show you how it's done. We shall be glad of assistance. Sosso has sent word. He's found your poet. I am to go and guide him through the marsh.'

He turned without a further word and led the way. I followed, taking care to plant my feet exactly where he'd planted his, until we came to more solid ground, where the two older children were busy doing something with a length of wool.

'Watch them,' said Tullio, and set off through the reeds.

It was not a complicated task, and not a pleasant one. The two boys were digging for worms and threading them lengthways along the coarse strand of home-spun yarn with the aid of a piece of sharpened bone. I watched them for a while, and then assisted in the provision of the worms. The threading exercise was more than I could bear. They, on the other hand, were quite adept at it, and very soon there was a sizeable length of worms, strung end to end, like so many squirming beads. My remarks and questions were ignored. Like the rest of the family, it seemed, these boys were used to working hard and speaking little.

'Enough,' the older one said suddenly. It was the first word that either child had addressed to me. He took the length of wool, tied the loose end firmly round a stick, and wound the string of worms around it so it formed a ball. Then he took it to the waterside, and plunged it in. 'You?' he said, and handed me the pole. He went back to his brother who, meanwhile, had pulled out another length of wool, and was beginning to create another string.

I was unsure what they expected me to do, but it soon became self-evident. There was a wriggling in the mud, a tug, and a moment later several eels – one of them quite large – were biting at the wool. I let out a howl of surprise and almost dropped my piece of wood, but the older boy was with me in a flash.

He looked scornfully at me and seized the stick, which he simply lifted to the shore. The eels, much to my surprise, clung on – too dedicated to their gruesome feast to let it go – until the younger boy came up with a sharpened stone and severed them just below the head. Even then the greedy, nasty little jaws remained clamped firmly to their prey, and had to be prised off with a piece of flint. I have never cared for eels very much, but this revolted me.

The carcasses were flung into a plaited basket waiting on the bank. 'A good spot for eels,' I said nervously.

The older boy gave me that look again. 'Better in the dark. You should see them in the season,' he said bitterly, and handed me the eeling pole again.

So that was how Tullio and Loquex found me, later on, standing by the river, trying to catch eels on a stick.

XXIII

Tullio acknowledged my offering with the briefest grunt of thanks. 'Here is your poet,' he said shortly. 'You stay here and talk to him – we'll take these eels home. Better if the boys don't overhear – the less they know, the happier their mother will be. This spot is safe enough. I'll come back and get you later on. Come, lads!' He signalled to his sons, and off they went.

Loquex looked at me suspiciously. 'What is the meaning of all this? What do you want with me? I was told that I was coming here to see a citizen, acting on behalf of Marcus Septimus, otherwise I would never have agreed to come. I thought I was being taken on a short cut to the villa, but instead I find myself brought here to a swamp, to talk to a fisherman.'

'I'm not a fisherman,' I said, belying the assertion as I spoke by picking up my stick and landing another wriggling eel on the end of it. I tossed the whole thing to the bank – the eel did not let go. 'Not by profession, anyway. I am indeed a citizen, a protégé of Marcus Septimus, and I was at the feast. I heard your poetry.'

I added this in the hope of flattering him, but the effect was unfortunate.

'And so did everyone. It isn't fair. I am invited to perform. I do my best, but nobody pays me what they promised me.

No time to claim it – I'm just hustled off and told to come back another day. And then what do I hear? His Excellency is under garrison arrest, and no communication is allowed. What happens to the money I am owed? It took me several hours to write that verse, and find out all the information too.'

'What information?'

'To write my tributes. People never think of that. Just scribble a few verses, that's what they think I do. They never think of all the work involved. I only recited a tiny bit of it, and wasn't paid an *as*.'

> 'Gaius Praxus came from Gaul
> He's very brave and very tall?'

I quoted. 'You must have needed a lot of information to write that?'

Loquex was oblivious of irony. 'You *were* there,' he said eagerly. 'You remember it?'

'Who could forget?' I muttered, softening the comment with a smile. Loquex was preening and I saw my chance. 'Would you like the opportunity to recite the rest? What was Marcus going to pay you for the task?'

'Six silver pieces.'

Six denarii. I could afford it, now that Julia had given me some coins, but it was an inflated sum. I thought quickly. 'Of course that was a fee for writing it, and declaiming it before an audience,' I said. 'I'll give you half as much if you'll recite it now.' I saw him hesitate and added swiftly, 'That way it won't be a total loss, and your fine verse will reach one listener, anyway.'

He looked around doubtfully. There was nothing to be

seen except the reeds, the eeling stick and the marshy ground.
'What, here?'

I nodded, and he cleared his throat. He took up a theatrical
stance and launched himself into his verse. 'Marcus Aurelius
Septimus, just and fair . . .' he began.

If I hoped to learn anything from this, I was disappointed.
The verse was every bit as bad as I recalled, and went on
even longer than I feared. Far from concentrating on the
most important guests, Loquex had managed a line or two
about every single one. I listened carefully, but apart from a
passing mention that the high priest of Jupiter had lands in
Gaul, Balbus's younger brother had been rising fast, and
Councillor Gaius had got himself a younger wife – none of
which fascinating facts had reached my ears – there was
nothing of significance in any part of it, just a series of
statements of the obvious. By the time he concluded the
final stanza – which even mentioned me – my eyes were
ready to glaze over. Loquex was looking at me expectantly.

'Quite a feat,' I said at last, trying to disguise my disappointment as I reached into my belt to find the coins. 'You did
well to remember all that without your scroll.'

'As you said earlier, citizen, it is not easy to forget –
especially when you have written it yourself. Of course,' he
added modestly, 'I'm slightly famous for my memory.'

'In that case, perhaps you can remember everything that
happened at the feast?' He looked about to launch into an
account, so I added hastily, 'After you left the dining room
that night?'

'Well, Marcus and the others cut me off, clapping before
I'd properly begun,' he said resentfully. 'I was ushered out,
into the court and round to the back door. That's all. I tried
to claim the money I was owed, but I was hurried to the

entrance by a slave and told to present my bill another time.'
He looked at me. 'I didn't hear until next day that Praxus
had been killed. I didn't murder him, if that is what you are
suggesting. Ask the slave who saw me out – he'll tell you the
same thing.'

I shook my head. The chances were the slave in question
was in custody, being interrogated by other men – and no
doubt by other methods. If there was anything to learn, the
authorities were probably aware of it by now. But I persisted
all the same. 'Did you see anything in the corridor, or court?
Anything at all unusual? Think carefully before you answer
me.'

He shook his head. 'Nothing. Not even servants from the
dining room carrying wine and dishes to and fro – except the
one who was accompanying me. He took me to the slave's
room to collect my coat, and when he picked me up again I
noticed he had a plate of something in his hand. Oh, and
there was a little bucket-boy as well, waiting outside the
vomitorium: he seemed to be in trouble of some kind when
I looked back into the court.'

I had difficulty keeping the excitement from my voice.
'You came back to the court?'

He shrugged. 'Not exactly. I intended to. The doorkeeper
had been told to let me out, but I was so enraged at being
hustled off halfway through my piece, without even being
paid, that I asked the man to wait, intending to burst in on
His Excellence and simply demand the money that was due.
But as soon as I put my head round the colonnade and heard
what was going on in the court I changed my mind and left.'

'What was going on?'

'The bucket-boy was being scolded for his idleness and
ordered to clean the place at once, on pain of being whipped,

because the feast would soon be over and the guests would want to visit the vomitorium again before they left for home. It all seemed very harsh to me – and quite unjustified. The room looked perfectly all right. But apparently his owner was seriously displeased.'

I found that I was standing like a statue, holding my breath. 'Go on.'

'It was all done very quietly, of course, so as not to disturb the guests, but sound always carries in a colonnade, especially a savage hiss like that, and obviously I could not help but overhear. Anyway, the lad got a savage cuff round the ear and was sent off to fill his bucket from a spring, which I gathered was outside in the grounds somewhere – without a torch-brand too, though it was clearly very cold and dark out there. I realised that if Marcus Septimus was in a mood like that, it obviously wasn't a good moment to insist on being paid, so I slipped back to the doorkeeper at once, said I'd thought better of my plan and disappeared before the bucket-boy came back. The doorman had me in his sight throughout – as I'm sure he could testify. I had no opportunity to murder anyone.'

I nodded. 'So who was hissing at the bucket-boy? A slave? Could you identify him again?'

'Of course I could. It was the same slave that had shown me out. The one they call Umbris. He seemed to be in charge of everything. You must have noticed him.'

I breathed out slowly and let this sink in, remembering what Golbo had said. It tallied perfectly. Umbris sent Golbo from the court, apparently on Marcus's command, at a moment of extreme convenience for anyone who had poisoned Praxus's meal and expected him to stagger out and die. If Marcus hadn't ordered that, who had? The slave could have no motive of his own, far less the money to buy poison with. Yet who else would Umbris take instruction from?

There was one obvious candidate, of course, suggested by something in Loquex's narrative which had struck me forcibly. I asked, with a pretence at casualness, 'Umbris talked about his "owner" ordering all this? He didn't say "the master" – you are sure of that?' Golbo, I remembered, had used the – same word.

Loquex looked bewildered, but he answered instantly. 'As I remember, citizen, "our owner" is what he said. Does it matter?'

'I don't know,' I said. I meant it. Of course, there was nothing remarkable in the choice of word itself: 'owner' is interchangeable with 'master' in most instances. But what of the mistress of the house? Julia was owner, but not master, of the slaves. She had loathed Praxus for his sexual overtures to her – could she have taken this revenge on him? She was in the house throughout with access to the kitchens day and night, and so had every chance to slip something into wine or food – and to ensure it reached the proper guest. After the murder she was soon upon the scene. Suspiciously quickly, when one thought about the facts. Suppose she had instructed Umbris to send the bucket-boy away, because she knew that Praxus had eaten poisoned food and would very soon be struggling out to die in a way that – given the amount he drank – would hardly seem suspicious in the least.

The more I thought of this, the more unfortunately possible it seemed. The servants would obey Julia's orders instantly, as unquestioningly as they would obey Marcus's own. They would protect her too, I thought suddenly. If Golbo suddenly had guessed that *she* had sent the order which removed him from the court, it might account for why he had changed his mind and run away. Could it even have been one of Julia's slaves who'd found Golbo in my dye-house on that fateful night, and silenced him in order to protect his mistress's name? Cilla had left the villa, as I knew. Would that explain why he had looked surprised, and not attempted to defend himself?

And what about that treasonable document? Julia was capable of scheming – she'd proved as much today – and she had 'co-operated' with the search which had disclosed that letter in his study. Had she written it and put it there for them to find? It was possible that she had used her husband's seal – Marcus wore his seal-ring every day, but it was likely that he took it off at night. Julia had more chance than anyone of using it, if she intended to discredit him. But why? Simply to draw suspicion from herself, because she'd murdered Praxus, and I had foolishly pointed out that his death was no mere accident?

But that made no sense, I realised with relief. Marcus was wearing the seal-ring when he was arrested, so Julia could not have used it later on to save herself. Nor could she have composed a convincing document: her grammar was erratic and she did not form her letters in the standard Roman army way, as Marcus and most educated writers did. That whole theory was impossible. I was creating illusions in the smoke like a Sibylline prophetess. Besides, although I could accept that Julia might wish pawing Praxus dead, I did not believe that she'd betray her husband and her child. I could more easily accept that Marcus had done the deed himself and written that incriminating letter too, trusting in the priest of Jupiter's prophecy and hoping to hasten the day when Pertinax would be Emperor of Rome. I shook my head.

The old poet was looking at me anxiously. 'I assure you, citizen . . .'

'It's all right, Loquex,' I said distractedly, handing him the coins. 'I don't doubt your word.'

He seized the money. 'Thank you, citizen.' Then, with a gleeful smile: 'I can't go until that fisherman comes back to guide me home. Would you like to hear my eulogy again?'

Since I did not know my own way back across the marsh, I really had very little choice. We had worked our way through the thing again, right down to the final verse about

'Libertus is a citizen, a mosaicist by trade
Who oftentimes has come to his good patron's aid'

before Tullio arrived to rescue me.

XXIV

Sosso was waiting when we reached the little roundhouse in the reeds. He looked so pleased and cunning, squatting in the smoky firelight beside the central hearth, that I felt my heart begin to stir with hope.

'You have something for me?' I demanded.

Sosso looked warningly towards the woman and the boys, and jerked a thumb in the direction of the door. All of them instantly withdrew.

'Money first,' he grunted. 'Five facts. That's five sestertii. That's what we said.'

In fact it was nothing of the kind, but as usual with Sosso it was hard to disagree, especially when he took that rough knife out again, and began to clean his fingernails with the point of it. I understood. It was not a threat, exactly, simply a reminder that the knife was there.

I thought quickly. 'I'll pay you one fact at a time – that way I can decide if it is worth the fee,' I said. I slipped my fingers into my makeshift purse and held out one sestertius.

He stretched out one misshapen arm and seized the coin. Then he threw back his head and produced that strange low owl-cry which I'd heard before, and a moment later Lercius came stooping through the entranceway, followed by Parva and Cornovacus.

I started. I had not seen anyone as I approached. No

wonder these people of the shadows had earned the nick-name 'ghosts'. Sosso gave his blackened grin at my discomfiture.

'Parva,' he commanded, and the girl edged closer to the flames so that the flickering fire lit her face, while the others took up station by the door. 'Speak!'

The pock-faced girl seemed to hesitate, but Sosso shook her roughly and she launched into her tale. 'Your pardon, citizen, it is only what I heard from the soldier who'd been on guard at the gate.'

'The villa?' I said eagerly.

She shook her head. 'The south gate of the town. Of course he was off duty by the time he talked to me. I'd arranged to meet him after it got dark under one of the arches near the market place – a sort of business arrangement, you understand.'

I nodded. I understood too well. Of course the girl had no licence from the town authorities, and was therefore acting outside the law. Her client should probably have been in barracks at that hour, too, but doubtless his colleagues on the watch could be persuaded to turn the other way. All the same, it was a risk. If Parva had anything to tell, she would have earned her money – more than once.

'He was the kind that likes to stand there gossiping,' Parva went on. 'They're not all like that – most of them want to do what they do, give you the money and get away, but one or two of them are different. They've left some girl behind, perhaps, or simply miss their homes and families and welcome an opportunity to talk. Others, like this one, simply want to boast and tell you what important men they are. Sosso always likes it if I make them talk – in case there are snippets we can pass on to Grossus, for a price.'

I glanced towards the ugly little dwarf, who was nodding judiciously.

Parva went on with her tale. 'Anyway, I'd had dealings with this one before. He's not too bad – a bit rough and inclined to bruise me, but he pays. And talks. He seemed a likely source of information on the garrison, so when I saw him on the gate I sidled up and let him make an assignation there and then.'

'Never mind all that. Get on with it!' Sosso was impatient.

Parva glanced at me with anxious eyes. Poor girl, I thought. She had been pretty once, and the thin body underneath the skimpy tunic showed only the first signs of womanhood. She would be lucky if disease and want allowed her to attain her twentieth year. 'Go on,' I said gently.

'I listened to him bragging about this and that, and then I asked him outright what he knew about your patron in the jail. Of course it is the gossip of the town, so he was not surprised at that. I flattered him, and said I bet he knew a thing or two. So he told me. Most of it was only what we already knew: Marcus was first arrested on a murder charge and has appealed to the Emperor, but after that his villa was searched and a treasonable document has come to light – under a seal which he owns is his. So the charge was altered to conspiracy and all his property is under guard.'

'And will doubtless be impounded by the Emperor once the trial has taken place in Rome,' I said bitterly. 'Unless we can avoid that in some way.'

She made a sympathetic face. 'It may be sooner than you think, too, citizen. The magistrates have sent a messenger to the Emperor, and Marcus will be following in a day or two. There's a suitable ship in Glevum dock. It came with olive oil and is almost ready to set sail again. When it does the prisoner and his guard will be aboard.'

I gulped. This was new information, and made things desperate. Once Marcus had embarked for Rome, there was precious little anyone could do.

'Is he well treated?' I could not help but ask.

She shrugged. 'I presume so. He comes from a wealthy family, after all, and of course he is a Roman citizen. It would be more than the commander's life was worth to let him come to any kind of harm, and no doubt he still has the wherewithal to pay for privilege. He was permitted to send a letter home, I hear – no doubt that was to ask for food and clothes.'

Of course, the letter that Julia received would have been longer than the extract which she'd quoted to me. Doubtless Marcus had requested some little luxuries as well as informing her about the second charge. But surely . . .? I frowned. 'Once that telltale document was found, I thought that communication was prohibited? Why did they allow a private letter to be sent?'

She shrugged. 'Presumably the commander read it first. That's usually the custom, so I'm told. I've heard of it before. A wealthy prisoner writes a letter and has it authorised – and the guards often sneak a look at it as well, since most of them can read. They laugh about the kind of abject things that people write.'

'But what if it was sealed? He had his seal-ring with him.' It distressed me to think of Marcus's message being sniggered over by licentious soldiery.

'It wouldn't be – not unless some special arrangement had been made. Anyway, my informant tells me that his ring has been taken from him – it is to be used as evidence, it seems, to prove that it matches the seal on the document they found. Your patron might possibly have managed to send sealed letters home, being as wealthy as he is, if this was a simple murder case – but now that there's conspiracy alleged . . .' She tailed off.

I knew what she meant. As I said before, the Emperor sees plots everywhere. 'So his seal-ring was taken and his letter would be read?'

She smiled assent. 'According to my customer, it was. He didn't know exactly what was in it, though – he wasn't there in person when it went. I don't know who did see it, but I could possibly find out. Do you want me to go back and try again?'

I shook my head. I had simply wanted to find out if Marcus had used his seal-ring on that note. It seemed that he had not. I knew what the letter said. At least I thought I did. Come to think of it, I had only Julia's word for that. Could she be trusted, in the light of what I knew? Perhaps, after all, it would be wise to check. 'What about the messenger who delivered it?' I said.

Parva was looking dubious. 'I don't know if he read it, citizen, or indeed if he could read at all. It wasn't a proper military messenger. It was a slave – and not one I've had any dealings with.' She smiled apologetically. 'I do have the occasional client who's a slave, of course, but mostly they haven't got the cash. Sometimes, if they get an *as* or two in tips, they come to me – they can't afford the licensed prostitutes – but even then they're always from the town. They don't come in from villas miles away.'

I stared at her. 'You are telling me that the slave who delivered the letter came from the *villa*?' In fact, I remembered vaguely, someone had spoken of a 'slave-messenger', but I'd not seen the significance of the word. 'One of Marcus's own slaves? You're sure of that? How did your customer know that, if he wasn't present at the time?'

'Oh,' Parva said lightly, 'he didn't tell me that. I heard it from . . .'

Sosso stepped forward, interrupting her. 'Different information. Another sestertius, citizen, I think.'

I had forgotten his presence in the room, but I would have parted with the aureus to hear the rest of this. I took out another coin and pressed it in her hand. 'You heard it from . . .?'

She looked enquiringly at the dwarf, who nodded his permission for her to go on. 'From one of those two lads up at the other gate the other day. They were complaining because it was so dull out there: nobody had come or gone since they arrived, except one silly handmaiden who kept wanting to go out for remedies and lady Julia's special messenger. Nobody from outside the house at all, they said, so it was very tedious to be on guard. Better to be on fatigue duty in the garrison, the younger one said – at least cleaning the latrines was something active to do. Then you turned up with your fertiliser cart.'

I thought of all the different ways in which we'd had communication with the villa in the last couple of days, and understood why Sosso smiled. 'Why didn't you tell me this before?' I said.

Parva met my eyes. 'You'd heard about the letter from your patron's wife – and you have spoken to her since. I didn't know it mattered who delivered it. It's the same messenger that she has used throughout.'

Julia had spoken of a messenger who took letters to Corinium and back. Someone with the freedom to come and go. Why hadn't it occurred to me before? 'I wonder who it was?' I muttered aloud.

Cornovacus unwound himself from his post beside the door, and stepped towards the fire. He jerked his head at Parva, and she scuttled off into the darkness, clasping her money to her breast.

'I can answer that, my fancy friend.' His eyes were glittering. 'Soon as I see the colour of that coin.'

I took out a sestertius, but he shook his head. 'Worth more than that, I think.' It was outrageous, but I had no choice. I looked at Sosso, but he didn't look at me. He was picking at his fingernails again.

I offered a denarius instead. Cornovacus tried the coin in his teeth then nodded as if satisfied. He must have put it somewhere, but I didn't see it go. 'All right,' he said. 'I'll tell you what I know. I got it from that twitching friend of yours – the one you spoke to near the fish market.'

'The military secretary with the tic?'

'That's him. Crept up behind him in an alleyway and forced him to tell me what he knew. Said I had seen him taking bribes from you and threatened to denounce him to the garrison. That frightened him enough, but when I said I knew what he got up to with unlicensed prostitutes, I thought the wretch would twitch himself to death. Offered me money straight away, so I knew I had him then. Sosso was right.'

'My suggestion.' Sosso grinned in answer to my glance. 'Thought he might be' – he paused – 'persuadable.'

'He talked like Apollo's fountain after that, non-stop burbling. Mostly it was all about this messenger – it was one of the slaves arrested at the feast. They had him in for questioning and then they let him go. I don't know exactly how it was arranged, and neither did your frightened little friend – he couldn't tell me, even when I picked him up and shook him like a leaf – though he thinks that sums of money were involved. All I know is, someone intervened on his behalf – that would be your patron, I presume – and the garrison commander agreed to let him go, explicitly to ferry messages, under penalty of being burned alive if he made any effort to escape, or didn't turn up if wanted at the trial.'

Freeing a potential witness in this way is most irregular, of course, but somehow when it was explained to me like this it didn't surprise me in the least. In fact, it accorded with what Parva had just said. Any wealthy prisoner would attempt to buy what privilege he could. And Marcus was a very wealthy man. 'So Marcus managed to bribe the prison governor to let him send a message to his wife – with someone he could trust?'

Cornovacus shrugged. 'I suppose it meant that military messengers were not involved, if there were any questions later on. Even the accusers were persuaded to agree – Great Mithras, it must have been a whopping bribe! Although Procurator Mellitus doesn't like it very much. He's keeping a close watch on the messenger, and insists that he'll produce him at the trial – but your patron's very gratified, of course.'

'So it was convenient to everyone.'

'Pluto only knows! Money opens doors, that's all I know.' Cornovacus had produced the denarius again, and was fingering the silver coin as he spoke, twisting it between his fingers like a conjuror. 'And the slave had already given what evidence he had about that wretched banquet – not that it amounted to a whore's dowry anyway. Now that this famous document has come to light, what happened on the evening of the feast doesn't really matter a moneylender's curse.'

Legally, the man was right. The murder case was trivial compared to the treason charge. But events that night had mattered to poor Golbo, I thought savagely. They had meant the difference between life and death to him. 'And what about the other villa slaves, who are still being marched off in tens for questioning?'

Cornovacus pocketed his denarius. 'Don't ask me, citizen. I'm not a soothsayer. I only know what I was told. They're following procedures, I suppose, and hoping for information about that document. That's all he told me, citizen. You've had your money's worth.' He turned as if to walk away.

I clutched his ragged sleeve. 'If this man gave evidence,' I said, 'did he mention a name, by any chance? A senior slave called Umbris, possibly?'

He stopped and looked at me. 'Umbris? The big black Nubian slave? That's the very man I'm talking of.'

I closed my eyes. Of course. I should have guessed, knowing my patron's ironic touch with names. Umbris, man of shadow, so called not because he moved so noiselessly, but because he was so dark.

That thought brought another, which I did not like. Umbris had taken a letter to the villa at about the time that Golbo was murdered. Suppose that he spotted the runaway in the woods? Did he follow him to my dye-house and then murder him? For reasons I'd refused to countenance? Julia's messenger, protecting Julia's name?

I shuddered, imagining a dark figure that suddenly emerged from the disguising smoke and shadows of the hut, uttering a soothing word or two perhaps, then seizing and wielding the heavy axe. That would account for the astonished look on that grotesque, discoloured face. And the big Nubian had the strength necessary to take a man's head off with a single blow, and do it at that particular angle too. That was no easy matter, as Molendinarius had pointed out. I was sure I was getting closer to the truth.

'He was at my roundhouse!' I exclaimed.

'Of course he was.' Lercius misinterpreted my words. 'I saw him. He's the one who gave me that message from your slave.'

So Umbris, carrying messages to and from Corinium, had come back to the roundhouse. Not to deliver a message, probably, but to see what had happened to the corpse. That explained the confusion of the message – Umbris had needed to think quickly of a way to explain his presence at my house to Lercius. I nodded. 'You said at the time that it was dark and shadowy and it was hard to see him. That was because he was dark and shadowy himself?'

'That's right, citizen. A big black messenger.' Lercius came over to the fire and squatted down, while Cornovacus went back to join the dwarf. 'I've got another message, too, but Sosso says I mustn't tell you till you've paid.'

Another sestertius changed hands. 'Another message? From my slave?' I was not very hopeful, if the message came from Umbris again, but it was worth a coin.

This time I was in for a surprise.

'Your slave said to say he saw Mellitus's shadow in Corinium again. He saw them together in the market place and discovered from the cake-seller that the shadow was Mellitus's own. That was the message. It didn't make much sense, but anyway he wanted you to know. Made me repeat it several times. It didn't mean anything to me.'

Shadow, I thought suddenly. Was it possible? Is that what Junio had said? He had seen Umbris in Corinium? Lercius had never heard the name and his Latin, though fluent, was inaccurate. Umbris *had* been to Corinium, I knew. But surely Junio would not send a message that concerned the messenger himself? Unless Julia had sent a different slave the second time, via the garrison, perhaps, as I'd heard her suggesting to the guard.

'A different messenger, I suppose?' I asked Lercius.

Lercius nodded.

I sighed. The message made no sense in any case. Umbris belonged to Marcus, not to Mellitus.

Or did he? The Nubian slave had been a gift to Marcus, a bribe from someone staying in the villa. Mellitus had visited before. What if he had 'given' Marcus what seemed a handsome gift? That would mean he had a spy within the household, someone who could watch and listen – and report to him. Someone who was well placed to poison another's food – and make sure that it reached the intended victim too.

I had decided long ago that Praxus's murderer must be a man of strength. Someone with sufficient size to seize him by the neck and throttle him when the dose of toxin proved not quite enough. From the beginning I had thought that only someone in Marcus's household could have done the deed. Umbris was the obvious candidate. I had not wished to countenance the thought, when I imagined Julia was involved – but supposing Umbris worked for Mellitus?

'That's it,' I said excitedly. 'That solves the mystery of Praxus's death, at least. Mellitus gets Umbris accepted in the house. Marcus is very pleased with him, and uses him at feasts. Then when Praxus comes along, and power is to be shared among the three, Mellitus sees a chance to murder him and seize more influence for himself. He provides the poison, Umbris serves it to Praxus in a dish – a very hefty dose of it no doubt. All this takes place in Marcus's house, so even if anything goes wrong suspicion won't fall on Mellitus – who makes very sure that he doesn't leave the banquet, or drink any of the wine. The only danger is the bucket-boy – who knows that Umbris ordered him away – so Umbris chases him and murders him, and hides the body to disguise that he's been there. Dear gods! Of course. That's why he talked of Marcus as his "owner" all the time – his real master was someone else! To Golbo, of course, master and owner were the same.'

They were all staring at me silently. Even the woman and her boys had clustered round the door, and were listening openly to this.

'Don't you see?' I said. 'It must have been Mellitus who arranged that Umbris should be freed and allowed to act as Marcus's messenger. The arrangement was presented as a concession to my patron, but of course it was nothing of the kind. Mellitus handled it very cleverly. He controlled the go-between! That gave him access to Marcus's messages – no wonder he allowed them to be sent!'

I looked around. They were still gazing at me, rapt.

'And of course, as procurator he had sufficient rank to co-opt Praxus's bodyguard,' I went on enthusiastically. 'When Praxus's death stopped looking like an accident he ordered that the villa should be searched – I heard him do it. No doubt he got the guard to plant that document. That way he turned events to his advantage. He made sure that Marcus was arraigned – so both of his rivals were accounted for! It was very neat. And when I started asking questions, he set Bullface's soldiers on to me. It all makes sense.'

I looked round the room triumphantly.

Then Sosso spoke. 'Good theory, citizen,' he grunted. 'Pity that not all of it is true.'

XXV

I stared at him, but Sosso shook his head. 'We can prove it,' he said. 'Lercius and me. Cost you a sestertius, of course.'

The story, once I had paid for it, was this. The dwarf had done exactly as I'd asked, and sent his gang around the town to find out where Mellitus had gone. One of them – the woman with the child – was sent to investigate a seedy inn just outside the city walls, intended for travellers who missed the closing of the gates.

'All your friends were on the lookout, then?' I interrupted in surprise.

'Still are. One at the garrison. Another begging outside Balbus's door . . .' He was checking on his stubby fingers as he spoke. 'One at your workshop too. You want to hear them all?'

I shook my head. Those few sestertii had been earned, I thought. 'Go on.'

'I can tell you,' Cornovacus said. 'The woman asked for water at the kitchen door and started talking to the slave who scrubbed the floors – you know the sort, searches the straw for bed-bugs every day. The silly sow had no more sense than boast about the "most important man" who had turned up in the middle of the night – in a litter with a page-boy at his side. Caused more sensation in a place like that than Jupiter arriving in a thundercloud. Anyway, the landlord turned his mistress out of bed and gave up his private room to Mellitus – he'd have offered to lick his sandals clean, by all accounts. I don't suppose the procurator was all that impressed, but the place was cheap enough and he agreed to stay. It was like a confounded henhouse there next day, it seems, everybody twittering about and sending off for bark-paper, ink – all kinds of luxuries – while Mellitus went off to the garrison.'

'Went there all right,' Sosso grunted, by way of confirmation of the tale. 'Our man saw him go.'

Capria chose that moment to come in with branches for the fire, and Cornovacus let her add them to the flames and leave again before he went on. 'Came back looking as self-satisfied as a hunter with a bear and ordered lunch. Then, suddenly, his page came back with a message in his hand, and suddenly Mellitus paid up and went. Left everything – didn't even stop to eat his lunch.' He sneered. 'The slave-girl finished off his pie herself, the stupid wench, and was soundly beaten when her owner learned of it.'

'So, we lost track of Mellitus again?' I said.

Sosso shook his head. 'Told the slave to order him a horse. All true. Lercius checked.'

The boy chimed in, eager to agree. 'There is a hiring stables right next door. The owner's got the order chalked up on the wall. Hire and escort to Corinium, he said – though I couldn't read the words, of course. Don't know any more, because he threw me out. I poked one of his horses with a stick and made it rear. Didn't it whinny, too?' He grinned happily at the memory.

'So Mellitus went home to Corinium. That's what Junio's message said. I wonder why? I've no doubt that the procurator organised events. The Nubian was here to act on his behalf. But something must have made him run away. It would be nice to know what made him change his mind like that.'

Sosso nodded. 'Exactly, citizen. That's why we brought you this.' He held out a scrap of folded bark. 'Lercius got it from the serving girl today. Had to twist her arm a bit.'

'A note?' I stretched out a hand for it, but Sosso snatched it back.

Lercius gave that manic laugh of his. 'Serves her right for boasting that she had a souvenir. The procurator tried to throw it in the fire, she said, but she went and rescued it. She wouldn't give it to me at first, but . . .' He mimed a savage twist.

'Worth a sestertius, citizen?' Sosso said.

I paid up with a sigh. At this rate, I would soon be penniless again. And although I was sure I knew who murdered Praxus now, that was only half the problem solved. The question of the document remained, and therefore what I knew so far would not help Marcus in the least. Even if I could persuade a court of law that Umbris and Mellitus were responsible for Praxus's death – and I had no proof – the ring-sealed letter condemned my patron on a greater charge. Though I had suspicions about that as well. Mellitus had ordered the guard to search the villa that night, which suggested that he knew what they would find. Had Umbris somehow stolen Marcus's ring earlier and planted the incriminating document in his study? Had they set Bullface after me as well?

'Going to read it?' Sosso broke into my thoughts.

I unfolded the little piece of bark. The message did not instantly incriminate Mellitus, as I had hoped. It was brief and very difficult to read, a few words scrawled in charcoal in an unformed hand, the spelling dreadful and the Latin worse, the whole thing scorched and blackened at the edge. All the same, I could discern the general drift. *New charges against Marcus . . . found a document . . . has taken charge of Praxus's bodyguard and might be dangerous. . . . back to Corinium and report.* That much I could make sense of, but the final line defeated me – though it was least affected by the flames. Try as I would, I could only read it as *The pig is in the drain.*

I tried to reason out what the note implied. The message was obviously from Umbris, and had reached Mellitus around midday – the serving girl was giving him lunch. From my experience at the garrison, when I was first admitted and then turned away, the second charge against my master had been laid while I was there, or immediately before, and that was in the morning. Marcus would have been permitted to write home at once, and Umbris was reporting to his master what the letter said – he must have read it as he carried it to Julia. The timings tallied. That all made sense.

Yet obviously Mellitus was not aware of the new charge, or why should Umbris write to him? *Who* had 'taken charge of Praxus's bodyguard and might be dangerous'? And above all, what did Umbris mean by 'the pig is in the drain'?

I looked at Sosso. 'What do you make of this?'

'Can't read it.' He shrugged. 'But if it says what Cilla says it says . . .'

'You've been inside the villa wall again?'

'Lercius did. The way he went before. How else could we discover what it said? Can't afford to pay the market scribes. Show him, Lercius.'

This time it was Lercius who put his hand inside his ragged robe and from a little leather pouch (I recognised my purse) produced an article for my inspection.

'There wasn't any pig that I could see, though I looked everywhere. Even the double-seat latrine. I was lucky there. There's a cesspit for the servants at the back, so no one is bothering much with the latrines now that your patron is away. I put my hand in right up to my arm, but there was no obstruction anywhere. The only thing I found was this. It looked as if it might have been pushed down beneath the seats. It was lying on the ledge above the stream. Here!' It was, by no imagination, like a pig – it was a small lump of something soft and pale, smelling not too dreadfully of drains. Lercius put it into my reluctant hand.

I looked at it with a kind of horrified fascination, but I didn't put it down. Slimy, soft and soggy. Where had I touched something of the kind before? 'Pigs,' I said, suddenly remembering. 'The almond-bread pigs that were served at the feast. That's what this is. A piece of almond bread. Of course. Umbris served the guest of honour first – so he could make sure which piglet Praxus ate! Later, this was in the water pail – I put my fingers on it. Umbris must have put it there when he was drowning Praxus in the vomitorium. Loquex told me he had been carrying something on a plate.'

Lercius was staring in astonishment.

'This is firm evidence!' I said. 'This is what poisoned Praxus at the feast. And Umbris served him – we have witnesses. The note connects the pig with Mellitus. Praxus must have tasted something odd and staggered out – so Umbris had to finish him by hand. We'll give this bread to the civic authorities. If they feed these remnants to a criminal, he'll die, and then the case is proved.'

'Not so, citizen.' Cornovacus stepped across the fire, and spoke urgently to me. 'Even if what you say is true, how could you convince a court that your wretched patron didn't hatch the plot? His food, his slave, his kitchens – and he had as much to gain as Mellitus. And, Dis take it, what about that document?'

I nodded. In my enthusiasm I had momentarily overlooked the fact that even if I had solved one half of the problem, a greater one remained.

Cornovacus gave a sour smile. 'You are a clever thinker, but you're wrong. Like one of Tullio's confounded eels, you've fallen into the trap they set for you.'

'They?' I said.

'The people who really did all this,' he said. 'Important people – I don't know their names – but I can show you who they are, and where they live. Both of them were there at Marcus's house that night. Great Mithras, man, don't look at me like that. Can't you see what's right in front of you? They *wanted* you to find the clues that led to Mellitus. Perhaps he did murder Praxus, I don't know, but if so they encouraged him, and if you hadn't worked it out probably they'd have "discovered" it themselves. They planned his downfall, don't you understand? – and your patron's too. With Praxus gone, that clears the way for them.'

I stared at him. 'How do you know all this?'

'They bribed your little twitching friend to help, that's how.' He laughed unpleasantly. 'Amazing what facts come tumbling out, when you shake a man hard enough.'

'The secretary to the garrison? But what could he have done? I can't believe . . .'

Cornovacus quelled me with a glance. 'Listen, citizen, I don't give a whore's dowry if your patron dies or not. You're paying me to help, and I am telling you. If you don't believe me, come and listen for yourself. I know where they meet. I'll take you there and you can see. Tomorrow, at first light, if you like. We'll lie in wait for them – I know a hiding place. I guarantee in half an hour you'll be convinced, and have all the evidence you need.' He shot me a look. 'If you're prepared to pay for it, of course.'

'You want a whole denarius again?'

He leaned closer. 'I want the aureus,' he said, and his tone was menacing. 'I know you've got it, citizen. I saw it earlier. But if this information frees your wretched patron, it's worth it, isn't it? Or shall I send to tell him that you grudged the fee? I'm sure Parva could find a way to let him know.'

I looked to Sosso for support, but the dwarf was cleaning his fingers with his knife again. 'Greedy,' he said, without looking up. 'But quite likely true. If Cornovacus says that you'll have evidence, you will.'

I sighed. I had no personal faith in Cornovacus as a guide, though I had to admire his abilities as a blackmailer and spy. I would not have put it past him to take me into town, steal my gold aureus and flee. But I did trust Sosso, and he seemed to think that it was worth my while. Besides, what did I have to lose? Without this promised evidence there was no chance my patron would be freed, and then there was no future for me here. At best I would have to leave Glevum with my wife and try to start again, selling my pavements somewhere else. Not an easy prospect, at my time of life. At worst . . .

I took a deep breath. 'Very well,' I said. 'You make sure I'm smuggled into town and I'll come with you as you suggest. But no money till I see the evidence.'

I thought that he might argue, but he simply smiled. 'Agreed.'

Sosso gave his owl-cry again and Tullio and his family, who had been hovering at the door, came in and huddled with us round the fire. The woman brought in the basketful of eels – all skinned and filleted by now – which she tipped into a pan. Soon she had fried enough to feed us all, before settling her children into bed and eating her own supper by the fire. She raked the embers around a sort of pot in which she set a round of dough to bake, and then – still silent – retired from the hearth.

Her husband grunted and got slowly to his feet, gesturing that she could go to bed. I lay down on my designated pile of reeds and tried to rest while Tullio went out into the dark and led Sosso and his gang back through the marsh.

I had so much to think about that sleep eluded me. Who were the two 'important people' who had planned the downfall of the proposed triumvirate? What was I missing that was self-evident? I gave it up at last, and must have fallen into fitful sleep, because I dreamt I was the high priest of Jupiter, dressed in a woman's mantle and a sack, helping Gaius the old ex-councillor thread piglets on a string, while Gwellia threw scraps of bark-paper in the fire.

'You've learned one useful thing from this,' Gwellia told me in my dream. 'If you can catch eels, at least we'll never starve.'

XXVI

I woke to a damp day and the smell of fresh-baked bread. The little house was full of steam and smoke, and when I raised myself on my arm to look out of the door, I saw that wisps of mist were rising from the river flats and joining a curtain of misty rain that hid the trees.

'Ah, citizen! You are awake.' Tullio's wife was already astir, fanning the fire into life and dusting ashes from the baking pot. 'Do you want food?' She gestured to where her boys were squatting on the floor. They had the iron skillet in which the meal had been fried the night before, and were mopping up the grease with chunks of flat bread from the loaf, which they stuffed hungrily into their mouths.

My stomach rebelled at the suggestion of more eels, but I accepted a morsel of the bread, washed down with a beaker of brackish rainwater. Capria waited patiently until I'd finished my feast before she said, 'My husband's waiting for you,' and gestured to the door.

I pulled on my sandals and my cloak, and stooped down through the door to go outside. Tullio was working in the rain, twisting wet osiers into a funnel shape which I recognised as another trap for fish. He straightened up as I approached, raindrops running down his face and dripping from his hair and nose. He put down his handiwork and

257

signalled that I should follow him. This was not a family of many words.

The mist seemed thicker as we picked our way across the marsh, and by the time we reached the path it was getting difficult to see, so when a sudden figure loomed up through the murk I was glad when it resolved itself into Cornovacus's lanky form.

I pressed a coin into Tullio's hand and set off with Cornovacus through the drizzling gloom, this time in the direction of the town. I tried to question him again, but he would not be drawn. 'Wait and see, for Pluto's sake! You won't believe me, anyway, unless you see it for yourself.'

He walked so quickly as he led the way that very soon I was too out of breath to talk, even when we reached the major road. There were few people on the move today, and even the handful that we passed were muffled up in cloaks and hoods and kept their heads down to avoid the rain. I had been apprehensive, thinking of the guard, but no one showed any interest in us.

I was concerned about how I was to pass the gate, but Cornovacus – or more likely Sosso – had a plan. As we approached, my companion drew me off the road, arranged my cloak to shield my face and stuck a length of rough branch in my hand. Then he instructed me to close my eyes, and led me by the hand. As we joined the little group of jostlers at the gate I heard him calling, 'Alms! Alms! Alms for the blind.' Once I even heard the chink of coins.

It was alarming to walk along like this without seeing where I was, and entirely in Cornovacus's care. I expected any moment that he'd seize my money-belt and leave me to the mercies of the guard, but nothing happened. There was no attempt to stop us entering the town and soon I could hear the sounds of commerce all around and feel fine paving underneath my feet.

Presently Cornovacus released my hand and hissed at me that we were safe. I was glad to open my eyes and find myself in one of the familiar alleyways behind the market place.

'Come on,' Cornovacus said, and we were off again. I made to throw away my stick but he prevented me, saying that I'd need it later.

He led on, past wretched pedlars huddling in doorways with their wares, but avoided the main streets as much as possible. By this time I half suspected where he was taking me and I was not surprised when he instructed me to close my eyes again and led me through the northern gate, to the alley where my ruined workshop was.

When I opened my eyes, Cornovacus turned to face me with a grin. 'Now do you believe me, citizen? You see the plan? Neat as a Vestal's girdle, isn't it? The guards have been withdrawn. Who'd look for dignitaries here? And even if they're found, they've only to look innocent and say you asked them here, to talk about your patron's case.'

In spite of myself, I was impressed. Marcus's enemies could hardly have chosen a safer place to meet. It was secluded, empty, and had been searched – and looted – days ago. One could hide small objects with impunity – a seal-ring, for instance, or even a document – as long as I was on the run. Best of all, the place belonged to me – if by some accident the guard came back and anything was found, blame would fall on a foolish pavement-maker, with known links to Marcus and interfering ways.

'Come on then, let's go,' I said, tightening my grip upon my staff.

He shook his head, and took it from me with a smile. 'Gently, citizen. We don't want to be seen. Fortunately there's nobody about.' It was true, I realised with surprise. The rain seemed to have cleared even the usual passers-by and donkeys from the street. 'We'll go and lie in wait for them, up on the sleeping floor. It isn't easy, since the ladder's burned, but there's enough floor left up there to hide. If you like I'll hoist you on my back.'

I led the way, with Cornovacus urging caution at my heels. I hurried past the stone heaps which were still outside the shop and was about to step inside when suddenly an urgent voice rang out. 'Don't go in there, master! It's a trap.'

I whirled round. A curly-headed figure had burst out from the building opposite. I stepped towards him. 'Junio? What are you doing here?'

'Look out!' he shouted, and I turned again.

Cornovacus was advancing on me with my staff. 'Confounded slave,' he muttered angrily, and aimed a blow me. But Junio's warning had alerted me and I dodged aside in time. The stick hit the ground with so much force it broke. Cornovacus gave a frustrated roar and lunged at me again, and at the same moment Bullface came from my workshop in a clattering run, while his half-dozen men emerged from the neighbouring businesses, weapons drawn, cutting off all prospect of escape. I understood now why the lane was so deserted when we entered it.

Junio had reached me by this time, and we stood back to back, although I had no knife to defend myself, and Junio wasn't armed.

Cornovacus approached us with the broken wood, his lips curled in his most unpleasant smile. 'Think that you could cheat me of my reward, did you, pavement-maker? We'll see what patterns blood and brains will make.'

Junio made a sudden move and tried to dive beneath his upraised arm to seize a missile from the pile of stones, but Cornovacus was too quick for him. With one hand he grabbed Junio by the neck and with the other he stabbed down viciously with the jagged stick.

What happened next was so confused that it is hard to give a true account of it. The first thing I saw was a lithe figure dropping from a roof, and grasping Cornovacus round the knees. The tall thief tumbled forward, and I was aware of Lercius grinning up at me before he sank his teeth into a leg, while Junio seized the chance to wriggle free and sit down on his erstwhile captor's head, forcing Cornovacus's face into the mud.

This was no more than a temporary respite, for Bullface and his men were closing in, forming an ugly circle round us now – though the sudden appearance of Lercius from above had startled them and halted their progress momentarily. Then all at once the air was full of shouts, and flying objects – pebbles, shoes, lumps of mud, even rotten fish and fruit – went whistling past our ears. Bullface ducked in time, and so did I, but several of the other guards were hit. One fell face downwards on the ground and lay there very still. The others turned, instinctively, to face the newcomers.

Sosso and several of his gang were loping towards us from the right, while the remainder were approaching from the left, all shouting, screaming, yelling at the limit of their lungs and hurling any missile that came to hand. Among them I saw Grossus, towering above the rest, and wielding a piece of timber that might have been a door. As I watched he brought it swinging down to fell another soldier.

The whole of the alley was in chaos now. The soldiers, unprepared for this attack, had lost formation and were skirmishing; but swords are little use against a hail of stones, and a faceful of stinking mud is not an encouragement to discipline. All the same they might have won the day, by regrouping in obedience to Bullface's roared commands, except that the inhabitants of the area – excited by the noise and being no lovers of the guard in any case – had poured into the street to join the fray. A woman threw a urine collection pot from an upper storey, covering Bullface with its contents as it fell; while someone from the candlemaker's overturned a vat of tallow in the lane to send a tide of slippery grease towards us all.

I looked around. Cornovacus had shaken Lercius off and tumbled Junio to the ground. He was on his haunches in a trice, ready to make another dart at me, but suddenly the dwarf was standing at his side. Something glittered, and Cornovacus gave a groan and rolled sideways in the mud. A soldier bore down on Sosso. Junio turned and fled.

I was the still centre of a heaving world, but it could not be for long. I darted towards the shelter of my shop, to my surprise I saw a figure in the gloom. I did not stop to think – I lowered my head and launched myself with all my might. I felt my head connect with a stomach, and the intruder fell backwards with an 'Ooff!' I imitated Junio's technique and sat down on my victim's chest, seizing my chisel and mallet from the toolbag on the floor. I placed the pointed metal on the skin between the eyes and saw for the first time who it was I'd caught.

Balbus. A different Balbus now. A white-faced Balbus with an uncertain voice, 'I beg you, citizen . . .'

'All right. Stand up and don't try anything.' When I relaxed my grip he did as he was told and struggled upright, back against the wall, still watching the mallet with terror in his eyes. I moved my chisel so that it was level with his heart. 'If those are your guards, call them off,' I said.

He nodded and ran a tongue around his lips. I allowed him to shuffle to the door and stood behind him with the mallet as he called, 'Enough! Disperse!' Over the hubbub he had to shout it twice. Even then it was a moment before it took effect.

The soldiers who were nearest to us stopped, though one who dropped his shield was caught by an apple in the face. There was a hush. People ceased to hurl things after that, and bit by bit the skirmishing decreased.

'Disperse!' Balbus roared again. Bullface and a couple of his men had fought their way out to the corner of the lane, and when they heard the order they took it as retreat. They immediately sheathed their weapons, formed up and marched away. The two guards still in the lane withdrew in disarray, taking their injured comrades with them – one of them hobbling, the other with black eyes and injured pride. The rioters vanished into doors and alleyways like smoke.

Suddenly the lane was empty, silent, littered with chunks of brick and stone and fruit. A helmet lay discarded in the mud. Only Cornovacus was still there, lying in the congealing tallow with a dark stain oozing from his back.

Now that the immediate danger from the crowd had passed, Balbus was recovering himself. 'This is an outrage, citizen,' he said, in something approaching his accustomed style. 'I call my soldiers to a riot in the street, and I am threatened with a pointed instrument. I shall bring a case against you for *injuria*, for the assault upon my dignity.'

'I think not, magistrate,' I said, gesturing him back into the shop. 'You have a better knowledge of the law. You failed to show the legally required "resentment" at the time – there are witnesses to that – and that is enough to bar the case.'

He attempted a sneer. 'Witnesses! A drunken rabble in defiance of the law. They will be caught and punished, all of them. And don't think you will get away unscathed. My personal servants have instructions to come here very soon, to escort me home. If any harm should come to me, you'll suffer for it, mark my words. To say nothing of that assault upon my guards.'

'*Your* guards?' I seized on the words. 'On whose authority?'

I still had the chisel and mallet in my hand, but he was swaggering now. 'That of Romnus Nonnius, Praxus's second in command. As leader of the council, I possess the right to request the use of soldiers if I choose, in the pursuit of justice and the maintenance of the law. And following the murder of his senior officer, he was anxious to oblige. He permitted me to use the bodyguard.'

'And the pursuit of justice involved arresting me?' It was clear now who had set Bullface on my trail. 'Or were there instructions that I should be killed?'

He flushed, and glanced towards the mallet. 'I gave no such instructions, naturally.'

'But if I happened to resist arrest?'

He shrugged.

'And you offered a reward, of course – which is why your informant told you where to look. I wondered how the guard had come to search the kindling-seller's hut. Cornovacus told them, naturally.'

'There is no law against it, citizen. And when your patron is accused of a crime against the state . . .'

'Ah yes, the famous document. You have seen it, I presume?'

'Naturally I have. I ordered Praxus's bodyguard to search the house, and that was when the letter came to light. There is no doubt about it, citizen. Only a few words, but it is enough. *I write in haste to urge you, dispose of that beast Praxus by any means you can. Your own brave Romnus Nonnius will take his place. Of course he will know nothing of events, but we shall see who is prepared to take a stand against that trumped-up idiot in Rome.* You see? It urges Praxus's murder and threatens revolt against the Emperor.'

'It didn't say who wrote it?'

'It did not need to. It was under Marcus's seal. I have the ring – I ordered it removed as soon as the document was brought to me – and it matches perfectly.'

'And was that the only document you seized?'

He looked impatient. 'What other did we need? That was evidence enough!'

'But how could you know that, magistrate? The document was sealed. Unless, of course, you took the ring and put my patron's seal on it yourself?' I said, remembering how I had remelted wax and resealed Julia's writing frame. 'And why, in any case, should Marcus urge someone else to topple Praxus, if he's supposed to have murdered him himself?' I raised the mallet as I spoke.

'You think you're very clever, citizen!' He was breathing hard. 'But you can't prove anything. Praxus's bodyguard will swear they found it, as I said.'

'And that's another thing,' I said. 'The bodyguard. On the authority of Romnus Nonnius you said. But where is Romnus Nonnius now? In Gaul? Only Praxus and his guard came ahead, I understand. So how did this authority arise?'

'I assure you, citizen, I have a document . . .'

'Another document? And when did that arrive? It would take days to send a messenger to Gaul and get an answer back. Or did you get it from a member of the bodyguard, perhaps? Along with a letter from your brother, Romnus Nonnius, urging you to find a way to bring down his senior officer so that he could take command instead, and further his plans to be a senator in Rome? Of course, he took care how he worded it in case the note was intercepted, as anyone with any wit would do, but I have no doubt it could be traced to him. Unfortunate that he mentioned his hatred of the Emperor as well.'

Balbus was looking wildly about, but he was a magistrate. He admitted nothing.

I leaned towards him. 'Why did you do it, Balbus?'

Silence.

'Very well, don't answer me, but I believe I know. Because, once it emerged that Praxus's death was not an accident, there was to be a search. Mellitus suggested it, not you. He was prepared to search the diners as they left. That must have frightened you. A most important person had just been killed, and there you were with a letter urging you to do that very thing. You must have had it on your person then. You'd just received it from a member of the bodyguard.'

'How did you . . .' he began to say, and then fell silent.

I was quite certain now that I was right. 'You must have done. As you came into the villa, probably. The bodyguard were posted at the gate. The banquet was the only chance you'd had, since Praxus and his party were staying out of town. And you had clearly read it, since you were so alarmed.'

'It was found by a guard in front of witnesses,' he said stubbornly. 'In Marcus's private rooms.'

'Of course. No doubt you seized a chance to slip it back to your brother's messenger, so that he could conveniently discover it. Then when it was duly brought to you, as senior magistrate, you confiscated Marcus's ring and used it to seal the document. Your friend who found it, naturally, would swear that it was sealed all along. One touch too many, Balbus. It was that which let you down. How could you know which document to seize if it was sealed?' I paused as there was a clatter in the street.

He was still defiant. One old man with a chisel is not much of a threat. 'You can prove nothing, citizen. Your word against a senior magistrate? Anyway, you will not have the chance! Here are my servants. They will take you under charge – and since you unfortunately attempted to resist . . .' He turned. The disturbance was not caused by his slaves. Lercius, Sosso and my servant Junio were standing at the door.

Balbus made a run for it. Sosso would have stopped him, but I shook my head.

'They will only feed you to the beasts,' I said, as we heard the councillor disappearing up the lane. 'And murdering Balbus won't save Marcus now. Our only hope is in a court of law. Though it will be difficult to prove.' I told them what I knew.

'But Balbus is right, master,' Junio said. 'He is the senior magistrate, now that Marcus is in jail. Your only witnesses are slaves and thieves. You are in danger too. You need a place to hide.'

I nodded. 'Corinium's not safe. Umbris and Mellitus are there, and they've been trying to kill me ever since that night – they think that Golbo might have told me what he knew. In fact, I'm sure that's why Umbris came back to the round-house twice: once when he found Golbo, and again when

Lercius was there. He came to kill me – not to bring a message to my home at all. I wonder why he decided to tell me what he did – that you were safe and Mellitus was in Corinium? The first thing he thought of, or just to make me feel secure, perhaps?'

'Remember that he played a double role,' Junio said anxiously. 'I sent the message, as he said I did. When he came to the house in Corinium, I asked him to tell you we were there, if he was able to. I hoped you'd know that we had got away – you found the bag?'

'I did,' I said. 'How did you manage that? You left before the soldiers ever came.'

'Gave it to the turnip-seller from whom I hired the cart,' Junio explained. 'The one that drove us to Corinium. I asked him if his household could see that it was hung up in the lane, if soldiers turned up at the roundhouse when I'd gone – said it was a votive offering to the gods. I had to pay him extra in the end, but he gave it to his daughter and said it would be done.' He grinned. 'I wasn't sure it would. Though they are a religious household – I could see that from the amulets they wore – I made sure that there was nothing worth stealing in the bag!'

I thought of the kindling-seller's wife, and smiled. 'All the same, I am surprised that Umbris passed on the message that Mellitus was in Corinium.'

'Perhaps that was to prove that he was not in Glevum when that letter came to light,' Junio said. 'If I understand the story rightly, as soon as that emerged, Mellitus turned and fled. He wanted to kill Praxus to gain himself more power, not get mixed up in army politics. No doubt he was delighted when Marcus was arraigned – but it's clear he wanted to have no part at all in that.'

'But why on earth did Umbris bring that second message here? That Mellitus and his shadow were in the market place?'

Junio grinned. 'He didn't bring that message. It was me. Once I realised the connection between the two, I was very worried. I didn't even know that you were safe. That's why I came back – to look for you.'

Lercius gave his idiotic grin. 'Told you yesterday I'd got a message from your slave. Found him at the roundhouse poking round.'

I sighed. Useless to remonstrate with him. I had not realised that Junio had come himself and Lercius had not enlightened me. I turned to Junio. 'I had to disappear. There were two lots of people hunting me, it seems – not just Mellitus and Umbris, though that was bad enough, but Balbus and the bodyguard.' I sighed. 'Sosso hid me in the swamp. But when you didn't find me, you thought I might be here, hidden in the workshop? That's what brought you here?'

'I thought there was a chance. But as soon as I arrived, I found the troops. I saw them clear the street and hide themselves in buildings round about. I let them hustle me along, with all the rest, and went into the pot-maker's – I've met the potter's slave before – and kept watch there. I had to make sure I wasn't seen, of course. I saw what happened to the skinny man.'

'The skinny man?' I said.

Sosso nodded. 'You know. Carried the light.' His voice was strangely cracked. 'That night. When we let you out.'

The wraith! I did remember, though it now seemed years ago. 'What did they do to him?'

'Stabbed him. Stuffed his body in a ditch,' Sosso said. I realised that the ugly little man was close to tears.

'Watching your workshop,' Lercius put in, 'but they got rid

of him. All bleeding round the neck, he was . . .' He stopped as he saw Sosso's face.

'Betrayed,' said the dwarf bitterly. He cleared his throat. 'By Cornovacus. Still, he paid.' Sosso had come to help me on the street, I saw, not for my sake, but for the skinny man who – even in that unhappy world – had been a friend. The wraith had died on my account, watching my workshop. It occurred to me that I didn't even know his name.

'If you get out me of this, I'll buy him a funeral,' I said. To be shovelled in a nameless pit is every man's worst fear.

Sosso managed a blackened grin. 'Cornovacus paid,' he said, more cheerfully, producing a handful of coins. They included a gold aureus. I saw.

I ran my hand across my makeshift purse. It was empty, naturally. Cornovacus had managed to rob me before he died.

To my eternal astonishment, Sosso took the aureus and pressed it in my hand. 'No use to us,' he said. 'Too big. You'll need it. We got a bargain. Get your patron free.'

'Not much hope of that,' I said, 'not without a wealthy man to speak for us. Pity I don't know anyone who would . . . or perhaps I do! Junio – get me a litter, quick. A curtained one for preference, before the guards come back.'

Junio stared. 'You're going to visit someone, master? In that state? What happened to your clothes?' He glanced at Sosso, who was still wearing my tunic, belt and shoes – though they were looking much the worse for wear by now. I was so used to it that I'd forgotten what a picture I must make.

'It's a long story,' I said. 'Just get that litter, quick. I'm going to see the high priest of Jupiter.'

XXVII

I was sitting in Marcus's dining room again, but this time the banquet was for me. There were no other guests, of course, except Gwellia and me, and poor old Councillor Gaius and his new young wife, but it was an honour all the same.

'Inspired,' Marcus was saying, gesturing to his slave to fill my cup. (The boy gave me a beaming smile: I had saved him from a painful questioning.) 'Simply inspired. It is doubtful if anyone other than the priest could have persuaded the court of magistrates to drop the charge. Saying it had been revealed in a dream – and that all the augurers agreed! Even Commodus couldn't argue with a fact like that, and once that bodyguard cracked under questioning . . .! Julia, my dear, I drink to you – inspired! Of course, Libertus, you were helpful too – stepping in and showing how it could all be rationally proved – but it was the high priest's intervention that really saved the day.'

'Mellitus got away with it, of course,' Gaius said. He was already getting flushed with wine. 'And that black slave of his.'

'Went into voluntary exile, certainly. But that might have been his sentence anyway. Though of course the murder charge against me was not the greatest threat.'

'Indeed not,' the ex-councillor agreed. 'Extraordinary that

there should have been two people planning to murder Praxus – and neither knew about the other one.'

'Or wanted to know,' Marcus said, with some asperity. 'Both of them were quite content to let me take the blame – Mellitus for the murder, and Balbus for that letter. I suppose that each of them believed that I *was* guilty of the other crime. Well, they are paying for it now. Mellitus is on his island, miles from anywhere. So much for his attempt to gain more power for himself. Of course he intended Praxus's death to look like an accident, but he was quite content to implicate me when he had the chance.'

Julia caught my eye. We had already discussed the possibility that Umbris would one day have used his poison upon Marcus too, but she said nothing. If my patron had not thought of it, there was nothing to be gained by mentioning it now.

'And Balbus?' Gaius's wife put the remains of a lark leg on her plate, and turned her attention to the watered wine. 'What's become of him? I understand he never did confess.'

'Silence won't help him when he gets to Rome. I hear his trial is to be heard next moon, but his brother has already fallen on his sword – so that will tell against him straight away,' Marcus said. 'I wonder what his punishment will be? Something unpleasant, I've no doubt. They say Commodus had a bald man pecked to death by birds for saying something displeasing.' He sounded remarkably dispassionate, considering that he had narrowly escaped a sentence at Commodus's hands himself. 'Clever of Libertus to spot that the *gens* name was the same, although of course there are a lot of men about with the cognomen Nonnius.'

Gwellia was looking ill at ease. She can never forget that she was once a slave, although her spell as a guest in Corinium had helped. She said nervously, 'I am glad that it has turned out to your satisfaction, Excellence. You have been most generous in restoring our affairs.'

Marcus beamed at her benevolently. 'Ensuring that your roundhouse was rebuilt? That seems the least I can do.'

Privately, I didn't disagree. Marcus, as usual, had found a way to give me the reward that made the least demand upon his purse, although with both his co-administrators gone he was now even more influential than before. He would soon be richer, too, if Balbus was found guilty at his trial – since Marcus would doubtless reap the usual reward for formally denouncing a conspirator.

However, I had no cause for complaint. He'd had his land slaves reconstruct the house for us and had provided some splendid furniture and pots, even a dozen chickens and a pig: it had all come from Mellitus's estate, which had already been seized. Marcus had also made it clear to the owner of my workshop in the town that some repairs were called for and – like any sensible man faced with suggestions from above – my landlord had instantly agreed. And I had a brand new toga and new shoes!

Marcus clapped his hands. 'Bring on the entertainment,' he decreed, and there was Lercius, in green underpants, contorting himself into unlikely shapes, walking on his hands, and generally performing lithe athletic feats. Gaius and Julia clapped him to the skies, although I was still conscious of the manic smile, and the way that Lercius looked hungrily towards the dog that was lying at the old councillor's feet.

Then it was Sosso, splendid in green silk, loping and cavorting round the room. The ladies shrieked, the pages sneered and Gaius and Marcus laughed uproariously. Gaius said, 'Bravo, Marcus. Where did you find them?'

Marcus smiled. 'They were making a nuisance in the town. I've given them a pardon, both of them. I believe they mean to work the fairs and banquet halls. They've got a girl with them, as well, who holds the purse. Over there, beside the door.'

'They should do well,' Gaius said enthusiastically. 'I'll have them the next time I host a feast.' He held out his goblet for more wine.

It had been Sosso's own idea, of course, that I should recommend him in this way, since there was no monetary reward to share. It seemed a sad thing to me, seeing him make an entertainment of himself, but with his shrewd brain no doubt he was right. At least he would make a living now, in heated dining rooms – no more scrabbling for soup or sleeping on the ground among the graves. I wondered how the other Ghosts of Glevum would survive now he had gone. With a little help from Grossus, possibly.

The entertainment over, it was time to go, and Junio was sent to fetch my cloak. He came, together with Gwellia's new slave – the female one she'd always wanted. This was a present from Julia, really meant for me.

'Are you ready, mistress?' Cilla said, helping my wife with her hood. 'I have a torch waiting. It's very dark outside.'

'It's very well for you, Libertus,' said Gaius grumpily. 'You've only got a little way to walk. The rest of us have got to go home in a litter in the rain. It's colder than the Styx out there tonight.'

I had to laugh. So much had happened since the banquet. But I had my wife and roundhouse back, and Gwellia was dyeing and spinning once again. Marcus had provided a new loom. I did not grudge the miller's wife the other one – nor the axe that Molendinarius had gained. Those were perhaps the best rewards that I could give them, in the circumstances, and I had seen that Tullio was paid in coin.

I looked at Junio walking down the path. He was chattering to Cilla as he went, and Gwellia turned to chide them. But I saw the look that passed between the slaves and smiled.

Everything was going to be all right.

Now you can buy any of these other bestselling Headline books from your bookshop or *direct from the publisher*.

FREE P&P AND UK DELIVERY
(Overseas and Ireland £3.50 per book)

The Slayers of Seth	Paul Doherty	£6.99
Corpse Candle	Paul Doherty	£6.99
The Devil's Acolyte	Michael Jecks	£6.99
The Sticklepath Strangler	Michael Jecks	£6.99
A Funeral in Blue	Anne Perry	£6.99
Southampton Row	Anne Perry	£6.99
The Legatus Mystery	Rosemary Rowe	£6.99
The Chariots of Calyx	Rosemary Rowe	£6.99
Smoke in the Wind	Peter Tremayne	£5.99
Our Lady of Darkness	Peter Tremayne	£6.99

TO ORDER SIMPLY CALL THIS NUMBER

01235 400 414

or visit our website: www.madaboutbooks.com

Prices and availability subject to change without notice.